CAPTURED BY TINY MEN

The warriors of Veltopismakus, scarce one-fourth of Tarzan's size, jumped their riding antelopes over every obstruction. One rider struck the ape-man head on in the pit of his stomach, sending him back a step. Another and another struck his legs and sides. Again and again the needlelike rapiers pierced his brown hide until he was red with his own blood. Always there were more than thousands bearing down upon him.

Again Tarzan was struck in the stomach by a charging rider and again the blow staggered him. Before he could recover himself, another struck him in the same place. This time he went down, and instantly he was covered, buried by warriors and beasts that swarmed over him, in countless numbers.

Tarzan tried to rise and that was the last he remembered before he sank into unconsciousness.

Edgar Rice Burroughs

TARZAN NOVELS

COMPLETE AND UNABRIDGED!

TARZAN AND THE ANT MEN

Edgar Rice Burroughs

BALLANTINE BOOKS • NEW YORK

ISBN 0-345-28997-8

This authorized edition published by arrangement with Edgar Rice Burroughs, Inc.

Manufactured in the United States of America

First U.S. Printing: July 1963
Eleventh U.S. Printing: July 1983

Cover art by Boris Vallejo

1

IN THE filth of a dark hut, in the village of Obebe the cannibal, upon the banks of the Ugogo, Esteban Miranda squatted upon his haunches and gnawed upon the remnants of a
half-cooked fish. About his neck was an iron slave collar from
which a few feet of rusty chain ran to a stout post set deep
in the ground near the low entranceway that let upon the
village street not far from the hut of Obebe himself.

For a year Esteban Miranda had been chained thus, like
a dog, and like a dog he sometimes crawled through the low
doorway of his kennel and basked in the sun outside. Two
diversions had he; and only two. One was the persistent idea
that he was Tarzan of the Apes, whom he had impersonated
for so long and with such growing success that, like the good
actor he was, he had come not only to act the part, but to live
it—to *be* it. He *was*, as far as he was concerned, Tarzan of the
Apes—there was no other—and he was Tarzan of the Apes
to Obebe, too; but the village witch doctor still insisted that he
was the river devil and as such, one to propitiate rather than
to anger.

It had been this difference of opinion between the chief
and the witch doctor that had kept Esteban Miranda from
the fleshpots of the village, for Obebe had wanted to eat him,
thinking him his old enemy the ape-man; but the witch doctor had aroused the superstitious fears of the villagers by half
convincing them that their prisoner was the river devil mas-
querading as Tarzan, and, as such, dire disaster would descend upon the village were he harmed. The result of this difference between Obebe and the witch doctor had been to pre-
serve the life of the Spaniard until the truth of one claim or
the other was proved—if Esteban died a natural death he was

Tarzan, the mortal, and Obebe the chief was vindicated; if he lived on forever, or mysteriously disappeared, the claim of the witch doctor would be accepted as gospel.

After he had learned their language and thus come to a realization of the accident of fate that had guided his destiny by so narrow a margin from the cooking pots of the cannibals he was less eager to proclaim himself Tarzan of the Apes. Instead he let drop mysterious suggestions that he was, indeed, none other than the river devil. The witch doctor was delighted, and everyone was fooled except Obebe, who was old and wise and did not believe in river devils, and the witch doctor who was old and wise and did not believe in them either, but realized that they were excellent things for his parishioners to believe in.

Esteban Miranda's other diversion, aside from secretly believing himself Tarzan, consisted in gloating over the bag of diamonds that Kraski the Russian had stolen from the ape-man, and that had fallen into the Spaniard's hands after he had murdered Kraski—the same bag of diamonds that the man had handed to Tarzan in the vaults beneath The Tower of Diamonds, in the Valley of The Palace of Diamonds, when he had rescued the Gomangani of the valley from the tyrannical oppression of the Bolgani.

For hours at a time Esteban Miranda sat in the dim light of his dirty kennel counting and fondling the brilliant stones. A thousand times had he weighed each one in an appraising palm, computing its value and translating it into such pleasures of the flesh as great wealth might buy for him in the capitals of the world. Mired in his own filth, feeding upon rotted scraps tossed to him by unclean hands, he yet possessed the wealth of a Croesus, and it was as Croesus he lived in his imaginings, his dismal hut changed into the pomp and circumstance of a palace by the scintillant gleams of the precious stones. At the sound of each approaching footstep he would hastily hide his fabulous fortune in the wretched loin cloth that was his only garment, and once again become a prisoner in a cannibal hut.

And now, after a year of solitary confinement, came a third diversion, in the form of Uhha, the daughter of Khamis the witch doctor. Uhha was fourteen, comely and curious. For a year now she had watched the mysterious prisoner from a distance until, at last, familiarity had overcome her fears and one day she approached him as he lay in the sun outside his hut. Esteban, who had been watching her half-timorous advance, smiled encouragingly. He had not a friend among the villagers. If he could make but one his lot would be much the easier and freedom a step nearer. At last Uhha came to a halt a few steps from him. She was a child, ignorant and a savage; but she was a woman-child and Esteban Miranda knew women.

"I have been in the village of the chief Obebe for a year," he said haltingly, in the laboriously acquired language of his captors, "but never before did I guess that its walls held one so beautiful as you. What is your name?"

Uhha was pleased. She smiled broadly. "I am Uhha," she told him. "My father is Khamis the witch doctor."

It was Esteban who was pleased now. Fate, after rebuffing him for long, was at last kind. She had sent him one who, with cultivation, might prove a flower of hope indeed.

"Why have you never come to see me before?" asked Esteban.

"I was afraid," replied Uhha simply.

"Why?"

"I was afraid—" she hesitated.

"Afraid that I was the river devil and would harm you?" demanded the Spaniard, smiling.

"Yes," she said.

"Listen!" whispered Esteban; "but tell no one. I am the river devil, but I shall not harm you."

"If you are the river devil why then do you remain chained to a stake?" inquired Uhha. "Why do you not change yourself to something else and return to the river?"

"You wonder about that, do you?" asked Miranda, sparring for time that he might concoct a plausible answer.

"It is not only Uhha who wonders," said the girl. "Many others have asked the same question of late. Obebe asked it first and there was none to explain. Obebe says that you are Tarzan, the enemy of Obebe and his people; but my father Khamis says that you are the river devil, and that if you wanted to get away you would change yourself into a snake and crawl through the iron collar that is about your neck. And the people wonder why you do not, and many of them are commencing to believe that you are not the river devil at all."

"Come closer, beautiful Uhha," whispered Miranda, "that no other ears than yours may hear what I am about to tell you."

The girl came a little closer and leaned toward him where he squatted upon the ground.

"I am indeed the river devil," said Esteban, "and I come

and go as I wish. At night, when the village sleeps, I am wandering through the waters of the Ugogo, but always I come back again. I am waiting, Uhha, to try the people of the village of Obebe that I may know which are my friends and which my enemies. Already have I learned that Obebe is no friend of mine, and I am not sure of Khamis. Had Khamis been a good friend he would have brought me fine food and beer to drink. I could go when I pleased, but I wait to see if there be one in the village of Obebe who will set me free. Thus may I learn which is my best friend. Should there be such a one, Uhha, fortune would smile upon him always, his every wish would be granted and he would live to a great age, for he would have nothing to fear from the river devil, who would help him in all his undertakings. But listen, Uhha, tell no one what I have told you! I shall wait a little longer and then if there be no such friend in the village of Obebe I shall return to my father and mother, the Ugogo, and destroy the people of Obebe. Not one shall remain alive."

The girl drew away, terrified. It was evident that she was much impressed.

"Do not be afraid," he reassured her. "I shall not harm you."

"But if you destroy all the people?" she demanded.

"Then, of course," he said, "I cannot help you; but let us hope that someone comes and sets me free so that I shall know that I have at least one good friend here. Now run along, Uhha, and remember that you must tell no one what I have told you."

She moved off a short distance and then returned.

"When will you destroy the village?" she asked.

"In a few days," he said.

Uhha, trembling with terror, ran quickly away in the direction of the hut of her father, Khamis, the witch doctor. Esteban Miranda smiled a satisfied smile and crawled back into his hole to play with his diamonds.

Khamis the witch doctor was not in his hut when Uhha his daughter, faint from fright, crawled into the dim interior. Nor were his wives. With their children, the latter were in the fields beyond the palisade, where Uhha should have been. And so it was that the girl had time for thought before she saw any of them again, with the result that she recalled distinctly, what she had almost forgotten in the first frenzy of fear, that the river devil had impressed upon her that she must reveal to no one the thing that he had told her.

And she had been upon the point of telling her father all!

What dire calamity then would have befallen her? She trembled at the very suggestion of a fate so awful that she could not even imagine it. How close a call she had had! But what was she to do?

She lay huddled upon a mat of woven grasses, racking her poor, savage little brain for a solution of the immense problem that confronted her—the first problem that had ever entered her young life other than the constantly recurring one of how most easily to evade her share of the drudgery of the fields. Presently she sat suddenly erect, galvanized into statuesque rigidity by a thought engendered by the recollection of one of the river devil's remarks. Why had it not occurred to her before? Very plainly he had said, and he had repeated it, that if he were released he would know that he had at least one friend in the village of Obebe, and that whoever releasd him would live to a great age and have every thing he wished for; but after a few minutes of thought Uhha drooped again. How was she, a little girl, to compass the liberation of the river devil alone?

"How, *baba*," she asked her father, when he had returned to the hut, later in the day, "does the river devil destroy those who harm him?"

"As the fish in the river, so are the ways of the river devil —without number," replied Khamis. "He might send the fish from the river and the game from the jungle and cause our crops to die. Then we should starve. He might bring the fire out of the sky at night and strike dead all the people of Obebe."

"And you think he may do these things to us, *baba?*"

"He will not harm Khamis, who saved him from the death that Obebe would have inflicted," replied the witch doctor.

Uhha recalled that the river devil had complained that Khamis had not brought him good food nor beer, but she said nothing about that, although she realized that her father was far from being so high in the good graces of the river devil as he seemed to think he was. Instead, she took another tack.

"How can he escape," she asked, "while the collar is about his neck—who will remove it for him?"

"No one can remove it but Obebe, who carries in his pouch the bit of brass that makes the collar open," replied Khamis; "but the river devil needs no help, for when the time comes that he wishes to be free he has but to become a snake and crawl forth from the iron band about his neck. Where are you going, Uhha?"

"I am going to visit the daughter of Obebe," she called back over her shoulder.

The chief's daughter was grinding maize, as Uhha should have been doing. She looked up and smiled as the daughter of the witch doctor approached.

"Make no noise, Uhha," she cautioned, "for Obebe, my father, sleeps within." She nodded toward the hut. The visitor sat down and the two girls chatted in low tones. They spoke of their ornaments, their coiffures, of the young men of the village, and often, when they spoke of these, they giggled. Their conversation was not unlike that which might pass between two young girls of any race or clime. As they talked, Uhha's eyes often wandered toward the entrance to Obebe's hut and many times her brows were contracted in much deeper thought than their idle passages warranted.

"Where," she demanded suddenly, "is the armlet of copper wire that your father's brother gave you at the beginning of the last moon?"

Obebe's daughter shrugged. "He took it back from me," she replied, "and give it to the sister of his youngest wife."

Uhha appeared crestfallen. Could it be that she had coveted the copper bracelet? Her eyes closely scrutinized the person of her friend. Her brows almost met, so deeply was she thinking. Suddenly her face brightened.

"The necklace of many beads that your father took from the body of the warrior captured for the last feast!" she exclaimed. "You have not lost it?"

"No," replied her friend. "It is in the house of my father. When I grind maize it gets in my way and so I laid it aside."

"May I see it?" asked Uhha. "I will fetch it."

"No, you will awaken Obebe and he will be very angry," said the chief's daughter.

"I will not awaken him," replied Uhha, and started to crawl toward the hut's entrance.

Her friend tried to dissuade her. "I will fetch it as soon as *baba* has awakened," she told Uhha, but Uhha paid no attention to her and presently was crawling cautiously into the interior of the hut. Once within she waited silently until her eyes became accustomed to the dim light. Against the opposite wall of the hut Obebe lay sprawled upon a sleeping mat. He snored lustily. Uhha crept toward him. Her stealth was the stealth of Sheeta the leopard. Her heart was beating like the tom-tom when the dance is at its height. She feared that its noise and her rapid breathing would awaken the old chief, of whom she was as terrified as of the river devil; but Obebe snored on.

Uhha came close to him. Her eyes were accustomed now to the half-light of the hut's interior. At Obebe's side and half beneath his body she saw the chief's pouch. Cautiously she reached forth a trembling hand and laid hold upon it. She tried to draw it from beneath Obebe's weight. The sleeper stirred uneasily and Uhha drew back, terrified. Obebe changed his position and Uhha thought that he had awakened. Had she not been frozen with horror she would have rushed into headlong flight, but fortunately for her she could not move, and presently she heard Obebe resume his interrupted snoring; but her nerve was gone and she thought now only of escaping from the hut without being detected. She cast a last frightened glance at the chief to reassure herself that he still slept. Her eyes fell upon the pouch. Obebe had turned away from it and it now lay within her reach, free from the weight of his body.

She reached for it only to withdraw her hand suddenly. She turned away. Her heart was in her mouth. She swayed dizzily and then she thought of the river devil and of the possibilities for horrid death that lay within his power. Once more she reached for the pouch and this time she picked it up. Hurriedly opening it she examined the contents. The brass key was there. She recognized it because it was the only thing the purpose of which she was not familiar with. The collar, chain and key had been taken from an Arab slave raider that Obebe had killed and eaten and as some of the old men of Obebe's village had worn similar bonds in the past, there was no difficulty in adapting it to its intended purpose when occasion demanded.

Uhha hastily closed the pouch and replaced it at Obebe's side. Then, clutching the key in a clammy palm, she crawled hurriedly toward the doorway.

That night, after the cooking fires had died to embers and been covered with earth and the people of Obebe had withdrawn into their huts, Esteban Miranda heard a stealthy movement at the entrance to his kennel. He listened intently. Someone was creeping into the interior—someone or something.

"Who is it?" demanded the Spaniard in a voice that he tried hard to keep from trembling.

"Hush!" responded the intruder in soft tones. "It is I, Uhha, the daughter of Khamis the witch doctor. I have come to set you free that you may know that you have a good friend in the village of Obebe and will, therefore, not destroy us."

Miranda smiled. His suggestion had borne fruit more quickly than he had dared to hope, and evidently the girl had obeyed his injunction to keep silent. In that matter he had reasoned wrongly, but of what moment that, since his sole aim in life—

freedom—was to be accomplished. He had cautioned the girl to silence believing this the surest way to disseminate the word he had wished spread through the village, where, he was positive, it would have come to the ears of some one of the superstitious savages with the means to free him now that the incentive was furnished.

"And how are you going to free me?" demanded Miranda.

"See!" exclaimed Uhha. "I have brought the key to the collar about your neck."

"Good," cried the Spaniard. "Where is it?"

Uhha crawled closer to the man and handed him the key. Then she would have fled.

"Wait!" demanded the prisoner. "When I am free you must lead me forth into the jungle. Whoever sets me free must do this if he would win the favor of the river god."

Uhha was afraid, but she did not dare refuse. Miranda fumbled with the ancient lock for several minutes before it at last gave to the worn key the girl had brought. Then he snapped the padlock again and carrying the key with him crawled toward the entrance.

"Get me weapons," he whispered to the girl and Uhha departed through the shadows of the village street. Miranda knew that she was terrified but was confident that this very terror would prove the means of bringing her back to him with the weapons. Nor was he wrong, for scarce five minutes had elapsed before Uhha had returned with a quiver of arrows, a bow and a stout knife.

"Now lead me to the gate," commanded Esteban.

Keeping out of the main street and as much in rear of the huts as possible Uhha led the fugitive toward the village gates. It surprised her a little that he, a river devil, should not know how to unlock and open them, for she had thought that river devils were all-wise; but she did as he bid and showed him how the great bar could be withdrawn, and helped him push the gates open enough to permit him to pass through. Beyond was the clearing that led to the river, on either hand rose the giants of the jungle. It was very dark out there and Esteban Miranda suddenly discovered that his new-found liberty had its drawbacks. To go forth alone at night into the dark, mysterious jungle filled him with a nameless dread.

Uhha drew back from the gates. She had done her part and saved the village from destruction. Now she wished to close the gates again and hasten back to the hut of her father, there to lie trembling in nervous excitement and terror against the morning that would reveal to the village the escape of the river devil.

Esteban reached forth and took her by the arm. "Come," he said, "and receive your reward."

Uhha shrank away from him. "Let me go!" she cried. "I am afraid."

But Esteban was afraid, too, and he had decided that the company of this little Negro girl would be better than no company at all in the depths of the lonely jungle. Possibly when daylight came he would let her go back to her people, but tonight he shuddered at the thought of entering the jungle without human companionship.

Uhha tried to tear herself free from his grasp. She struggled like a little lion cub, and at last would have raised her voice in a wild scream for help had not Miranda suddenly clapped his palm across her mouth, lifted her bodily from the ground and running swiftly across the clearing disappeared into the jungle.

Behind them the warriors of Obebe the cannibal slept in peaceful ignorance of the sudden tragedy that had entered the life of little Uhha and before them, far out in the jungle, a lion roared thunderously.

2

THREE persons stepped from the veranda of Lord Greystoke's African bungalow and walked slowly toward the gate along a rose-embowered path that swung in a graceful curve through the well-ordered, though unpretentious, grounds surrounding the ape-man's rambling, one-story home. There were two men and a woman, all in khaki, the older man carrying a flier's helmet and a pair of goggles in one hand. He was smiling quietly as he listened to the younger man.

"You wouldn't be doing this now if mother were here," said the latter, "she would never permit it."

"I'm afraid you are right, my son," replied Tarzan; "but only this one flight alone and then I'll promise not to go up again until she returns. You have said yourself that I am an apt pupil and if you are any sort of an instructor you should have perfect confidence in me after having said that I was perfectly competent to pilot a ship alone. Eh, Meriem, isn't that true?" he demanded of the young woman.

She shook her head. "Like My Dear, I am always afraid for you, *mon pere*," she replied. "You take such risks that one would think you considered yourself immortal. You should be more careful."

The younger man threw his arm about his wife's shoulders. "Meriem is right," he said; "you *should* be more careful, Father."

Tarzan shrugged. "If you and mother had your way my nerves and muscles would have atrophied long since. They were given me to use and I intend using them—with discretion. Doubtless I shall be old and useless soon enough, and long enough, as it is."

A child burst suddenly from the bungalow, pursued by a perspiring governess, and raced to Meriem's side.

"Muvver," he cried, "Dackie doe? Dackie doe?"

"Let him come along," urged Tarzan.

"Dare!" exclaimed the boy, turning triumphantly upon the governess; "Dackie do doe yalk!"

Out on the level plain, that stretched away from the bunga-low to the distant jungle the verdant masses and deep shadows of which were vaguely discernible to the northwest, lay a bi-plane, in the shade of which lolled two Waziri warriors who had been trained by Korak, the son of Tarzan, in the duties of mechanicians, and, later, to pilot the ship themselves; a fact that had not been without weight in determining Tarzan of the Apes to perfect himself in the art of flying, since, as chief of the Waziri, it was not mete that the lesser warriors of his tribe should excel him in any particular. Adjusting his helmet and goggles Tarzan climbed into the cockpit.

"Better take me along," advised Korak.

Tarzan shook his head, smiling good-naturedly.

"Then one of the boys, here," urged his son. "You might develop some trouble that would force you to make a landing and if you have no mechanician along to make repairs what are you going to do?"

"Walk," replied the ape-man. "Turn her over, Andua!" he directed one of the blacks.

A moment later the ship was bumping over the veldt, from which, directly, it rose in smooth and graceful flight, circled, climbing to a greater altitude, and then sped away in an air line, while on the ground below the six strained their eyes until the wavering speck that it had dwindled to disappeared entirely from their view.

"Where do you suppose he is going?" asked Meriem.

Korak shook his head. "He isn't supposed to be going anywhere in particular," he replied; "just making his first practice flight alone; but, knowing him as I do, I wouldn't be surprised to learn that he had taken it into his head to fly to London and see mother."

"But he could never do it!" cried Meriem.

"No ordinary man could, with no more experience than he has had; but then, you will have to admit, father is no ordinary man."

For an hour and a half Tarzan flew without altering his course and without realizing the flight of time or the great distance he had covered, so delighted was he with the ease with which he controlled the ship, and so thrilled by this new power that gave him the freedom and mobility of the birds, the only denizens of his beloved jungle that he ever had had cause to envy.

Presently, ahead, he discerned a great basin, or what might better be described as a series of basins, surrounded by wooded hills, and immediately he recognized to the left of it the winding Ugogo; but the country of the basins was new to him and he was puzzled. He recognized, simultaneously, another fact; that he was over a hundred miles from home, and he determined to put back at once; but the mystery of the basins lured him on—he could not bring himself to return home without a closer view of them. Why was it that he had never come upon this country in his many wanderings? Why had he never even heard of it from the natives living within easy access to it. He dropped to a lower level the better to inspect the basins, which now appeared to him as a series of shallow craters of long extinct volcanoes. He saw forests, lakes and rivers, the very existence of which he had never dreamed, and then quite suddenly he discovered a solution of the seeming mystery that there should exist in a country with which he was familiar so large an area of which he had been in total ignorance, in common with the natives of the country surrounding it. He recognized it now—the so-called Great Thorn Forest. For years he had been familiar with that impenetrable thicket that was supposed to cover a vast area of territory into which only the smallest of animals might venture, and now he saw it was but a relatively narrow fringe encircling a pleasant, habitable country, but a fringe so cruelly barbed as to have forever protected the secret that it held from the eyes of man.

Tarzan determined to circle the long hidden land of mystery before setting the nose of his ship toward home, and, to obtain a closer view, he accordingly dropped nearer the earth. Beneath him was a great forest and beyond that an open veldt that ended at the foot of precipitous, rocky hills. He saw that absorbed as he had been in the strange, new country he had permitted the plane to drop too low. Coincident with the realization and before he could move the control within his hand, the ship touched the leafy crown of some old monarch of the jungle, veered, swung completely around and crashed downward through the foliage amidst the snapping and rending of broken branches and the splintering of its own woodwork. Just for a second this noise and then silence.

Along a forest trail slouched a mighty creature, manlike in its physical attributes, yet vaguely inhuman; a great brute that walked erect upon two feet and carried a club in one horny, calloused hand. Its long hair fell, unkempt, about its shoulders, and there was hair upon its chest and a little upon its arms and legs, though no more than is found upon many males of civilized races. A strip of hide about its waist supported the ends of a narrow G-string as well as numerous rawhide strands to the lower ends of which were fastened round stones from one to two inches in diameter. Close to each stone were attached several small feathers, for the most part of brilliant hues. The strands supporting the stones being fastened to the belt at intervals of one to two inches and the strands themselves being about eighteen inches long the whole formed a skeleton skirt, fringed with round stones and feathers, that fell almost to the creature's knees. Its large feet were bare and its white skin tanned to a light brown by exposure to the elements. The illusion of great size was suggested more by the massiveness of the shoulders and the development of the muscles of the back and arms than by height, though the creature measured close to six feet. Its face was massive, with a broad nose, and a wide, full-lipped mouth; the eyes, of normal size, were set beneath heavy, beetling brows, topped by a wide, low forehead. As it walked it flapped its large, flat ears and occasionally moved rapidly portions of its skin on various parts of its head and body to dislodge flies, as you have seen a horse do with the muscles along its sides and flanks.

It moved silently, its dark eyes constantly on the alert, while the flapping ears were often momentarily stilled as the woman listened for sounds of quarry or foe.

She stopped now, her ears bent forward, her nostrils, ex-

panded, sniffing the air. Some scent or sound that our dead
sensitory organs could not have perceived had attracted her
attention. Warily she crept forward along the trail until, at
a turning, she saw before her a figure lying face downward
in the path. It was Tarzan of the Apes. Unconscious he lay
while above him the splintered wreckage of his plane was
wedged among the branches of the great tree that had caused
its downfall.

The woman gripped her club more firmly and approached.
Her expression reflected the puzzlement the discovery of this
strange creature had engendered in her elementary mind, but
she evinced no fear. She walked directly to the side of the
prostrate man, her club raised to strike; but something stayed
her hand. She knelt beside him and fell to examining his clothing. She turned him over on his back and placed one of her
ears above his heart. Then she fumbled with the front of his
shirt for a moment and suddenly taking it in her two mighty
hands tore it apart. Again she listened, her ear this time against
his naked flesh. She arose and looked about, sniffing and listening, then she stooped and lifting the body of the ape-man she
swung it lightly across one of her broad shoulders and continued along the trail in the direction she had been going. The
trail, winding through the forest, broke presently from the
leafy shade into an open, parklike strip of rolling land that
stretched at the foot of rocky hills, and, crossing this, disappeared within the entrance of a narrow gorge, eroded by the
elements from the native sandstone fancifully as the capri-
cious architecture of a dream, among whose grotesque domes
and miniature rocks the woman bore her burden.

A half mile from the entrance to the gorge the trail entered
a roughly circular amphitheater, the precipitous walls of which
were pierced by numerous cave-mouths before several of
which squatted creatures similar to that which bore Tarzan
into this strange, savage environment.

As she entered the amphitheater all eyes were upon her, for
their large, sensitive ears had warned them of her approach
long before she had arrived within scope of their vision. Immediately they beheld her and her burden several of them arose
and came to meet her. All females, these, similar in physique
and scant garb to the captor of the ape-man, though differing
in proportions and physiognomy as do the individuals of all
races differ from their fellows. They spoke no words nor
uttered any sounds, nor did she whom they approached, as she
moved straight along her way which was evidently directed
toward one of the cave-mouths, but she gripped her bludgeon

firmly and swung it to and fro, while her eyes, beneath their scowling brows, kept sullen surveillance upon the every move of her fellows.

She had approached close to the cave, which was quite evidently her destination, when one of those who followed her darted suddenly forward and clutched at Tarzan. With the quickness of a cat the woman dropped her burden, turned upon the temerarious one, and swinging her bludgeon with lightning-like celerity felled her with a heavy blow to the head, and then, standing astride the prostrate Tarzan, she glared about her like a lioness at bay, questioning dumbly who would be next to attempt to wrest her prize from her; but the others slunk back to their caves, leaving the vanquished one lying, unconscious, in the hot sand and the victor to shoulder her burden, undisputed, and continue her way to her cave, where she dumped the ape-man unceremoniously upon the ground just within the shadow of the entranceway, and, squatting beside him, facing outward that she might not be taken unaware by any of her fellows, she proceeded to examine her find minutely. Tarzan's clothing either piqued her curiosity or aroused her disgust, for she began almost immediately to divest him of it, and having had no former experience of buttons and buckles, she tore it away by main force. The heavy, cordovan boots troubled her for a moment, but finally their seams gave way to her powerful muscles.

Only the diamond-studded, golden locket that had been his mother's she left untouched upon its golden chain about his neck.

For a moment she sat contemplating him and then she arose and tossing him once more to her shoulder she walked toward the center of the amphitheater, the greater portion of which was covered by low buildings constructed of enormous slabs of stone, some set on edge to form the walls while others, lying across these, constituted the roofs. Joined end to end, with occasional wings at irregular intervals running out into the amphitheater, they enclosed a rough oval of open ground that formed a large courtyard.

The several outer entrances to the buildings were closed with two slabs of stone, one of which, standing on edge, covered the aperture, while the other, leaning against the first upon the outside, held it securely in place against any efforts that might be made to dislodge it from the interior of the building.

To one of these entrances the woman carried her unconscious captive, laid him on the ground, removed the slabs that closed the aperture and dragged him into the dim and gloomy interior, where she deposited him upon the floor and clapped her palms together sharply three times with the result that there presently slouched into the room six or seven children of both sexes, who ranged in age from one year to sixteen or seventeen. The very youngest of them walked easily and seemed as fit to care for itself as the young of most lower orders at a similar age. The girls, even the youngest, were armed with clubs, but the boys carried no weapons either of offense or defense. At sight of them the woman pointed to Tarzan, struck her head with her clenched fist and then gestured toward herself, touching her breast several times with a calloused thumb. She made several other motions with her hands, so eloquent of meaning that one entirely unfamiliar with her sign language could almost guess their purport, then she turned and left the building, replaced the stones before the entrance, and slouched back to her cave, passing, apparently without notice, the woman she had recently struck down and who was now rapidly regaining consciousness.

As she took her seat before her cave-mouth her victim suddenly sat erect, rubbed her head for a moment and then, after looking about dully, rose unsteadily to her feet. For just an instant she swayed and staggered, but presently she mastered herself, and with only a glance at the author of her hurt moved off in the direction of her own cave. Before she had reached it her attention, together with that of all the others of this strange community, or at least of all those who were in the open, was attracted by the sound of approaching footsteps. She halted in her tracks, her great ears up-pricked, listening, her eyes directed toward the trail leading up from the valley. The others were similarly watching and listening and a moment later their vigil was rewarded by sight of another of their kind as she appeared in the entrance of the amphitheater. A huge creature this, even larger than she who captured the ape-man —broader and heavier, though little, if any, taller—carrying upon one shoulder the carcass of an antelope and upon the other the body of a creature that might have been half-human and half-beast, yet, assuredly, not entirely either the one or the other.

The antelope was dead, but not so the other creature. It wriggled weakly—its futile movements could not have been termed struggles—as it hung, its middle across the bare brown shoulder of its captor, its arms and legs dangling limply before and behind, either in partial unconsciousness or in the paralysis of fear.

The woman who had brought Tarzan to the amphitheater rose and stood before the entrance of her cave. We shall have to call her The First Woman, for she had no name; in the muddy convolutions of her sluggish brain she never had sensed even the need for a distinctive specific appellation and among her fellows she was equally nameless, as were they, and so, that we may differentiate her from the others, we shall call her The First Woman, and, similarly, we shall know the creature that she felled with her bludgeon as The Second Woman, and she who now entered the amphitheater with a burden upon each shoulder, as The Third Woman. So The First Woman rose, her eyes fixed upon the newcomer, her ears up-pricked. And The Second Woman rose, and all the others that were in sight, and all stood glaring at The Third Woman who moved steadily along with her burden, her watchful eyes ever upon the menacing figures of her fellows. She was very large, this Third Woman, so for a while the others only stood and glared at her, but presently The First Woman took a step forward and turning, cast a long look at The Second Woman, and then she took another step forward and stopped and looked again at The Second Woman, and this time she pointed at herself, at The Second Woman and then at The Third Woman who now quickened her pace in the direction of her cave, for she understood the menace in the attitude of The First Woman. The Second Woman understood, too, and moved forward now with The First Woman. No word was spoken, no sound issued from those savage lips; lips that never had parted to a smile; lips that never had known laughter, nor ever would.

As the two approached her The Third Woman dropped her spoils in a heap at her feet, gripped her cudgel more firmly and prepared to defend her rights. The others, brandishing their own weapons, charged her. The remaining women were now but onlookers, their hands stayed, perhaps, by some ancient tribal custom that gauged the number of attackers by the quantity of spoil, awarding the right of contest to whoever initiated it. When The First Woman had been attacked by The Second Woman the others had all held aloof, for it had been The Second Woman that had advanced first to try conclusively for the possession of Tarzan. And now The Third Woman had come with two prizes, and since The First Woman and The Second Woman had stepped out to meet her the others had held back.

As the three women came together it seemed inevitable that The Third Woman would go down beneath the bludgeons of the others, but she warded both blows with the skill and celerity of a trained fencer and stepping quickly into the opening she had dealt The First Woman a terrific blow upon the head that stretched her motionless upon the ground, where a little pool of blood and brains attested the terrible strength of the wielder of the bludgeon the while it marked the savage, unmourned passing of The First Woman.

And now The Third Woman could devote her undivided attention to The Second Woman, but The Second Woman seeing the fate of her companion did not wait to discuss the matter further, and instead of remaining to continue the fight she broke and ran for the cave, while the creature that The Third Woman had been carrying along with the carcass of the antelope apparently believing that it saw a chance for escape while its captor was engaged with her assailants was crawling stealthily away in the opposite direction. Its attempt might have proved successful had the fight lasted longer; but the skill and ferocity of The Third Woman had terminated the whole thing in a matter of seconds, and now, turning about, she espied a portion of her prey seeking to escape and sprang quickly after it. As she did so The Second Woman wheeled and darted back to seize the carcass of the antelope, while the crawling fugitive leaped to its feet and raced swiftly down the trail that led through the mouth of the amphitheater toward the valley.

As the thing rose to its feet it became apparent that it was a man, or at least a male, and evidently of the same species as the women of this peculiar race, though much shorter and of proportionately lighter build. It stood about five feet in height, had a few hairs on its upper lip and chin, a much lower forehead than the women, and its eyes were set closer together. Its legs were much longer and more slender than those of the women, who seemed to have been designed for strength rather than speed, and the result was that it was apparent from the start that The Third Woman could have no hope of overhauling her escaping quarry, and then it was that the utility of the strange skirt of thongs and pebbles and feathers became apparent. Seizing one of the thongs she disengaged it easily and quickly from the girdle that supported them about her hips, and grasping the end of the thong between a thumb and forefinger she whirled it rapidly in a vertical plane until the feathered pebble at its end was moving with great rapidity— then she let go the thong. Like an arrow the missile sped toward the racing fugitive, the pebble, a fairly good-sized one as large as an English walnut, struck the man upon the back of his head dropping him, unconscious, to the ground. Then The

Third Woman turned upon The Second Woman who, by this time, had seized the antelope, and brandishing her bludgeon bore down upon her. The Second Woman, possessing more courage than good sense, prepared to defend her stolen flesh and took her stand, her bludgeon ready. As The Third Woman bore down upon her, a veritable mountain of muscle, The Second Woman met her with threatening cudgel, but so terrific was the blow dealt by her mighty adversary that her weapon, splintered, was swept from her hands and she found herself at the mercy of the creature she would have robbed. Evidently she knew how much of mercy she might expect. She did not fall upon her knees in an attitude of supplication—not she. Instead she tore a handful of the pebble-missiles from her girdle in a vain attempt to defend herself. Futilest of futilities! The huge, destroying bludgeon had not even paused, but swinging in a great circle fell crushingly upon the skull of The Second Woman.

The Third Woman paused and looked about questioningly as if to ask: "Is there another who wishes to take from me my antelope or my man? If so, let her step forward." But no one accepted the gage and presently the woman turned and walked back to the prostrate man. Roughly she jerked him to his feet and shook him. Consciousness was returning slowly and he tried to stand. His efforts, however, were a failure and so she threw him across her shoulder again and walked back to the dead antelope, which she flung to the opposite shoulder and, continuing her interrupted way to her cave, dumped the two unceremoniously to the ground. Here, in the cave-mouth, she kindled a fire, twirling a fire stick dexterously amidst dry tinder in a bit of hollowed wood, and cutting generous strips from the carcass of the antelope ate ravenously. While she was thus occupied the man regained consciousness and sitting up looked about, dazed. Presently his nostrils caught the aroma of the cooking meat and he pointed at it. The woman handed him the rude stone knife that she had tossed back to the floor of the cave and motioned toward the meat. The man seized the implement and was soon broiling a generous cut above the fire. Half-burned and half-raw as it was he ate it with seeming relish, and as he ate the woman sat and watched him. He was not much to look at, yet she may have thought him handsome. Unlike the women, who wore no ornaments, the man had bracelets and anklets as well as a necklace of teeth and pebbles, while in his hair, which was wound into a small knot above his forehead, were thrust several wooden skewers ten or twelve inches long, which protruded in various directions in a horizontal plane.

When the man had eaten his fill the woman rose and seizing him by the hair dragged him into the cave. He scratched and bit at her, trying to escape, but he was no match for his captor.

Upon the floor of the amphitheater, before the entrances to the caves, lay the bodies of The First Woman and The Second Woman and black upon them swarmed the circling scavengers of the sky. Ska, the vulture, was first always to the feast.

3

WITHIN the dim interior of the strange rocky chamber where he had been so ruthlessly deposited, Tarzan immediately became the center of interest to the several Alali young that crowded about him. They examined him carefully, turned him over, pawed him, pinched him, and at last one of the young males, attracted by the golden locket removed it from the ape-man's neck and placed it about his own. Lowest, perhaps, in the order of human evolution nothing held their interest overlong, with the result that they soon tired of Tarzan and trooped out into the sunlit courtyard, leaving the ape-man to regain consciousness as best he could, or not at all. It was immaterial to them which he did. Fortunately for the Lord of the Jungle the fall through the roof of the forest had been broken by the fortuitous occurrence of supple branches directly in the path of his descent, with the happy result that he suffered only from a slight concussion of the brain. Already he was slowly regaining consciousness, and not long after the Alali young had left him his eyes opened, rolled dully inspecting the dim interior of his prison, and closed again. His breathing was normal and when again he opened his eyes it was as though he had emerged from a deep and natural slumber, the only reminder of his accident being a dull aching of the head.

Sitting up, he looked about him, his eyes gradually accustoming themselves to the dim light of the chamber. He found himself in a rude shelter constructed of great slabs of rock. A single opening led into what appeared to be another similar chamber the interior of which, however, was much lighter than that in which he lay. Slowly he rose to his feet and crossed to the opening. Across the second chamber he beheld another doorway leading into the fresh air and the sunshine. Except for filthy heaps of dead grasses on the floor both the rooms were unfurnished and devoid of any suggestion that they were utilized as places of human habitation. From the second doorway, to which he crossed, he looked out upon a narrow courtyard walled by great slabs of stone, the lower ends of which, embedded in the ground, caused them to remain erect. Here he saw the young Alali squatting about, some in the sun, others in the shadow. Tarzan looked at them in evident puzzlement. What were they? What was this place in which he was, all too evidently, incarcerated? Were these his keepers or were they his fellow prisoners? How had he come hither?

Running his fingers through his shock of black hair in a characteristic gesture of perplexity, he shook his head. He recalled the unfortunate termination of the flight; he even remembered falling through the foliage of the great tree; but beyond that all was blank. He stood for a moment examining the Alali, who were all-unconscious of his near presence or his gaze upon them, and then he stepped boldly out into the courtyard before them, as a lion, fearless, ignores the presence of jackals.

Immediately they saw him, they rose and clustered about him, the girls pushing the boys aside and coming boldly close, and Tarzan spoke to them, first in one native dialect and then in another, but they seemed not to understand, for they made no reply, and then, as a last resort, he addressed them in the primitive language of the great apes, the language of Manu the monkey, the first language that Tarzan had learned when, as a babe, he suckled at the hairy breast of Kala, the she-ape, and listened to the gutturals of the savage members of the tribe of Kerchak; but again his auditors made no response—at least no audible response, though they moved their hands and shoulders and bodies, and jerked their heads in what the ape-man soon recognized as a species of sign language, nor did they utter any vocal sounds that might indicate that they were communicating with one another through the medium of a spoken language. Presently they again lost interest in the newcomer and resumed their indolent lounging about the walls of the courtyard while Tarzan paced to and fro its length, his keen eye searching for whatever avenue of escape chance might provide, and he saw it in the height of the walls, to the top of which a long, running jump would take his outstretched fingers, he was sure; but not yet—he must wait for darkness to shield his attempt from those within the enclosure and those without. And as darkness approached the actions of the other occupants of the courtyard became noticeably altered; they walked back and forth, constantly passing and repassing the entrance to the shelter at the end of the courtyard, and occasionally entering the first room and often passing to the second room where they listened for a moment before the great slab that closed the outer aperture; then back into the courtyard again and back and forth in restless movement. Finally one stamped a foot upon the ground and this was taken up by the others until, in regular cadence, the thud, thud, thud of their naked feet must have been audible for some distance beyond the confines of their narrow prison yard.

Whatever this procedure might have been intended to accomplish, nothing, apparently, resulted, and presently one of the girls, her sullen face snarling in anger, seized her bludgeon more firmly in her two hands and stepping close to one of the walls began pounding violently upon one of its huge stone slabs. Instantly the other girls followed her example, while the young males continued beating time with their heels.

For a while Tarzan was puzzled for an explanation of their behavior, but it was his own stomach that at last suggested an answer—the creatures were hungry and were attempting to attract the attention of their jailers; and their method of doing so suggested something else, as well, something of which his past brief experience with them had already partially convinced him—the creatures were without speech, even totally unvocal, perhaps.

The girl who had started the pounding upon the wall suddenly stopped and pointed at Tarzan. The others looked at him and then back at her, whereupon she pointed at her bludgeon and then at Tarzan again, after which she acted out a little pantomime, very quicky, very briefly, but none the less realistically. The pantomime depicted the bludgeon falling upon Tarzan's head, following which the pantomimist, assisted by her fellows, devoured the ape-man. The bludgeons ceased to fall upon the wall; the heels no longer smote the earth; the assemblage was interested in the new suggestion. They eyed Tarzan hungrily. The mother who should have brought them food, The First Woman, was dead. They did not know this; all they knew was that they were hungry and that The First Woman had brought them no food since the day before. They were not cannibals. Only in the last stages of hunger, would they have devoured one another, even as shipwrecked sailors of civilized races have been known to do; but they did not look upon the stranger as one of their own kind. He was as unlike them as some of the other creatures that The First Woman had brought them to feed upon. It was no more wrong to devour him than it would have been to devour an antelope. The thought, however, would not have occurred to most of them; the older girl it was who had suggested it to them, nor would it have occurred to her had there been other food, for she knew that he had not been brought here for that purpose— he had been brought as the mate of The First Woman, who in common with the other women of this primitive race hunted a new mate each season among the forests and the jungles where the timid males lived their solitary lives except for the brief weeks that they were held captive in the stone corrals of the dominant sex, and where they were treated with great brutality and contempt even by the children of their temporary spouses.

Sometimes they managed to escape, though rarely, but eventually they were turned loose, since it was easier to hunt a new one the following season than to feed one in captivity for a whole year. There was nothing approximating love in the family relations of these savage half-brutes. The young, conceived without love, knowing not their own fathers, possessed not even an elemental affection for one another, nor for any other living thing. A certain tie bound them to their savage mothers, at whose breasts they suckled for a few short months and to whom they looked for food until they were sufficiently developed to go forth into the forests and make their own kills or secure whatever other food bountiful Nature provided for them.

Somewhere between the ages of fifteen and seventeen the young males were liberated and chased into the forest, after which their mothers knew them not from any other male and at a similar age the females were taken to the maternal cave, where they lived, accompanying their mothers on the daily hunt, until they had succeeded in capturing a first mate. After that they took up their abodes in separate caves and the tie between parent and child was cut as cleanly as though it never had existed, and they might, the following season, even become rivals for the same man, or at any time quarrel to the death over the spoils of the chase.

The building of the stone shelters and corrals in which the children and the males were kept was the only community activity in which the women engaged and this work they were compelled to do alone, since the men would have escaped into

the forest at the first opportunity had they been released from
the corrals to take part in the work of construction, while the
children as soon as they had become strong enough to be of
any assistance would doubtless have done likewise; but the
great shes were able to accomplish their titanic labors alone.

Equipped by nature with mighty frames and thews of steel
they quarried the great slabs from a sidehill overlooking the
amphitheater, slid them to the floor of the little valley and
pulled and pushed them into position by main strength and
awkwardness, as the homely saying of our forefathers has it.

Fortunately for them it was seldom necessary to add to the
shelters and corrals already built since the high rate of mor-
tality among the females ordinarily left plenty of vacant enclosures for maturing girls. Jealousy, greed, the hazards of the
hunt, the contingencies of intertribal wars all took heavy toll
among the adult shes. Even the despised male, fighting for his
freedom, sometimes slew his captor.

The hideous life of the Alalus was the natural result of the
unnatural reversal of sex dominance. It is the province of the
male to initiate love and by his masterfulness to inspire first
respect, then admiration in the breast of the female he seeks
to attract. Love itself developed after these other emotions.
The gradually increasing ascendency of the female Alalus over
the male eventually prevented the emotions of respect and
admiration for the male from being aroused, with the result
that love never followed.

Having no love for her mate and having become a more
powerful brute, the savage Alalus woman soon came to treat
the members of the opposite sex with contempt and brutality
with the result that the power, or at least the desire, to initiate
love ceased to exist in the heart of the male—he could not love
a creature he feared and hated, he could not respect or admire
the unsexed creatures that the Alali women had become, and
so he fled into the forests and the jungles and there the dominant females hunted him lest their race perish from the earth.

It was the offspring of such savage and perverted creatures
that Tarzan faced, fully aware of their cannibalistic intentions.
The males did not attack him at once, but busily engaged themselves in fetching dry grass and small pieces of wood from
one of the covered chambers, and while the three girls, one of
them scarce seven years of age, approached the ape-man warily
with ready bludgeons, they prepared a fire over which they expected soon to be broiling juicy cuts from the strange creature
that their hairy dam had brought them.

One of the males, a lad of sixteen, held back, making excited

signs with hands, head and body. He appeared to be trying to
dissuade or prevent the girls from the carrying-out of their
plan, he even appealed to the other boys for backing, but they
merely glanced at the girls and continued their culinary preparations. At last however, as the girls were deliberately approaching the ape-man he placed himself directly in their path
and attempted to stop them. Instantly the three little demons
swung their bludgeons and sprang forward to destroy him.
The boy dodged, plucked several of the feathered stones from
his girdle and flung them at his assailants. So swift and so accurate did the missiles speed that two girls dropped, howling, to
the ground. The third missed, striking one of the other boys
on the temple, killing him instantly. He was the youth who
had stolen Tarzan's locket, which, being like all his fellow
males a timid creature, he had kept continually covered by a
palm since the ape-man's return to consciousness had brought
him out into the courtyard among them.

The older girl, nothing daunted, leaped forward, her face
hideous in a snarl of rage. The boy cast another stone at her
and then turned and ran toward the ape-man. What reception
he expected he himself probably did not know. Perhaps it
was the recrudescence of a long dead emotion of fellowship
that prompted him to place himself at Tarzan's side—possibly
Tarzan himself in whom loyalty to kind was strong had in-
spired this reawakening of an atrophied soul-sense. However
that may be the fact remains that the boy came and stood at
Tarzan's side while the girl, evidently sensing danger to herself in this strange, new temerity of her brother, advanced
more cautiously.

In signs she seemed to be telling him what she would do to
him if he did not cease to interpose his weak will between her
and her gastronomic desires; but he signed back at her defiantly and stood his ground. Tarzan reached over and patted
him on the back, smiling. The boy bared his teeth horribly, but
it seemed evident that he was trying to return the ape-man's
smile. And now the girl was almost upon them. Tarzan was
quite at a loss as to how to proceed against her. His natural
chivalry restrained him from attacking her and made it seem
most repellant to injure her even in self-preservation; but he
knew that before he was done with her he might even possibly
have to kill her and so, while looking for an alternative, he
steeled himself for the deed he loathed; but yet he hoped to
escape without that.

The Third Woman, conducting her new mate from the cave
to the corral where she would keep him imprisoned for a week

or two, had heard the cadenced beating of naked heels and heavy bludgeons arising from the corral of The First Woman and immediately guessed their import. The welfare of the offspring of The First Woman concerned her not as an individual. Community instinct, however, prompted her to release them that they might search for food and their services not be lost to the tribe through starvation. She would not feed them, of course, as they did not belong to her, but she would open their prison gate and turn them loose to fend for themselves, to find food or not to find it, to survive or to perish according to the inexorable law of the survival of the fittest.

But The Third Woman took her time. Her powerful fingers entangled in the hair of her snarling spouse she dragged the protesting creature to her corral, removed the great slab from before the entrance, pushed the man roughly within, accelerating his speed with a final kick, replaced the slab and turned leisurely toward the nearby corral of The First Woman. Removing the stone door she passed through the two chambers and entered the corral at the moment that the oldest girl was advancing upon Tarzan. Pausing by the entranceway she struck her bludgeon against the stone wall of the shelter, evidently to attract the attention of those within the corral. Instantly all looked in her direction. She was the first adult female, other than their own dam, that the children of The First Woman had seen. They shrunk from her in evident terror. The youth at Tarzan's side slunk behind the ape-man, nor did Tarzan wonder at their fear. The Third Woman was the first adult Alalus he had seen, since all of the time that he had been in the hands of The First Woman he had been unconscious.

The girl who had been threatening him with her great club seemed now to have forgotten him, and instead stood with snarling face and narrowed eyes confronting the newcomer. Of all the children she seemed the least terrified.

The ape-man scrutinized the huge, brutish female standing at the far end of the corral with her savage eyes upon him. She had not seen him before as she had been in the forest hunting at the time that The First Woman had brought her prize back to the amphitheater. She had not known that The First Woman had any male in her corral other than her own spawn. Here, indeed, was a prize. She would remove him to her own corral. With this idea in mind, and knowing that, unless he succeeded in dodging past her and reaching the entranceway ahead of her, he could not escape her, she moved very slowly toward him, ignoring now the other occupants of the corral.

Tarzan, not guessing her real purpose, thought that she was about to attack him as a dangerous alien in the sacred precincts of her home. He viewed her great bulk, her enormous muscular development and the huge bludgeon swinging in her hamlike hand and compared them with his own defenseless nakedness.

To the jungle-born flight from useless and uneven combat carries with it no stigma of cowardice, and not only was Tarzan of the Apes jungle-born and jungle-raised, but the stripping of his clothes from him had now, as always before, stripped also away the thin and unnatural veneer of his civilization. It was, then, a savage beast that faced the oncoming Alalus woman—a cunning beast as well as a powerful one—a beast that knew when to fight and when to flee.

Tarzan cast a quick glance behind him. There crouched the Alalus lad, trembling in fear. Beyond was the rear wall of the corral, one of the great stone slabs of which tilted slightly outward. Slow is the mind of man, slower his eye by comparison with the eye and the mind of the trapped beast seeking escape. So quick was the ape-man that he was gone before The Third Woman had guessed that he was contemplating flight, and with him had gone the eldest Alalus boy.

Wheeling, all in a single motion Tarzan had swung the young male to his shoulder, leaped swiftly the few paces that had separated him from the rear wall of the corral, and, catlike, run up the smooth surface of the slightly tilted slab until his fingers closed upon the top, drawn himself over without a single backward glance, dropped the youth to the ground upon the opposite side, following him so quickly that they alighted almost together. Then he glanced about. For the first time he saw the natural amphitheater and the caves before several of which women still squatted. It would soon be dark. The sun was dropping behind the crest of the western hills. Tarzan saw but a single avenue of escape—the opening at the lower end of the amphitheater through which the trail led down into the valley and the forest below. Toward this he ran, followed by the youth.

Presently a woman, sitting before the entrance of her cave, saw him. Seizing her cudgel she leaped to her feet and gave immediate chase. Attracted by her another and another took up the pursuit, until five or six of them thundered along the trail.

The youth, pointing the way, raced swiftly ahead of the ape-man, but swift as he was, he could not outdistance the lithe muscles that had so often in the past carried their master safely from the swift rush of a maddened Numa, or won him a meal against the fleetness of Bara the deer. The heavy, lumbering women behind them had no chance of overhauling this swift pair if they were to depend entirely upon speed, but that they had no intention of doing. They had their stone missiles with which, almost from birth, they had practiced until approximate perfection was attained by each in casting them at either stationary or moving targets. But it was growing dark, the trail twisted and turned and the speed of the quarry made them elusive marks at which to cast an accurate missile that would be so timed as to stun rather than to kill. Of course more often than not a missile intended to stun did actually kill, but the quarry must take that chance. Instinct warned the women against killing the males, though it did not warn them against treating them with the utmost brutality. Had Tarzan realized why the women were pursuing him he would have run even faster than he did, and when the missiles began to fly past his head perhaps he did accelerate his speed a trifle.

Soon the ape-man reached the forest and as though he had dissolved into thin air disappeared from the astonished view of his pursuers, for now, indeed, was he in his own element. While they looked for him upon the ground he swung swiftly through the lower terraces, keeping in view the Alalus boy racing along the trail beneath him.

But with the man escaped, the women stopped and turned back toward their caves. The youth they did not want. For two or three years he would roam the forests unmolested by his own kind, and if he escaped the savage beasts and the spears and arrows of the ant people he would come to man's estate and be fair prey for any of the great shes during the mating season. For the time being, at least, he would lead a comparatively safe and happy existence.

His chances of survival had been materially lessened by his early escape into the forest. Had The First Woman lived she would have kept him safely within the walls of her corral for another year at least, when he would have been better fitted to cope with the dangers and emergencies of the savage life of the forest and the jungle.

The boy, his keen ears telling him that the women had given up the pursuit, halted and looked back for the strange creature that had freed him from the hated corral, but he could see only a short distance through the darkness of the growing forest night. The stranger was not in sight. The youth pricked up his great ears and listened intently. There was no sound of human footsteps other than the rapidly diminishing ones of the retreating women. There were other sounds, however, unfamiliar forest sounds that filled his muddy brain with vague terrors—sounds that came from the surrounding underbrush; sounds that came from the branches above his head, and, too, there were terrifying odors.

Darkness, complete and impenetrable, had closed in upon him with a suddenness that left him trembling. He could almost feel it weighing down upon him, crushing him and at the same time leaving him exposed to nameless terrors. He looked about him and could see naught, so that it seemed to him that he was without eyes, and being without a voice he could not call out either to frighten his enemies or attract the attention of the strange creature that had befriended him, and whose presence had so strangely aroused in his own breast an inexplicable emotion—a pleasurable emotion. He could not explain it; he had no word for it who had no word for anything, but he felt it and it still warmed his bosom and he wished in his muddy way that he could make a noise that would attract that strange creature to him again. He was lonely and much afraid.

A crackling of the bushes nearby aroused him to new and more intimate terror. Something large was approaching through the black night. The youth stood with his back against a great tree. He dared not move. He sniffed but what movement of the air there was took course from him in the direction of the thing that was creeping upon him out of the terrible forest, and so he could not identify it; but his instinct told him that the creature had identified him and was doubtless creeping closer to leap upon him and devour him.

He knew naught of lions, unless instinct carries with it a picture of the various creatures of which the denizens of the wild are instinctively afraid. In all his life he had never been outside the corral of The First Woman and as his people are without speech his dam could have told him nothing of the outside world, yet when the lion roared he knew that it was a lion.

4

E STEBAN MIRANDA, clinging tightly to the wrist of little Uhha, crouched in the darkness of another forest twenty miles away and trembled as the thunderous notes of another lion reverberated through the jungle.

The girl felt the trembling of the body of the big man at her side and turned contemptuously upon him.

"You are not the river devil!" she cried. "You are afraid. You are not even Tarzan, for Khamis, my father, has told me that Tarzan is afraid of nothing. Let me go that I may climb a tree—only a coward or a fool would stand here dead with terror waiting for the lion to come and devour him. Let me go, I say!" and she attempted to wrench her wrist free from his grasp.

"Shut up!" he hissed. "Do you want to attract the lion to us?" But her words and struggles had aroused him from his paralysis and stooping he seized her and lifted her until she could grasp the lower branches of the tree beneath which they stood. Then, as she clambered to safety, he swung himself easily to her side.

Presently, higher up among the branches, he found a safer and more comfortable resting place, and there the two settled down to await the coming of the dawn, while below them Numa the lion prowled for a while, coughing and grunting, and occasionally voicing a deep roar that shook the jungle.

When daylight came at last the two, exhausted by a sleepless night, slipped to the ground. The girl would have delayed, hoping that the warriors of Obebe might overtake them; but the man harbored a fear rather than a hope of the same contingency and was, therefore, for hastening on as rapidly as possible that he might put the greatest possible distance between himself and the black cannibal chief.

He was completely lost, having not the remotest idea of where he should search for a reasonably good trail to the coast, nor, at present, did he care; his one wish being to escape recapture by Obebe, and so he elected to move northward, keeping always an eye open for any indication of a well-marked trail toward the west. Eventually, he hoped, he might discover a village of friendly natives who would aid him upon his journey toward the coast, and so the two moved as rapidly as they could in a northerly direction, their way skirting The Great Thorn Forest along the eastern edge of which they traveled.

The sun beating down upon the hot corral of The First Woman found it deserted of life. Only the corpse of a youth lay sprawled where it had fallen the previous evening. A speck appeared in the distant blue. It grew larger as it approached until it took upon itself the form of a bird gliding easily upon motionless wings. Nearer and nearer it came, now and again winging great, slow circles, until at last it swung above the corral of The First Woman. Once again it circled and then dropped to earth within the enclosure—Ska, the vulture, had come. Within the hour the body of the youth was hidden by a mantle of the great birds. It was a two-days feast, and when they left, only the clean picked bones remained, and entangled about the neck of one of the birds was a golden chain from which depended a diamond-encrusted locket. Ska fought the bauble that swung annoyingly beneath him when he flew and impeded his progress when he walked upon the ground, but it was looped twice about his neck and he was unable to dislodge it, and so he winged away across The Great Thorn Forest, the bright gems gleaming and scintillating in the sun.

Tarzan of the Apes, after eluding the women that had chased him and the Alalus youth into the forest, halted in the tree beneath which the frightened son of The First Woman had come to a terrified pause. He was there, close above him, when Numa charged, and reaching quickly down had seized the youth by the hair and dragged him to safety as the lion's raking talons embraced thin air beneath the feet of the Alalus.

The following day the ape-man concerned himself seriously in the hunt for food, weapons and apparel. Naked and unarmed as he was it might have gone hard with him had he been other than Tarzan of the Apes, and it might have gone hard with the Alalus had it not been for the ape-man. Fruits and nuts Tarzan found, and birds' eggs, but he craved meat and for meat he hunted assiduously, not alone because of the flesh of the kill, but for the skin and the gut and the tendons, that he could use in the fabrication of the things he required for the safety and comfort of his primitive existence.

As he searched for the spoor of his prey he searched also for the proper woods for a spear and for bow and arrows, nor were they difficult to find in this forest of familiar trees, but the day was almost done before the gentle wind, up which he had been hunting, carried to his sensitive nostrils the scent spoor of Bara the deer.

Swinging into a tree he motioned the Alalus to follow him, but so inept and awkward was the creature that Tarzan was compelled to drag him to a place among the branches, where, by signs, he attempted to impart to him the fact that he wished him to remain where he was, watching the materials that the ape-man had collected for his weapons, while the latter continued the hunt alone.

That the youth understood him he was not at all sure, but at least he did not follow when Tarzan swung off silently through the branches of the forest along the elusive trail of the ruminant, the scent of which was always translated to the foster son of Kala the she-ape as Bara the deer, though in fact, as practically always, the animal was an antelope. But strong are the impressions of childhood and since that long-gone day up-on which he had pored over the colored alphabet primer in the far-off cabin of his dead father beside the landlocked harbor on the West Coast, and learned that "D stands for Deer," and had admired the picture of the pretty animal, the thing that most closely resembled it, with which he was familiar in his daily life, the antelope, became for him then, and always remained, Bara the deer.

To approach sufficiently close to Bara to bring him down with spear or arrow requires cunning and woodcraft far be-yond the limited range of civilized man's ability. The native hunter loses more often than he wins in this game of wits and percipience. Tarzan, however, must excel them both and the antelope, too, in the keenness of his perceptive faculties and in coordination of mind and muscles if he were to lay Bara low with only the weapons with which nature had endowed him.

As Tarzan sped silently through the jungle, guided by his nostrils, in the direction of Bara the deer increasing strength of the familiar effluvium apprised him that not far ahead Bara foregathered in numbers, and the mouth of the savage ape-man watered in anticipation of the feast that but awaited his com-ing. And as the strength of the scent increased, more warily went the great beast, moving silently, a shadow among the shadows of the forest, until he came at last to the verge of an opening in which he saw a dozen antelope grazing.

Squatting motionless upon a low hanging limb the ape-man watched the movements of the herd against the moment that one might come close enough to the encircling trees to give a charge at least a shadow of a chance for success. To wait patiently, oftentimes hour upon hour, for the quarry to expose itself to more certain death is a part of the great game that the hunters of the wild must play. A single ill-timed or thoughtless movement may send the timorous prey scampering off into the far distance from which they may not return for days.

To avoid this Tarzan remained in statuesque immobility waiting for chance to send one of the antelope within striking distance, and while he waited there came to his nostrils, faintly, the scent of Numa the lion. Tarzan scowled. He was down-wind from Bara and the lion was not between him and the ante-lope. It must, therefore, be upwind from the quarry as well as from himself; but why had not the sensitive nostrils of the

Herbivora caught the scent of their archenemy before it had
reached the ape-man; that they had not was evidenced by their
placidity as they grazed contentedly, their tails switching and
occasionally a head raised to look about with up-pricked ears
though with no symptom of the terror that would immediately
follow the discovery of Numa in their vicinity.

The ape-man concluded that one of those freaks of the air
currents that so often leaves a motionless pocket of air directly
in the path of the flow had momentarily surrounded the antelope, insulating them, as it were, from their immediate surroundings. And while he was thinking these things and wishing
that Numa would go away he was shocked to hear a sudden
crashing in the underbrush upon the opposite side of the clearing beyond the antelope, who were instantly upon the alert
and poised for flight. Almost simultaneously there broke into
view a young lion which, upon coming in sight of the antelope,
set up a terrific roaring as it charged. Tarzan could have torn
his hair in rage and disappointment. The blundering stupidity
of a young lion had robbed him of his meat—the ruminants
were scattering in all directions. The lion, charging futilely,
had lost his own meat and Tarzan's too; but wait! what was
this? A terrified buck, blind to all save the single thought of
escape from the talons of the dread carnivore, was bolting
straight for the tree in which Tarzan sat. As it came beneath
him a sleek brown body shot headforemost from the foliage,
steel fingers gripped the throat of the buck, strong teeth
fastened in its neck. The weight of the savage hunter carried
the quarry to its knees and before it could stumble to its feet
again a quick wrench with those powerful hands had twisted
and broken its neck.

Without a backward glance the ape-man threw the carcass
to his shoulder and leaped into the nearest tree. He had no need
to waste time in looking back to know what Numa would be
doing, for he realized that he had leaped upon Bara full in the
sight of the king of beasts. Scarce had he drawn himself to
safety ere the great cat crashed across the spot where he had
stood.

Numa, baffled, roared terribly as he returned to glare up at
the ape-man perched above him. Tarzan smiled.

"Son of Dango, the hyena," he taunted, "go hungry until you
learn to hunt," and casting a broken branch contemptuously in
the lion's face the ape-man vanished among the leafy branches
bearing his kill lightly across one broad shoulder.

It was still daylight when Tarzan returned to where the
Alalus was awaiting him. The youth had a small stone knife

and with this the ape-man hacked off a generous portion of the antelope for the whelp of The First Woman and another for himself. Into the raw flesh, hungrily, sank the strong white teeth of the English lord, while the Alalus youth, gazing at him in surprise, sought materials for fire making. Amused, Tarzan watched him until the other had succeeded in preparing his food as he thought it should be prepared—the outside burned to a cinder, the inside raw, yet it was cooked food and doubtless imparted to its partaker a feeling of great superiority over the low beasts that devoured their meat raw, just as though he had been a civilized epicure eating decaying game and putrid cheeses at some fashionable club in London.

Tarzan smiled as he thought how vague, after all, the line that separates primitive from civilized man in matters pertaining to their instincts and their appetites. Some of his French friends, with whom he was dining upon a certain occasion, were horrified when they learned that in common with many of the African tribes and the apes he ate catepillars, and they voiced their horror between mouthfuls of the snails they were eating with relish at the time. The provincial American scoffs at the French for eating frogs' legs, the while he munches upon the leg of a pig! The Esquimaux eat raw blubber, the Amazonians, both white and native, eat the contents of the stomachs of parrots and monkeys and consider them delicacies, the Chinese coolie asks not how his meat came by its death, nor how long since, and there is a man in New York, an estimable and otherwise harmless man, who eats Limburger cheese on Bartlett pears.

The following day, with sufficient meat to last them several days, Tarzan set to work upon his weapons and his loincloth. Showing the Alalus how to scrape the antelope hide with his stone knife, the ape-man set to work, with nothing more in the way of tools than bits of stone picked from the bed of a stream, to fashion weapons with which to cope successfully with the Alali women, the great carnivores and whatever other enemies time might reveal to him.

And as he worked he watched the Alalus youth and wondered of what use the poor creature could be to him in finding his way through the encircling thorn forest that he must pass to reach familiar country and the trail for home. That the poor thing was timid had been evidenced by its manner when fleeing from the Alali women and its terror when confronted by Numa. Its speechlessness made it useless as a companion and it was entirely without woodcraft other than a certain crude, instinctive kind that was of no use to Tarzan. But it had placed itself at his side during the altercation in the corral and although it could not have been of any help to him yet it had won a right to his consideration by its act. Moreover it was evident, quite evident, that the creature had attached itself to Tarzan and intended to remain with him.

An idea occurred to Tarzan as he worked upon his weapons and thought upon the Alalus—he would make similar weapons for the youth and teach him how to use them. He had seen that the crude weapons of the Alali would be no match against one armed with a bow and arrows, or even a good spear. Accurately they could not hope to throw their missiles as far as a good bowman could speed his shaft and their bludgeons were helpless in the face of a well-thrown spear.

Yes, he would make weapons for the youth and train him in their use and then he could be made of service in the hunt and, if necessary, in the fight, and as Tarzan of the Apes thought upon the matter the Alalus suddenly paused in his work and bent an ear close to the ground, then he lifted his head and turned his eyes upon Tarzan, pointing at him, at his ear, and then at the ground. The ape-man understood that he was to listen as the other had and when he did so he distinctly heard approaching footsteps resounding upon the hard-worn trail.

Gathering up his belongings he carried them high among the trees to a safe cache with the remnants of Bara the deer and then returning helped the youth into the tree beside him.

Slowly, already, the Alalus was becoming more at ease in the trees and could help himself to a greater extent in climbing into them, but he was still practically helpless in Tarzan's estimation.

The two had not long to wait before there swung down the trail one of the terrible women of the amphitheater, and behind her at ten or fifteen paces another, and behind the second a third. It was not often that they traveled thus, for theirs was a solitary existence, the Alali being almost devoid of gregarious instincts, yet they did occasionally start out upon their hunts together, especially when they were hunting some dangerous beast that had encroached upon their rights, or when, failing to collect sufficient men from the forest during the mating season, the unfortunate ones banded together to make a raid upon the corrals of a neighboring tribe.

The three, slouching along the trail, passed directly beneath the tree from which Tarzan and the youth watched them. The great, flat ears flapped lazily, the dark eyes wandered from side to side, and from time to time they moved rapidly the skin upon some portions of their bodies as they sought to dislodge annoying insects.

The two in the tree remained motionless while the three brute-women passed along down the trail to be presently lost to their view at a turning of the forest highway, then, after a short interval of listening, they descended to the ground and resumed their interrupted labors. The ape-man smiled as he idly pondered the events of the past few minutes—Tarzan of the Apes, Lord of the Jungle, hiding among the trees to escape the notice of three women! But such women! He knew little about them or their ways as yet, but what he did know was sufficient to convince him that they were as formidable foes as ever he had encountered and that while he remained weaponless he was no match against their great bludgeons and swift-thrown missiles.

The days passed; the ape-man and his silent companion perfected the weapons that would more easily give them food, the latter working mechanically, following the instructions of his master, until at last the time came when Tarzan and the Alalus were fully equipped and then they hunted together, the man training the youth in the use of bow and spear and the long grass rope that from boyhood had formed a unique feature of the ape-man's armament.

During these days of hunting there came over the Alalus youth, quite suddenly, a great change. It had been his habit to glide stealthily through the forest, stopping often to look this way and that, fearful, apparently, of every creature that roamed the shadowed trails; his one great fear the ferocious females of his kind; but suddenly all this changed as by magic. Slowly he was mastering the bow and the spear; with deep interest and a sense of awe and respect he had watched Tarzan bring down many animals, great and small, for food, and once he had seen him dispatch Sabor the lioness with a single thrust of his great spear when Sabor had caught the ape-man in a clearing too far from the sanctuary of his beloved trees, and then his own day came. He and Tarzan were hunting when the former disturbed a small herd of wild pigs, bringing down two with his arrows. The others scattered in all directions and one of these, a boar, sighting the Alalus, charged him. The youth was of a mind to flee, for ages of inherited instinct prompted him to flight. Always the male Alalus fled from danger, and between fleeing from carnivorous animals and from their own women they had become very swift, so swift that no dangerous enemy could overtake them—an Alalus man could be captured only by craft. He could have escaped the boar by flight and for an instant he was upon the verge of flight, but a sudden thought checked him—back flew his spear hand as the ape-man had taught him and then forward with all the weight of his body behind the cast. The boar was coming straight for him. The spear struck in front of the left shoulder and ranged downward through the heart. Horta the boar dropped in his tracks.

A new expression came into the eyes and spread over the countenance of the Alalus. He no longer wore that hunted expression; he no longer slunk through the forest casting fearful glances from side to side. Now he walked erect, boldly and with fearless mien, and, perhaps, instead of dreading the appearance of a female he rather courted the event. He was the personification of avenging manhood. Within him rankled countless ages of contemptuous treatment and abuse at the hands of his shes. Doubtless he never thought of the matter in this way at all, but the fact remained, and Tarzan realized it, that the first woman unfortunate enough to stumble upon this youth was going to get the surprise of her life.

And while Tarzan and the Alalus roamed the strange land hemmed in by The Great Thorn Forest and the ape-man sought for an avenue of escape, Esteban Miranda and little Uhha, daughter of Khamis the witch doctor, wandered along the forest's outer verge in search of a trail toward the west and the coast.

5

WITH doglike devotion the Alalus youth clung to Tarzan. The latter had mastered the meager sign language of his protégé giving them a means of communication that was adequate for all their needs. The former, gaining confidence with a growing familiarity with his new weapons, became more independent, with the result that the two more often separated for the hunt, thus insuring a more fully stocked larder.

It was upon one of these occasions that Tarzan came suddenly upon a strange sight. He had been following the scent spoor of Bara the deer when it was suddenly crossed by that of one of the great female Alali. That probably meant that another would attempt to rob him of his prey. The savage instinct of the jungle beast predominated in the guidance of the breech-clouted ape-man. It was not the polished Lord Greystoke of London whose snarling upper lip revealed two gleaming fighting fangs—it was a primordial hunting-brute about to be robbed of its quarry.

Taking to the trees he moved rapidly in the direction of the Alalus woman, but before he came within sight of her a new scent impinged upon his nostrils—a strange, new scent that puzzled him. It was the scent of man, yet strange and unfamiliar to a degree. Never before had anything like it arrested his attention. It was very faint and yet, somehow, he knew that it was close, and then, ahead of him, he heard voices, low musical voices, that came faintly to his ears; and though they were low and musical there was something in the quality and pitch of them that suggested excitement. Now Tarzan went more carefully, Bara, the deer, all but forgotten.

As he drew nearer he realized that there were many voices and much commotion and then he came upon a large plain that stretched away to distant hills, and in the foreground, not a hundred yards from him, he looked upon a sight that might well have caused him to doubt the veracity of his own eyes. The only familiar figure was a giant Alalus woman. Surrounding her was a horde of diminutive men—tiny white warriors—mounted upon what appeared to be a form of the Royal Antelope of the West Coast. Armed with lances and swords they repeatedly charged at the huge legs of the Alalus, who, backing slowly toward the forest, kicked viciously at her assailants and struck at them with her heavy bludgeon.

It quickly became evident to Tarzan that they were attempting to hamstring her and had they been successful they might easily have slain her then; but though there must have been fully a hundred of them their chances of success appeared small, since, with a single kick of her mighty foot the woman could lay low a dozen or more of her assailants at a time. Already fully half the force was *hors de combat*, their bodies with those of many of their mounts being scattered out onto the plain marking the trail of the combat up to the time that Tarzan had come upon the scene.

The courage of the survivors, however, filled Tarzan with admiration as he watched them hurl themselves upon almost certain death in their stubborn efforts to bring down the female, and then it was that the ape-man saw the reason, or the apparent reason, for the mad sacrifice of life—in her left hand the Alalus clutched one of the tiny warriors. It was to rescue him, evidently, that the others were maintaining this forlorn hope.

If the warriors filled Tarzan with admiration to scarcely a lesser extent did their courageous and agile mounts. Always had he thought of the Royal Antelope, the smallest known member of its family, as the most timid of creatures, but not so these cousins of theirs. Slightly larger, standing perhaps fifteen inches at the withers, they were in all other outward respects identical; yet, at the guidance of their riders, they leaped fearlessly into close range of those enormous feet and the great, slashing bludgeon. Perfectly reined were they, too; so perfectly that their muscles seemed to have coordinated with the minds of their riders. In and out they bounded, scarcely touching the ground before they were out of harm's way again. Ten or a dozen feet they covered at a leap, so that Tarzan wondered not only at their agility but at the almost marvelous riding ability of the warriors who could keep their seats so perfectly upon these leaping, bounding, turning, twisting mounts.

It was a pretty sight and an inspiring one, and however unreal it had at first appeared to him he was not long in realizing that he was looking upon a race of real pygmies—not members of the black tribe with which all African explorers are more or less familiar, but with that lost white race of diminutive men reference to which is occasionally to be found in ancient manuscript of travel and exploration, of myth and legend.

While the encounter interested him and he viewed it at first as a disinterested neutral he soon found his sympathies gravitating to the tiny warriors and when it became evident that the Alalus woman was going to make good her escape into the forest with her captive, the ape-man decided to take a hand in the affair himself.

As he stepped from the concealment of the forest the little warriors were the first to see him. Evidently they mistook him at first for another of their giant enemies, for a great cry of disappointment rose from them, and they fell back for the first time since Tarzan had been watching the unequal struggle. Wishing to make his intentions clear before the little men set upon him he moved quickly in the direction of the woman, who, the instant that her eyes fell upon him, made imperative

signs for him to join her in dispatching the balance of the pygmies. She was accustomed to being feared and obeyed by her
mankind, when she had them in her power. Perhaps she wondered a little at the temerity of this he, for as a rule they all
ran from her; but she needed him badly and that was the idea
that dominated her thoughts.

As Tarzan advanced he commanded her in the sign language
he had learned from the youth that she was to release her
captive and go away, molesting the little men no more. At
this she made an ugly grimace and raising her bludgeon came
forward to meet him. The ape-man fitted an arrow to his bow.

"Go back!" he signed her. "Go back, or I will kill you. Go
back, and put down the little man."

She snarled ferociously and increased her pace. Tarzan
raised the arrow to the level of his eye and drew it back until
the bow bent. The pygmies, realizing that for the moment at
least this strange giant was their ally, sat their mounts and
awaited the outcome of the duel. The ape-man hoped that the
woman would obey his commands before he was compelled
to take her life, but even a cursory glance at her face revealed
anything but an intention to relinquish her purpose, which now
seemed to be to annihilate this presumptuous meddler as well.

On she came. Already she was too close to make further
delay safe and the ape-man released his shaft. Straight into
her savage heart it drove and as she stumbled forward Tarzan
leaped to meet her, seizing the warrior from her grasp before
she might fall upon the tiny body and crush it, and as he did
so the other warriors, evidently mistaking his intentions,
spurred forward with loud shouts and brandishing weapons;
but before they had reached him he had set the rescued man
upon the ground and released him.

Instantly the attitude of the charging pygmies changed again
and from war cries their tones turned to cheers. Riding forward
they drew rein before the warrior that Tarzan had rescued and
several of their number leaped from their mounts and, kneeling, raised his hand to their lips. It was evident then to the
ape-man that he had rescued one who stood high among them,
their chief, perhaps; and now he wondered what would be
their attitude toward him, as, with a look of amused tolerance
upon his grim features, he watched them as one might watch
the interesting doings of a swarm of ants.

As they felicitated their fellow upon his miraculous escape
Tarzan had an opportunity to inspect them more closely. The
tallest of them stood about eighteen inches in height, their

white skins were tanned by exposure to a shade a trifle darker than his own, yet there was no question but that they were white men; their features were regular and well proportioned, so that by any standards of our race they would have been considered handsome. There were, of course, variations and exceptions; but on the whole those that he saw before him were fine-looking men. All were smooth-faced and there seemed to be no very old men among them, while he whom Tarzan had saved from the Alalus woman was apparently younger than the average, and much younger than those who had dismounted to do him homage.

As Tarzan watched them the young man bade the others rise and then addressed them for a moment after which he turned toward the ape-man and directed his remarks to him, none of which, of course, Tarzan could understand. By his manner, however, he guessed that the other was thanking him and possibly too asking his further intentions toward them and in reply the ape-man endeavored to assure them that he desired their friendship. Further to emphasize his peaceful intentions he cast his weapons aside and took a step toward them, his arms thrown slightly outward, his open palms in their direction.

The young man seemed to understand his friendly overtures, for he too advanced, offering his hand to Tarzan. The ape-man knew that the other meant that he should kiss it, but this he did not do, preferring to assume a role of equality with their highest. Instead, he kneeled upon one knee that he might more easily reach the proffered hand of the pygmy and pressing the tiny fingers gently, inclined his head slightly in a formal bow which carried no suggestion of servility. The other seemed satisfied, returned the bow with equal dignity and then attempted to convey to the ape-man that he and his party were about to ride off across the plain, inviting him to accompany them.

Rather curious to see more of these remarkable little people Tarzan was nothing loath to accept the invitation. Before the party set out, however, they dispersed to gather up their dead and wounded and to put out of their misery any of the injured antelope that were too severely hurt to travel. This they did with the relatively long, straight sword which was part of the armament of each. Their lances they left resting in cylindrical boots attached to the right side of their saddles. For other weapons Tarzan could discover nothing but a tiny knife carried in a scabbard at the right side by each warrior. The blade, like the blade of the rapier, was two edged but only about an inch and a half long, with a very sharp point.

Having gathered the dead and wounded, the latter were examined by the young leader of the party, who was accompanied by the five or six who had gathered about him at the time that Tarzan had released him. These Tarzan took to be lieutenants, or underchiefs. He saw them question the wounded and in three cases, each evidently a hopeless one, the leader ran his sword quickly through the hearts of the unhappy men.

While this seemingly cruel, yet unquestionably sound, military measure was being carried out, the balance of the warriors, directed by underofficers, were excavating a long trench beside the dead, of which there were twenty, their tool being a stout shovel blade carried attached to the saddle and which could be quickly fitted to the butt of the spear or lance. The men worked with extreme rapidity and under a plan that seemed to abhor lost motion, of which there was the absolute minimum, until in an incredibly short time they had excavated a trench fifty inches in length, eighteen inches wide and nine inches deep, the equivalent of which to men of normal size would have been nearly seventeen feet long, six feet wide and three feet deep. Into this they packed the dead like sardines and in two layers. They then shoveled back sufficient earth to fill the interstices between the bodies and to come to a level with the top of the upper layer, after which loose stones were rolled in until the bodies were entirely covered by two inches of stones. The remaining earth from the excavation was then piled over all.

By the time this work was completed the loose antelope had been caught and the wounded strapped to their backs. At a word from their commander the party formed with military precision, a detail started ahead with the wounded and a moment later the balance of the troop was mounted and on the way. The method of mounting and taking up the march was unique and a source of considerable interest to Tarzan. The dismounted warriors were standing in line facing the young leader who was mounted, as were the several officers who accompanied him. Each warrior held his mount by the bridle. The commander made a rapid signal with the raised point of his sword—there was no spoken word of command—immediately after which he dropped the point quickly at his side simultaneously wheeling his mount, which leaped quickly off in the direction that the troop was facing, the mounts of his officers wheeling with him as though actuated by a single brain, and at the same instant the mount of each alternate warrior in the line leaped forward and as it leaped its rider swung to his saddle, vaulting to his seat as lightly as a feather. The instant the first line had cleared them the antelopes of the second line leaped in pursuit, their riders mounted as had the others before them and with a second and longer leap the intervals were closed and the whole troop raced forward in a compact line. It was a most clever and practical evolution and one that made it possible to put mounted troops in motion as rapidly as foot troops; there was no long delay caused by taking distance, mounting and closing ranks.

As the troop galloped away ten warriors wheeled from the left flank and, following one of the officers who had detached himself from the party of the commander of the troop, returned to Tarzan. By signs the officer conveyed to the ape-man the intelligence that he was to follow this party which would guide him to their destination. Already the main body was far away across the open plain, their lithe mounts clearing as many as five or six feet in a single bound. Even the swift Tarzan could not have kept pace with them.

As the ape-man started away under the guidance of the detachment his thoughts reverted for an instant to the Alalus youth who was hunting alone in the forest behind them, but he soon put the creature from his mind with the realization that it was better equipped to defend itself than any of its kind, and that when he had made his visit to the country of the pygmies he could doubtless return and find the Alalus, if he so desired.

Tarzan, inured to hardship and to long and rapid marches, fell into a dogtrot such as he could keep up for hours at a time without rest, while his guides, trotting their graceful mounts, kept just ahead of him. The plain was more rolling than it had appeared from the verge of the forest, with here and there a clump of trees; the grass was plentiful and there were occasional bands of the larger species of antelope grazing at intervals. At sight of the approaching riders and the comparatively giantlike figure of Tarzan they broke and ran. Once they passed a rhinoceros, the party making only a slight detour to avoid it, and later, in a clump of trees, the leader halted his detachment suddenly and seizing his lance advanced again slowly toward a clump of bushes at the same time transmitting an order to his men which caused them to spread and surround the thicket.

Tarzan halted and watched the proceedings. The wind was

blowing from him in the direction of the thicket, so that he could not determine what manner of creature, if any, had attracted the attention of the officer; but presently, when the warriors had completely surrounded the bushes and those upon the other side had ridden into it, their spears couched and ready, he heard an ugly snarl issuing from the center of the thicket and an instant later an African wildcat sprang into view, leaping directly at the officer waiting with ready spear to receive it. The weight and momentum of the beast all but unseated the rider, the point of whose spear had met the cat full in the chest. There were a few spasmodic struggles before death ensued, during which, had the spear broken, the man would have been badly mauled and perhaps killed, for the cat was relatively as formidable a beast as is the lion to us. The instant that it died four warriors leaped forward and with their sharp knives removed the head and skin in an incredibly short time.

Tarzan could not but note that everything these people did was accomplished with maximum efficiency. Never did there seem to be any lost motion, never was one at a loss as to what to do, never did one worker get in the way of another. Scarcely ten minutes had elapsed from the moment that they had encountered the cat before the detachment was again moving, the head of the beast fastened to the saddle of one of the warriors, the skin to that of another.

The officer who commanded the detachment was a young fellow, not much, if any, older than the commander of the troop. That he was courageous Tarzan could bear witness from the manner in which he had faced what must have been, to so diminutive a people, a most deadly and ferocious beast; but then, the entire party's hopeless attack upon the Alalus woman had proved that they all were courageous, and the ape-man admired and respected courage. Already he liked these little men, though it was at times still difficult for him to accept them as a reality, so prone are we to disbelieve in the possibility of the existence of any form of life with which we are not familiar by association or credible repute.

They had been traveling for almost six hours across the plain, the wind had changed and there was borne to Tarzan's nostrils clearly the scent of Bara the deer, ahead. The ape-man, who had tasted no food that day, was ravenous, with the result that the odor of meat aroused all the savage instincts fostered by his strange upbringing. Springing forward abreast the leader of the detachment that was escorting him he signed them to halt and then as clearly as he could through the comparatively laborious and never quite satisfactory medium of further signs explained that he was hungry, that there was meat ahead and that they should remain in the rear until he had stalked his prey and made his kill.

The officer having understood and signified his assent Tarzan crept stealthily forward toward a small clump of trees beyond which his keen scent told him there were several antelope, and behind Tarzan followed the detachment, so noiselessly that even the keen ears of the ape-man heard them not.

Sheltered by the trees Tarzan saw a dozen or more antelope grazing a short distance beyond, the nearest being scarce a hundred feet from the small grove. Unslinging his bow and taking a handful of arrows from his quiver, the ape-man moved noiselessly to the tree nearest the antelope. The detachment was not far behind him, though it had stopped the moment the officer saw the game that Tarzan was stalking, lest it be frightened away.

The pygmies knew naught of bows and arrows and so they watched with deep interest every move of the ape-man. They saw him fit an arrow to his bow, draw it far back and release it almost all in a single movement, so quick with this weapon was he, and they saw the antelope leap to the impact of the missile which was followed in rapid succession by a second and a third, and as he shot his bolts Tarzan leaped forward in pursuit of his prey; but there was no danger that he would lose it. With the second arrow the buck was upon his knees and when Tarzan reached him he was already dead.

The warriors who had followed close behind Tarzan the instant that there was no further need for caution were already surrounding the antelope, where they were talking with much more excitement than Tarzan had seen them display upon any previous occasion, their interest seemingly centered about the death-dealing projectiles that had so easily laid the great animal low, for to them this antelope was as large as would be the largest elephant to us; and as they caught the ape-man's eye they smiled and rubbed their palms together very rapidly with a circular motion, an act which Tarzan assumed to be in the nature of applause.

Having withdrawn his arrows and returned them to his quiver Tarzan signed to the leader of the detachment that he would borrow his rapier. For an instant the man seemed to hesitate and all his fellows watched him intently, but he drew the sword and passed it hilt foremost to the ape-man. If you are going to eat flesh raw while it is still warm you do not bleed the carcass, nor did Tarzan in this instance. Instead he merely cut off a hind quarter, sliced off what he wanted and fell to devouring it hungrily.

The little men viewed his act with surprise not unmixed with horror and when he offered them some of the flesh they refused it and drew away. What their reaction was he could not know, but he guessed that they held a strong aversion to the eating of raw meat. Later he was to learn that their revulsion was due to the fact that within the entire range of their experience, heretofore, the only creatures that devoured raw meat devoured the pygmies as well. When, therefore, they saw this mighty giant eating the flesh of his kill raw they could not but draw the conclusion that should he become sufficiently hungry he would eat them.

Wrapping some of the meat of the antelope in its own skin Tarzan secured it to his back and the party resumed its journey. The warriors now seemed troubled and as they conversed in low tones they cast many backward glances in the direction of the ape-man. They were not afraid for themselves, for these warriors scarcely knew the meaning of fear. The question that caused them apprehension related to the wisdom of leading among their people such a huge devourer of raw flesh, who, at a single hurried meal, had eaten the equivalent of a grown man.

The afternoon was drawing to a close when Tarzan discerned in the far distance what appeared to be a group of symmetrical, dome-shaped hillocks and later, as they approached these, he saw a body of mounted warriors galloping to meet them. From his greater height he saw these before the others saw them, and attracting the officer's attention made signs apprising the latter of his discovery, but the oncoming warriors were hidden from the view of their fellows by the inequalities of the ground.

Realizing this Tarzan stooped and, before the officer could guess his intention, had gathered antelope and rider gently in his powerful hands and lifted them high above the ground. For an instant consternation held the remaining warriors. Swords flashed and a warning cry arose and even the plucky pygmy in his grasp drew his own diminutive weapon; but a smile from the ape-man reassured them all, and an instant later the officer saw why Tarzan had raised him aloft. He called down to the others below him then and from their manner as from that of him whom he held the ape-man guessed

that the approaching party was composed of friends of his
escort, and so, a few minutes later, it proved when he was
surrounded by several hundreds of the pygmies, all friendly,
eager and curious. Among them was the leader whom he had
rescued from the Alalus woman and him he greeted with
a handshake.

A consultation now took place between the leader of the
detachment that had escorted the ape-man, the young commander of the larger party and several older warriors. By the
expressions of their faces and the tone of their voices Tarzan
judged that the matter was serious and that it concerned
him he was sure from the numerous glances that were cast in
his direction. He could not know, though, that the subject of
their discussion was based upon the report of the commander
of the escort that their mighty guest was an eater of raw flesh
and the consequent danger of bringing him among their
people.

The chief among them, the young commander, settled the
question, however, by reminding them that though the giant
must have been very hungry to have devoured as much flesh
as they told him he had, nevertheless he had traveled for many
hours with only a small number of their warriors always within easy reach of him and had not offered to molest them.
This seemed a conclusive argument of his good intentions and
consequently the cavalcade set forth without further delay in
the direction of the hillocks that were now in plain view a
mile or two away.

As they neared them Tarzan saw what appeared to be
literally innumerable little men moving about among the hillocks, and as he came nearer still he realized that these seeming hillocks were symmetrical mounds of small stones quite
evidently built by the pygmies themselves and that the hordes
of pygmies moving about among them were workers, for here
was a long line all moving in one direction, emerging from a
hole in the ground and following a well-defined path to a half-
completed hillock that was evidently in course of construction.
Another line moved, empty-handed, in the opposite direction,
entering the ground through a second hole, and upon the
flanks of each line and at frequent intervals, marched armed
warriors, while other similar lines of guarded workers moved
in and out of openings in each of the other domelike struc-
tures, carrying to the mind of the ape-man a suggestion of ants
laboring about their hills.

6

S KA, the vulture, winged his way leisurely in great circles far above the right bank of the Ugogo. The pendant locket, sparkling in the sun light, had ceased to annoy him while on the wing, only when he alighted and walked upon the ground did it become an incumbrance; then he stepped upon it and tripped, but long since had he ceased to fight it, accepting it now as an inescapable evil. Beneath him he presently descried the still, recumbent form of Gorgo, the buffalo, whose posture proclaimed that he was already fit food for Ska. The great bird dropped, alighting in a nearby tree. All was well, no foes were in evidence. Satisfied of this, Ska flapped down to the fallen beast.

Miles away a giant white man crouched in the concealment of a dense thicket with a little black girl. The fingers of one of the man's hands were across her mouth, those of the other held a knife at her heart. The man's eyes were not upon the girl, but were straining through the dense foliage toward a game trail along which two ebon warriors were advancing. Succor was close at hand for Uhha, the daughter of Khamis the witch doctor, for the two approaching were hunters from the village of Obebe, the chief; but she dared not call aloud to attract them lest the sharp point of Miranda's knife slip into her young heart, and so she heard them come and go until, their voices lost in the distance, the Spaniard arose and dragged her back upon the trail, where they took up, what seemed to Uhha, their endless and fruitless wanderings through the jungle.

In the village of the ant men Tarzan found a warm welcome and having decided to remain for a while that he might study them and their customs he set to work, as was his wont when thrown among strange peoples, to learn their language as quickly as possible. Having already mastered several languages and numerous dialects the ape-man never found it difficult to add to his linguistic attainments, and so it was only a matter of a comparatively short time before he found it possible to understand his hosts and to make himself understood by them. It was then that he learned that they had at first thought that he was some form of Alalus and had consequently believed that it ever would be impossible to communicate with him by other means than signs. They were greatly delighted therefore when it had become apparent that he could utter vocal sounds identical to theirs, and when they comprehended that he desired to learn their tongue, Adendrohahkis, the king, placed several instructors at his disposal and gave orders that all his people, with whom the giant stranger might come in contact, should aid him to an early understanding of their language.

Adendrohahkis was particularly well inclined toward the ape-man because of the fact that it had been the king's son, Komodoflorensal, whom Tarzan had rescued from the clutches of the Alalus woman, and so it was that everything was done to make the giant's stay among them a pleasant one. A hundred slaves brought his food to him where he had taken up his abode beneath the shade of a great tree that grew in lonely majesty just outside the city. When he walked among the group of dome-houses a troop of cavalry galloped ahead to clear a path for him, lest he trod upon some of the people of the city; but always was Tarzan careful of his hosts, so that no harm ever befell one of them because of him.

As he mastered the language he learned many things concerning these remarkable people. Prince Komodoflorensal almost daily took it upon himself to assist in the instruction of his colossal guest and it was from him that Tarzan learned most. Nor were his eyes idle as he strolled around the city. Particularly interesting was the method of construction used in erecting the comparatively gigantic dome-houses which towered high above even the great Tarzan. The first step in the construction was to outline the periphery of the base with bowlders of uniform size and weighing, perhaps, fifty pounds each. Two slaves easily carried such a bowlder when it was slung in a rope hammock and as thousands of slaves were employed the work progressed with rapidity. The circular base, with a diameter of one hundred and fifty to two hundred feet, having been outlined, another, smaller circle was laid about ten feet inside the first, four openings being left in each circle to mark the location of the four entrances to the completed building and corresponding to the four principal cardinal points of the compass. The walls of the entrances were then outlined upon the ground with similar large bowlders, these being a little more carefully selected for uniformity, after which the four enclosures thus formed were packed closely with bowlders. The corridors and chambers of the first floor were then outlined and the spaces between filled with bowlders, each being placed with the utmost care and nicety in relation to those touching it and those that should rest upon it when the second course was laid, for these were to support a tremendous weight when the edifice was completed. The corridors were generally three feet wide, the equivalent of twelve feet by our standards, while the chambers, varied in dimensions according to the uses to which they were to be put. In the exact center of the building a circular opening was left that measured ten feet in diameter and this was carried upward as the building progressed until the whole formed an open shaft from ground floor to roof in the completed edifice.

The lower course having been built up in this manner to a height of six inches wooden arches were placed at intervals the lengths of the corridors which were now ceiled over by the simple expedient of fastening thin wooden strips lengthways of the corridors from arch to arch until the corridors were entirely roofed. The strips, or boards, which overlapped one another, were fastened in place by wooden dowels driven through them into the peripheries of the arches. As this work was progressing the walls of the various chambers and the outer wall of the building were raised to a height of twenty-four inches, bringing them to the level of the ceilings of the arched corridors, and the spaces between chambers and corridors were packed with bowlders, the interstices between which were filled with smaller stones and gravel. The ceiling beams were then placed across the other chambers, timbers six inches square hewn from a hard, tough wood being used, and in the larger chambers these were further supported, at intervals, by columns of the same dimensions and material. The ceiling beams being in place they were covered over with tight-fitting boards, doweled to place. The ceilings of the chambers now projected six inches above the surrounding course of the structure, and at this juncture hundreds of cauldrons were brought in which a crude asphaltum was heated until it became liquid and the interstices of the next six inch course were filled with it, bringing the entire completed course to the same level at a height of thirty inches, over all of which a second six inch course of rock and asphaltum was laid, and the second story laid out and completed in a similar manner.

The palace of Adendrohahkis, constructed in this way, was two hundred twenty feet in diameter, and one hundred ten feet high, with thirty-six floors capable of housing eighty thousand people, a veritable anthill of humanity. The city consisted of ten similar domes, though each slightly smaller than the king's, housing a total of five hundred thousand people, two-thirds of whom were slaves; these being for the most part the artisans and body servants of the ruling class. Another half million slaves, the unskilled laborers of the city, dwelt in the subterranean chambers of the quarries from which the building material was obtained. The passageways and chambers of these mines were carefully shored and timbered as the work progressed, resulting in fairly commodious and comfortable quarters for the slaves upon the upper levels at least, and as the city was built upon the surface of an ancient ground moraine, on account of the accessibility of building material, the drainage was perfect, the slaves suffering no inconvenience because of their underground quarters.

The domes themselves were well ventilated through the large central air shaft and the numerous windows that pierced the outer walls at frequent intervals at each level above the ground floor, in which, as previously explained, there were but four openings. The windows, which were six and one-quarter inches wide by eighteen and a half inches high, admitted a certain amount of light as well as air; but the interior of the dome, especially the gloomy chambers midway between the windows and the central light and air shaft, was illuminated by immense, slow-burning, smokeless candles.

Tarzan watched the construction of the new dome with keenest interest, realizing that it was the only opportunity that he ever would have to see the interior of one of these remarkable, human hives, and as he was thus engaged Komodoflorensal and his friends hastened to initiate him into the mysteries of their language; and while he learned the language of his hosts he learned many other things of interest about them. The slaves, he discovered, were either prisoners of war or the descendants of prisoners of war. Some had been in bondage for so many generations that all trace of their origin had become lost and they considered themselves as much citizens of Trohanadalmakus, the city of King Adendrohahkis, as did any of the nobility. On the whole they were treated with kindness and were not overworked after the second generation. The recent prisoners and their children were, for the most part, included in the caste of unskilled labor from which the limit of human endurance was exacted. They were the miners, the quarriers and the builders and fully fifty per cent of them were literally worked to death. With the second generation the education of the children commenced, those who showed aptitude for any of the skilled crafts being immediately transferred from the quarries to the domes, where they took up the relatively easy life of a prosperous and in- dulged middle class. In another manner might an individual escape the quarries—by marriage, or rather by selection as they choose to call it, with a member of the ruling class. In a community where class consciousness was such a charac- teristic of the people and where caste was almost a fetish it was rather remarkable that such connections brought no odium upon the inferiors, but, on the contrary, automatically elevated the lesser to the caste of the higher contracting party.

"It is thus, Deliverer of the Son of Adendrohahkis," ex- plained Komodofiorensal, in reply to Tarzan's inquiry rela- tive to this rather peculiar exception to the rigid class distinc- tions the king's son had so often impressed upon him: "Ages ago, during the reign of Klamataamorosal in the city of Tro- hanadalmakus, the warriors of Veltopishago, king of the city of Veltopismakus, marched upon our fair Trohanadalmakus and in the battle that ensued the troops of our ancestors were all but annihilated. Thousands of our men and women were carried away into slavery and all that saved us from being totally wiped out was the courageous defense that our own slaves waged for their masters. Klamataamorosal, from whom I am descended, fighting in the thick of the fray noted the greater stamina of the slaves; they were stronger than the war- riors of either city and seemed not to tire at all, while the high caste nobility of the fighting clans, though highly courageous, became completely exhausted after a few minutes of fighting.

"After the battle was over Klamataamorosal called together all the chief officers of the city, or rather all who had not been killed or taken prisoner, and pointed out to them that the rea- son our city had been defeated was not so much because of the greater numbers of the forces of the king Veltopishago as due to the fact that our own warriors were physical weaklings, and he asked them why this should be and what could be done to remedy so grievous a fault. The youngest man among them, wounded and weak from loss of blood, was the only one who could offer a reasonable explanation, or suggest a means of correcting the one obvious weakness of the city.

"He called their attention to the fact that of all the race of Minunians the people of the city of Trohanadalmakus were the most ancient and that for ages there had been no infusion of new blood, since they were not permitted to mate outside their own caste, while their slaves, recruited from all the cities of Minuni, had interbred, with the result that they had become strong and robust while their masters, through in-breeding, had grown correspondingly weaker.

"He exhorted Klamataamorosal to issue a decree elevating to the warrior class any slave that was chosen as mate by either a man or woman of that class, and further to obligate each and every warrior to select at least one mate from among their slaves. At first, of course, the objections to so iconoclastic a suggestion were loud and bitter; but Klamataamorosal was quick to sense the wisdom of the idea and not only did he issue the decree, but he was the first to espouse a slave woman, and what the king did all were anxious to do also.

"The very next generation showed the wisdom of the change and each succeeding generation has more than fulfilled the expectations of Klamataamorosal until now you see in the people of Trohanadalmakus the most powerful and warlike of the Minunians.

"Our ancient enemy, Veltopismakus, was the next city to adopt the new order, having learned of it through slaves taken in raids upon our own community, but they were several generations behind us. Now all the cities of Minuni wed their warriors with their slave women. And why not? Our slaves are all descended from the warrior class of other cities from which their ancestors were captured. We all are of the same race, we all have the same language and in all important respects the same customs.

"Time has made some slight changes in the manner of the selection of these new mates and now it is often customary to make war upon another city for the sole purpose of capturing their noblest born and most beautiful women.

"For us of the royal family it has been nothing less than salvation from extinction. Our ancestors were transmitting disease and insanity to their progeny. The new, pure, virile blood of the slaves has washed the taint from our veins and so altered has our point of view become that whereas, in the past, the child of a slave woman and a warrior was without caste, the lowest of the low, now they rank highest of the high, since it is considered immoral for one of the royal family to wed other than a slave."

"And your wife?" asked Tarzan. "You took her in a battle with some other city?"

"I have no wife," replied Komodoflorensal. "We are preparing now to make war upon Veltopismakus the daughter of whose king, we are told by slaves from that city, is the most beautiful creature in the world. Her name is Janzara, and as she is not related to me, except possibly very remotely, she is a fit mate for the son of Adendrohahkis."

"How do you know she is not related to you?" asked the ape-man.

"We keep as accurate a record of the royal families of Veltopismakus and several others of the nearer cities of Minuni as we do of our own," replied Komodoflorensal, "obtaining our information from captives, usually from those who are chosen in marriage by our own people. For several generations the kings of Veltopismakus have not been sufficiently powerful or fortunate to succeed in taking royal princesses from us by either force of arms or strategy, though they never have ceased attempting to do so, and the result has been that they have been forced to find their mates in other and oftentimes distant cities.

"The present king of Veltopismakus, Elkomoelhago, the father of the princess Janzara, took his mate, the mother of the princess, from a far distant city that has never, within historic times, taken slaves from Trohanadalmakus, nor have our warriors visited that city within the memory of any living man. Janzara, therefore, should make me an excellent mate."

"But what about love—suppose you should not care for one another?" asked Tarzan.

Komodoflorensal shrugged his shoulders. "She will bear me a son who will some day be king of Trohanadalmakus," he replied, "and that is all that can be asked."

While the preparations for the expedition against Veltopismakus were being carried on Tarzan was left much to his own devices. The activities of these diminutive people were a never ending source of interest to him. He watched the endless lines of slaves struggling with their heavy burdens toward the new dome that was rising with almost miraculous speed, or he strolled to the farmlands just beyond the city where other slaves tilled the rich soil, which they scratched with tiny plows drawn by teams of diadets, the diminutive antelope that was their only beast of burden. Always were the slaves accompanied by armed warriors if they were slaves of the first or second generation, lest they should attempt escape or revolution, as well as a protection against beasts of prey and human enemies, since the slaves were not permitted to bear arms and, consequently, could not protect themselves. These slaves of the first and second generations were always easily recognizable by the vivid green tunic, reaching almost to the knees, which was the single garment of their caste, and which carried upon both its front and back an emblem or character in black that denoted the city of the slave's birth and the individual to whom he now belonged. The slaves employed upon public works all belonged to the king, Adendrohahkis, but in the fields many families were represented by their chattels.

Moving about the city upon their various duties were thousands of white-tunicked slaves. They exercised the mounts of their masters, they oversaw much of the more menial and laborious work of the lower caste slaves, they plied their trades and sold their wares in perfect freedom; but like the other slaves they wore but a single garment, together with rough sandals which were common to both classes. On their breasts and backs in red were the emblems of their masters. The second generation slaves of the green tunics had a similar emblem, these having been born in the city and being consequently considered a part of it. There were other, though minor, distinguishing marks upon the tunics of the higher caste slaves; small insignia upon one shoulder or upon both, or upon a sleeve, denoting the occupation of the wearer. Groom, body servant, major-domo, cook, hairdresser, worker in gold and silver, potter—one could tell at a glance the vocation of each—and each belonged, body and soul, to his master, who was compelled to feed and clothe these dependents, the fruits of whose labors belonged exclusively to him.

The wealth of one warrior family might lie in the beauty and perfection of the gold and silver ornaments it sold to its wealthy fellows and in such an instance all its skilled slaves, other than those required for personal and household duties, would be employed in the designing and fabrication of these articles. Another family might devote its attention to agriculture, another to the raising of diadets; but all the work was done by the slaves, with the single exception of the breaking of the diadets that were bred for riding, an occupation that was not considered beneath the dignity of the warrior class, but rather, on the contrary, looked upon as a fitting occupation for nobles. Even the king's son broke his own diadets.

As an interested spectator Tarzan whiled the lazy days away. To his repeated queries as to the possibility of a way out of this bizarre, thorn-infested world, his hosts replied that it was naught to penetrate the forest of thorn trees, but that as it continued indefinitely to the uttermost extremities of matter it was quite useless to attempt to penetrate it at all, their conception of the world being confined to what they actually had seen—a land of hills, valleys and forest, surrounded by thorn trees. To creatures of their size the thorn forest was far from impenetrable, but Tarzan was not their size. Still he never ceased to plan on a means of escape, though he was in no great haste to attempt it, since he found the Minunians interesting and it suited his present primitive mood to loll in lazy ease in the city of Trohanadalmakus.

But of a sudden a change came, early of a morning, just as the first, faint promise of dawn was tinging the eastern sky.

7

THE Alalus youth, son of The First Woman, ranged the forest in search of the ape-man, the only creature that ever had stirred within his savage, primitive breast any emotion even slightly akin to affection; but he did not find him. Instead he fell in with two older males of his own species, and these three hunted together, as was occasionally the custom of these inoffensive creatures. His new acquaintances showed little interest in his strange armament—they were quite content with a stick and a stone knife. To the former an occasional rodent fell and the latter discovered many a luscious grub and insect beneath the mold that floored the forest or hidden under the bark of a tree. For the most part, however, they fed upon fruits, nuts and tubers. Not so the son of The First Woman, however. He brought in many birds and an occasional antelope, for he was becoming daily more proficient with the bow and the spear, and as he often brought in more than he could eat and left the remainder to his two fellows, they were permanently attached to him, or at least until such time as some fearsome woman should appear upon the scene to shatter their idyllic existence and drag one of them away to her corral.

They wondered a little at him in their slow and stupid minds, for he seemed to differ in some vague, intangible way from them and all others of their sex that they had known. He held his chin higher for one thing and his gaze was far less shifty and apologetic. He strode with a firmer step and with less caution; but perhaps they smiled inwardly as they cogitated muddily upon that inevitable moment that would discover one of their coarse, brutal, hairy shes felling him with her bludgeon and dragging him off toward the caves by the hair of his head.

And then one day the thing happened, or at least a part of it happened—they met a huge she suddenly in an open place in the forest. The two who accompanied the son of The First Woman turned in flight, but when they had reached the vantage ground of close-growing timber they paused and looked back to see if the woman was pursuing them and what had become of their companion. To their relief they saw that the woman was not following them and to their consternation that their fellow had not fled, but was facing her defiantly, and motioning her to go away, or be killed. Such crass stupidity! He must have been whelped without brains. It never occurred to them to attribute his act to courage. Courage was for the shes; the male spent his life in fleeing danger and the female of his species.

But they were grateful to him, for his rash act would save them since the she would take but one of them and that one would be he who thus foolishly remained behind to defy her.

The woman, unaccustomed to having her rights challenged by mere man, was filled with surprise and righteous anger. Her surprise brought her to a sudden halt twenty paces from the man and her anger caused her to reach for one of the stone missiles hanging at her girdle. That was her undoing. The son of The First Woman, standing before her with an arrow already fitted to his bow, waited not to discover her further intentions, but even as the woman's fingers loosed the feathered messenger of defeat from the leather thong of her girdle, he drew the shaft to his cheek and released it.

His two companions, watching from the seclusion of the wood, saw the woman stiffen, her face contorted in a spasm of pain; they saw her clutch frantically at a feathered shaft protruding from her chest, sink to her knees and then sprawl to earth, where she lay kicking with her feet and clutching with her fingers for a brief moment before she relapsed into eternal quiet; then they emerged from their concealment, and as the son of The First Woman approached his victim and wrenched the arrow from her heart they joined him, half-stunned as they were by surprise, and gazed first at the corpse of the she with expressions of incredulity and then at him with what was closely akin to awe and reverence.

They examined his bow and arrows and again and again they returned to the wound in the woman's chest. It was all quite too amazing. And the son of The First Woman? He held his head high and his chest out and strutted proudly. Never before had he or any other man been cast in the role of hero and he enjoyed it. But he would impress them further. Seizing the corpse of the woman he dragged it to a nearby tree where he propped it in a sitting posture against the bole; then he walked away some twenty feet and, signing his fellows to observe him closely, he raised his heavy spear and hurled it at his realistic target, through which it passed to embed itself in the tree behind.

The others were greatly excited. One of them wanted to attempt this wondrous feat and when he had thrown, and missed, his fellow insisted upon having a turn. Later they craved practice with the bow and arrow. For hours the three remained before their grisly target, nor did they desist until hunger prompted them to move on and the son of The First Woman had promised to show them how to fashion weapons similar to his own—a momentous occurrence in the history of the Alali, though these three sensed it as little as did the hundreds of Alalus women repairing to their caves that night in blissful ignorance of the blow that had been struck at their supremacy by the militant suffragists of Minuni.

And as suddenly, with more immediate results, the even tenor of Tarzan's existence in the city of Trohanadalmakus was altered and a series of events initiated that were to lead to the maddest and most unbelievable denouement.

The ape-man lay upon a bed of grasses beneath a great tree that grew beside the city of King Adendrohahkis. Dawn was flushing the sky above the forest to the east of Trohanadalmakus, when Tarzan, his ear close to the ground, was suddenly awakened by a strange reverberation that seemed to come faintly from the bowels of the earth. It was such a dim and distant sound that it would scarce have been appreciable to you or to me had we placed an ear flat against the ground after having been told that the noise existed; but to Tarzan it was an interruption of the ordinary noises of the night and, therefore, however slight, of sufficient import to impinge upon his consciousness even in sleep.

Awakened, he still lay listening intently. He knew that the sound did not come from the bowels of the earth, but from the surface and he guessed that it originated at no great distance, and also, he knew, that it was coming closer rapidly. For just a moment it puzzled him and then a great light dawned upon him and he sprang to his feet. The dome of the king, Adendrohahkis, lay a hundred yards away and toward it he bent his steps. Just before the south entrance he was challenged by a tiny sentinel.

"Take word to your king," the ape-man directed him, "that Tarzan hears many diadets galloping toward Trohanadalmakus and that unless he is much mistaken each carries a hostile warrior upon its back."

The sentinel turned and hallooed down the corridor leading from the entrance, and a moment later an officer and several other warriors appeared. At sight of Tarzan they halted.

"What is wrong?" demanded the officer.

"The King's Guest says that he heard many diadets approaching," replied the sentinel.

"From what direction?" demanded the officer, addressing Tarzan.

"From that direction the sounds appeared to come," replied the ape-man, pointing toward the west.

"The Veltopismakusians!" exclaimed the officer, and then, turning to those who had accompanied him from the interior of the king's dome: "Quick! arouse Trohanadalmakus—I will warn the king's dome and the king," and he wheeled and ran quickly within, while the others sped away to awaken the city.

In an incredibly short space of time Tarzan saw thousands of warriors streaming from each of the ten domes. From the north and the south doors of each dome rode mounted men, and from the east and west marched the foot soldiers. There was no confusion; everything moved with military precision and evidently in accordance with a plan of defense in which each unit had been thoroughly drilled.

Small detachments of cavalry galloped quickly to the four points of the compass—these were scouts each detail of which spread fanwise just beyond the limits of the domes until the city was encircled by a thin line of mounted men that would halt when it had reached a predetermined distance from the city, and fall back with information before an advancing enemy. Following these, stronger detachments of mounted men moved out to north and south and east and west to take positions just inside the line of scouts. These detachments were strong enough to engage the enemy and impede his progress as they fell back upon the main body of the cavalry which might by this plan be summoned in time to the point at which the enemy was making his boldest effort to reach the city.

And then the main body of the cavalry moved out, and in this instance toward the west, from which point they were already assured the foe was approaching; while the infantry, which had not paused since it emerged from the domes, marched likewise toward the four points of the compass in four compact bodies of which by far the largest moved toward the west. The advance foot troops took their stations but a short distance outside the city, while within the area of the domes the last troops to emerge from them, both cavalry and infantry, remained evidently as a reserve force, and it was with these troops that Adendrohahkis took his post that he might be centrally located for the purpose of directing the defense of his city to better advantage.

Komodoflorensal, the prince, had gone out in command of the main body of cavalry that was to make the first determined stand against the oncoming foe. This body consisted of seven thousand five hundred men and its position lay two miles outside the city, half a mile behind a cavalry patrol of five hundred men, of which there were four, one at each point of the compass, and totaling two thousand men. The balance of the ten thousand advance troops consisted of the five hundred mounted scouts or vedettes who, in turn, were half a mile in advance of the picket patrols, at two hundred foot intervals, entirely surrounding the city at a distance of three miles. Inside the city fifteen thousand mounted men were held in reserve.

In the increasing light of dawn Tarzan watched these methodical preparations for defense with growing admiration for the tiny Minunians. There was no shouting and no singing, but on the face of every warrior who passed close enough for the ape-man to discern his features was an expression of exalted rapture. No need here for war cries or battle hymns to bolster the questionable courage of the weak—there were no weak.

The pounding of the hoofs of the advancing Veltopismakusian horde had ceased. It was evident that their scouts had discovered that the intended surprise had failed. Were they altering the plan or point of attack, or had they merely halted the main body temporarily to await the result of a reconnaissance? Tarzan asked a nearby officer if, perchance, the enemy had abandoned his intention of attacking at all. The man smiled and shook his head.

"Minunians never abandon an attack," he said.

As Tarzan's eyes wandered over the city's ten domes, illuminated now by the rays of the rising sun, he saw in each of the numerous window embrasures, that pierced the domes at regular intervals at each of their thirty odd floors, a warrior stationed at whose side lay a great bundle of short javelins, while just to his rear was piled a quantity of small, round stones. The ape-man smiled.

"They overlook no possible contingency," he thought. "But the quarry slaves! what of them? Would they not turn against their masters at the first opportunity for escape that an impending battle such as this would be almost certain to present to them?" He turned again to the officer and put the question to him.

The latter turned and pointed toward the entrance to the nearest quarry, where Tarzan saw hundreds of white-tunicked slaves piling rocks upon it while a detachment of infantry leaned idly upon their spears as their officers directed the labor of the slaves.

"There is another detachment of warriors bottled up inside the quarry entrance," explained the officer to Tarzan. "If the enemy gains the city and this outer guard is driven into the domes or killed or captured, the inner guard can hold off an entire army, as only one man can attack them at a time. Our slaves are safe, therefore, unless the city falls and that has not happened to any Minunian city within the memory of man. The best that the Veltopismakusians can hope for now is to pick up a few prisoners, but they will doubtless leave behind as many as they take. Had their surprise been successful they might have forced their way into one of the domes and made way with many women and much loot. Now, though, our forces are too well disposed to make it possible for any but a greatly superior force to seriously threaten the city itself. I even doubt if our infantry will be engaged at all."

"How is the infantry disposed?" asked Tarzan.

"Five thousand men are stationed within the windows of the domes," replied the officer; "five thousand more comprise the reserve which you see about you, and from which detachments have been detailed to guard the quarries. A mile from the city are four other bodies of infantry; those to the east, north and south having a strength of one thousand men each, while the one to the west, facing the probable point of attack, consists of seven thousand warriors."

"Then you think the fighting will not reach the city?" asked Tarzan.

"No. The lucky men today are in the advance cavalry— they will get whatever fighting there is. I doubt if an infantry-man draws a sword or casts a spear; but that is usually the case—it is the cavalry that fights, always."

"I take it that you feel unfortunate in not being attached to a cavalry unit. Could you not be transferred?"

"Oh, we must all take our turns of duty in each branch," explained the officer. "We are all mounted except for defense of the city and for that purpose we are assigned to the foot troops for four moons, followed by five moons in the cavalry" —the word he used was *diadetax*—"five thousand men being transferred from one to the other the night of each new moon."

Tarzan turned and looked out across the plain toward the west. He could see the nearer troops standing at ease, awaiting the enemy. Even the main body of cavalry, two miles away, he could discern, because there were so many of them; but the distant pickets and vedettes were invisible. As he stood leaning upon his spear watching this scene, a scene such as no other man of his race ever had witnessed, and realized the seriousness of these little men in the business of war that confronted them, he could not but think of the people of his own world lining up their soldiers for purposes usually far less momentous to them than the call to arms that had brought the tough little warriors of Adendrohahkis swarming from their pallets in the defense of home and city.

No chicanery of politics here, no thinly veiled ambition of some potential tyrant, no mad conception of hairbrained dreamers seized by the avaricious criminal for self-aggrandizement and riches; none of these, but patriotism of purest strain energized by the powerful urge of self-preservation. The perfect fighters, the perfect warriors, the perfect heroes these. No need for blaring trumpets; of no use to them the artificial aids to courage conceived by captains of the outer world who send unwilling men to battle for they know not what, deceived by lying propaganda, enraged by false tales of the barbarity of the foe, whose anger has been aroused against them by similar means.

During the lull that followed the departure from the city of the last of the advance troops Tarzan approached Adendrohahkis where he sat astride his diadet surrounded by a number of his high officers. The king was resplendent in golden jerkin, a leathern garment upon which small discs of gold were sewn, overlapping one another. About his waist was a wide belt of heavy leather, held in place by three buckles of gold, and of such dimensions as to have almost the appearance of a corset. This belt supported his rapier and knife, the scabbards of which were heavily inlaid with gold and baser metals in intricate and beautiful designs. Leather cuisses protected his upper legs in front covering the thighs to the knees, while his forearms were encased in metal armlets from wrists almost to elbows. Upon his feet were strapped tough sandals, with a circular golden plate protecting each anklebone. A well-shaped leather casque fitted his head closely.

As Tarzan stopped before him the king recognized the ape-man with a pleasant greeting. "The captain of the guard reports that it is to you we owe the first warning of the coming of the Veltopismakusians. Once again have you placed the people of Trohanadalmakus under deep obligations. However are we to repay our debt?"

Tarzan gestured deprecatively. "You owe me nothing, King of Trohanadalmakus," he replied. "Give me your friendship and tell me that I may go forward and join your noble son, the prince; then all the obligations shall be upon my head."

"Until the worms of death devour me I shall be your friend always, Tarzan," returned the king graciously. "Go where you will and that you choose to go where there should be fighting surprises me not."

It was the first time that any Minunian had addressed him by his name. Always had he been called Saviour of the Prince, Guest of the King, Giant of the Forest and by other similar impersonal appellations. Among the Minunians a man's name is considered a sacred possession, the use of which is permitted only his chosen friends and the members of his family, and to be called Tarzan by Adendrohahkis was equivalent to an invitation, or a command, to the closest personal friendship with the king.

The ape-man acknowledged the courtesy with a bow. "The friendship of Adendrohahkis is a sacred honor, ennobling those who wear it. I shall guard it always with my life, as my most treasured possession," he said in a low voice; nor was the Lord of the Jungle moved by any maudlin sentimentality as he addressed the king. For these little people he had long since acknowledged to himself a keen admiration and for the personal character of Adendrohahkis he had come to have the most profound respect. Never since he had learned their language had he ceased his inquiries concerning the manners and the customs of these people, and he had found the personality of Adendrohahkis so inextricably interwoven with the lives of his subjects that in receiving the answers to his questions he could not but absorb unquestionable evidence of the glories of the king's character.

Adendrohahkis seemed pleased with his words, which he acknowledged graciously, and then the ape-man withdrew and started toward the front. On the way he tore a leafy branch from a tree that grew beside his path for the thought had occurred to him that such a weapon might be useful against Minunians and he knew not what the day might hold.

He had just passed the advanced infantry when a courier sped by him on a mad race toward the city. Tarzan strained his eyes ahead, but he could see no sign of battle and when he reached the main cavalry advance there was still no indication of an enemy as far ahead as he could see.

Prince Komodoflorensal greeted him warmly and looked a little wonderingly, perhaps, at the leafy branch he carried across one shoulder.

"What news?" asked Tarzan.

"I have just sent a messenger to the king," replied the prince, "reporting that our scouts have come in touch with those of the enemy, who are, as we thought, the Veltopismakusians. A strong patrol from the outpost in our front pushed through the enemy's scout line and one courageous warrior even managed to penetrate as far as the summit of the Hill of Gartolas, from which he saw the entire main body of the enemy forming for attack. He says there are between twenty and thirty thousand of them."

As Komodoflorensal ceased speaking, a wave of sound came rolling toward them from the west.

"They are coming!" announced the prince.

8

S KA, perched upon the horn of dead Gorgo, became suddenly aware of a movement in a nearby thicket. He turned his head in the direction of the sound and saw Sabor the lioness emerge from the foliage and walk slowly toward him. Ska was not terrified. He would leave, but he would leave with dignity. He crouched to spring upward, and extended his great wings to aid him in taking off. But Ska, the vulture, never rose. As he essayed to do so, something pulled suddenly upon his neck and held him down. He scrambled to his feet and, violently this time, strove to fly away. Again he was dragged back. Now Ska was terrified. The hateful thing that had been dangling about his neck for so long was holding

him to earth—the swinging loop of the golden chain had
caught around the horn of Gorgo, the buffalo. Ska was trapped.

He struggled, beating his wings. Sabor stopped to regard
him and his wild antics. Ska was flopping around in a most
surprising manner. Sabor had never seen Ska behave thus before, and lions are sensitive, temperamental animals; so Sabor
was not surprised only, she was inclined to be frightened. For
another moment she watched the unaccountable antics of Ska
and then she turned tail and slunk back into the undergrowth,
turning an occasional growling countenance back upon the
vulture, as much as to say; "Pursue me at your peril!" But Ska
had no thought of pursuing Sabor. Never again would Ska,
the vulture, pursue aught.

"They are coming!" announced Komodoflorensal prince of
Trohanadalmakus.

As Tarzan looked out across the rolling country in the
direction of the enemy, he presently saw, from his greater
height, the advance of the Veltopismakusians.

"Our scouts are falling back," he announced to Komodoflorensal.

"You can see the enemy?" demanded the prince.

"Yes."

"Keep me advised as to their movements."

"They are advancing in several long lines, deployed over a
considerable front," reported the ape-man. "The scouts are
falling back upon the outpost which seems to be standing its
ground to receive them. It will be overwhelmed—if not by the
first line then by those that succeed it."

Komodoflorensal gave a short command. A thousand
mounted men leaped forward, urging their diadets into bounding leaps that cleared five, six and even seven feet at a time.
Straight for the outpost ahead of them they raced, deploying as
they went.

Another thousand moved quickly toward the right and a
third toward the left of the advance cavalry's position following Tarzan's announcement that the enemy had divided into
two bodies just before it engaged the outpost, and that one of
these was moving as though with the intention of turning the
right flank of the main cavalry of Trohanadalmakus, while the
other circled in the direction of the left flank.

"They are striking boldly and quickly for prisoners," said
the prince to Tarzan.

"Their second and third lines are ploying upon the center
and moving straight for us," said Tarzan. "They have reached

the outpost, which is racing forward with them, giving battle vigorously with rapiers."

Komodoflorensal was dispatching messengers toward the rear. "It is thus that we fight," he said, evidently in explanation of the action of the outpost. "It is time that you returned to the rear, for in another few moments you will be surrounded by the enemy if you remain. When they reach us we, too, will turn and fight them hand-to-hand back toward the city. If it still is their intention to enter the city the battle will resemble more a race than aught else, for the speed will be too great for effective fighting; but if they have abandoned that idea and intend contenting themselves with prisoners there will be plenty of fighting before we reach the infantry, past which I doubt if they will advance.

"With their greatly superior numbers they will take some prisoners, and we shall take some—but, quick! you must get back to the city, if already it is not too late."

"I think I shall remain here," replied the ape-man.

"But they will take you prisoner, or kill you."

Tarzan of the Apes smiled and shook his leafy branch. "I do not fear them," he said, simply.

"That is because you do not know them," replied the prince. "Your great size makes you overconfident, but remember that you are only four times the size of a Minunian and there may be thirty thousand seeking to overthrow you."

The Veltopismakusians were driving swiftly forward. The prince could give no more time to what he saw was but a futile attempt to persuade Tarzan to retreat, and while he admired the strange giant's courage he likewise deplored his ignorance. Komodoflorensal had grown fond of their strange guest and he would have saved him had it been possible, but now he must turn to the command of his troops, since the enemy was almost upon them.

Tarzan watched the coming of the little men on their agile, wiry mounts. Line after line poured across the rolling country toward him, carrying to his mind a suggestion of their similarity to the incoming rollers of the ocean's surf, each drop of which was soft and harmless, but in their countless numbers combined into a relentless and terrifying force of destruction, and the ape-man glanced at his leafy bough and smiled, albeit a trifle ruefully.

But now his whole attention was riveted by the fighting in the first two lines of the advancing horde. Racing neck and neck with the Veltopismakusian warriors were the men of Adendrohahkis' outpost and the thousands who had reinforced them. Each had selected an enemy rider whom he sought to strike from his saddle, and at top speed each duel was carried on with keen rapiers, though here and there was a man wielding his spear, and sometimes to good effect. A few riderless diadets leaped forward with the vanguard, while others, seeking to break back or to the flanks, fouled the racing ranks, often throwing beasts and riders to the ground; but more frequently the warriors leaped their mounts entirely over these terrified beasts. The riding of the Minunians was superb, and their apparently effortless control of their swift and nervous steeds bordered upon the miraculous. Now a warrior, lifting his mount high into the air, cleared an adversary and as he rose above him cut down viciously with his rapier at his foeman's head, striking him from the saddle; but there was scarce time to catch more than a fleeting, kaleidoscopic impression of the swift-moving spectacle before the great horde swarmed down upon him.

With his leafy bough, Tarzan had thought to sweep the little men from his path, but now friend and foe were so intermingled that he dared not attempt it for fear of unseating and injuring some of the warriors of his hosts. He raised the bough above their heads and waited until the first lines should have passed him and then, with only the enemies of Adendrohahkis about him, he would brush them aside and break the center of their charge.

He saw the surprised expressions upon the faces of the men of Veltopismakus as they passed near him—surprise, but no fear—and he heard their shouts as one more fortunate than his fellows was able to rein closer to him and cut viciously at his legs as he sped past. Then indeed it became naught other than a matter of self-preservation to attempt to fend these off with his bough, nor was this impossible as the first lines moved past in loose ranks; but presently the solid mass of the Veltopismakusian cavalry was upon him. There was no veering aside to avoid him. In unbroken ranks, file after file, they bore down upon him. He threw his useless bough before him to impede their progress and grappled them with his fingers, tearing the riders from their mounts and hurling them back upon their onrushing fellows; but still they came.

They jumped their diadets over every obstruction. One rider, leaping straight for him, struck him head on in the pit of the stomach, half winding him and sending him back a step. Another and another struck his legs and sides. Again and again the needlelike points of their rapiers pierced his brown hide until from hips to feet he was red with his own blood, and always there were more thousands bearing down upon him. His weapons, useless against them, he made no attempt to use and though he wrought havoc among them with his bare hands there were always a hundred to take the place of each that he disposed of.

He smiled grimly as he realized that in these little people, scarce one-fourth his size, he, the incomparable Tarzan, the Lord of the Jungle, had met his Wellington. He realized that he was entirely surrounded by the Veltopismakusians now, the warriors of Trohanadalmakus having engaged the advancing enemy were racing onward with them toward the seven thousand dismounted men who were to receive the brunt of that terrific charge. Tarzan wished that he might have witnessed this phase of the battle, but he had fighting enough and to spare to engage all his attention where he was.

Again he was struck in the stomach by a charging rider and again the blow staggered him. Before he could recover himself another struck him in the same place and this time he went down, and instantly he was covered, buried by warriors and diadets, swarming over him, like ants, in countless numbers. He tried to rise and that was the last he remembered before he sank into unconsciousness.

Uhha, daughter of Khamis the witch doctor of the tribe of Obebe the cannibal, lay huddled upon a little pile of grasses in a rude thorn shelter in an open jungle. It was night but she was not asleep. Through narrowed lids she watched a giant white man who squatted just outside the shelter before a tiny fire. The girl's lids were narrowed in hate as her smoldering eyes rested upon the man. There was no fear of the supernatural in her expression—just hate, undying hate.

Long since had Uhha ceased to think of Esteban Miranda as The River Devil. His obvious fear of the greater beasts of the jungle and of the black men-beasts had at first puzzled and later assured her that her companion was an impostor; River Devils do not fear anything. She was even commencing to doubt that the fellow was Tarzan, of whom she had heard so many fabulous stories during her childhood that she had come to look upon him as almost a devil himself—her people had no gods, only devils—which answer just as good a purpose among the ignorant and superstitious as do gods among the educated and superstitious.

And when Esteban Miranda quite conclusively proved by his actions that he feared lions and that he was lost in the jungle these things did not square at all with her preconceived estimate of the powers and attributes of the famous Tarzan.

With the loss of her respect for him she lost, also, nearly all her fear. He was stronger than she and brutal. He could and would hurt her if she angered him, but he could not harm her in any other way than physically and not at all if she could keep out of his clutches. Many times had she rehearsed plans for escape, but always she had hesitated because of the terrible fear she had of being alone in the jungle. Recently, however, she had been coming to realize more and more clearly that the white man was little or no protection to her. In fact, she might be better off without him, for at the first hint of danger it had been Miranda's habit to bolt for the nearest tree, and where trees were not numerous this habit of hers had always placed Uhha under a handicap in the race for self-preservation, since Esteban, being stronger, could push her aside if she impeded his progress towards safety.

Yes, she would be as well off alone in the jungle as in the company of this man whom she thoroughly despised and hated, but before she left him she must, her savage little brain assured her, revenge herself upon him for having tricked her into aiding him in his escape from the village of Obebe the chief as well as for having forced her to accompany him.

Uhha was sure that she could find her way to the village, albeit they had traveled long and far, and she was sure too that she could find the means for subsistence along the way and elude the fiercer beasts of prey that might beset the way. Only man she feared; but in this she was not unlike all other created things. Man alone of all the creations of God is universally hated and feared and not only by the lower orders but by his own kind, for of them all man alone joys in the death of others —the great coward who, of all creation, fears death the most.

And so the little Negro girl lay watching the Spaniard and her eyes glittered, for in his occupation she saw a means to her revenge. Squatting before his fire, leaning far forward, Esteban Miranda, gloated over the contents of a small buckskin bag which he had partially emptied into the palm of one of his hands. Little Uhha knew how highly the white man prized these glittering stones, though she was entirely ignorant of their intrinsic worth. She did not even know them for diamonds. All she knew was that the white man loved them, that he valued them more highly than his other possessions and that he had repeatedly told her that he would die sooner than he would part with them.

For a long time Miranda played with the diamonds and for

a long time Uhha watched him; but at last he returned them to their bag, which he fastened securely inside his loincloth. Then he crawled beneath the thorn shelter, dragged a pile of thorns into the entrance to close it against the inroads of prowling beasts, and lay down upon the grasses beside Uhha.

How was this little girl going to accomplish the theft of the diamonds from the huge, Tarzanian Spaniard? She could not filch them by stealth, for the bag that contained them was so fastened inside his loincloth that it would be impossible to remove it without awakening him; and certainly this frail child could never wrest the jewels from Esteban by physical prowess. No, the whole scheme must die where it was born—inside Uhha's thick little skull.

Outside the shelter the fire flickered, lighting the jungle grasses about it and casting weird, fantastic shadows that leaped and danced in the jungle night. Something moved stealthily among the lush vegetation a score of paces from the tiny camp. It was something large, for the taller grasses spread to its advance. They parted and a lion's head appeared. The yellow-green eyes gazed uneasily at the fire. From beyond came the odor of man and Numa was hungry; too, upon occasion he had eaten of man and found him good—also of all his prey the slowest and the least able to protect himself; but Numa did not like the looks of things here and so he turned and disappeared from whence he had come. He was not afraid of the fire. Had he been he would have been afraid of the sun by day, for the sun he could not even look at without discomfort, and to Numa the fire and the sun might have been one, for he had no way of knowing which was sixty feet away and which ninety-three million miles. It was the dancing shadows that caused his nervous apprehension. Huge, grotesque creatures of which he had had no experience seemed to be leaping all about him, threatening him from every side.

But Uhha paid no attention to the dancing shadows and she had not seen Numa the lion. She lay very still now, listening. The fire flared less high as the slow minutes dragged their leaden feet along. It was not so very long that she lay thus, but it seemed long to Uhha, for she had her plan all matured and ready for execution. A civilized girl of twelve might have conceived it, but it is doubtful that she would have carried it to its conclusion. Uhha, however, was not civilized and being what she was she was not hampered by any qualms of conscience.

Presently the Spaniard's breathing indicated that he was asleep. Uhha waited a little longer to make assurance doubly sure, then she reached beneath the grasses just beside her and when she withdrew her hand again she brought forth a short, stout cudgel. Slowly and cautiously she rose until she knelt beside the recumbent form of the sleeping Spaniard. Then she raised her weapon above her head and brought it down once, heavily, upon Esteban's skull. She did not continue to beat him —the one blow was enough. She hoped that she had not killed him, for he must live if her scheme of revenge was to be realized; he must live and know that Uhha had stolen the bag of pebbles that he so worshiped. Uhha appropriated the knife that swung at Miranda's hip and with it she cut away his loincloth and took possession of the buckskin bag and its contents. Then she removed the thorns from the entrance to the shelter, slipped out into the night and vanished into the jungle. During all her wanderings with the Spaniard she had not once lost her sense of the direction which pointed toward her home, and now, free, she set her face resolutely toward the southwest and the village of Obebe the cannibal. An elephant trail formed a jungle highway along which she moved at a swinging walk, her way lighted by the rays of a full moon that filtered through the foliage of a sparse forest. She feared the jungle night and the nocturnal beasts of prey, but she knew that she must take this chance that she might put as great a distance as possible between herself and the white man before he regained consciousness and started in pursuit.

A hundred yards ahead of her, in the dense thicket that bordered the trail, Numa the lion sniffed, and listened with up-pricked ears bent in her direction. No dancing shadows here to suggest menacing forms to Numa's high-strung nervous system—only the scent of man coming closer and closer—a young she-man, most tender of its kind. Numa licked his slavering jowls and waited.

The girl came rapidly along the trail. Now she was abreast the lion, but the king of beasts did not spring. There is something in the scent of the man-thing and the sight of the man-thing that awakens strange terrors in the breast of Numa. When he stalks Horta the boar or Bara the deer there is nothing in the near presence of either that arouses a similar sensation in the savage carnivore; then he knows no hesitancy when the instant comes to spring upon his prey. It is only the man-thing, helpless and leaden-footed, that causes him to pause in indecision at the crucial moment.

Uhha passed, ignorant of the fact that a great lion, hunting and hungry, stood within two paces of her. When she had passed Numa slunk into the trail behind her, and there he followed, stalking his tender quarry until the moment should come when the mists of his indecision should be dispelled. And so they went through the jungle night—the great lion, creeping on stealthy, noiseless pads, and just ahead of him the little black girl, unconscious of the grim death stalking her through the dappled moonlight.

9

WHEN TARZAN of the Apes regained consciousness he found himself lying upon an earthen floor in a large chamber. As he first opened his eyes, before complete consciousness returned, he noticed that the room was well, but not brilliantly, lighted, and that there were others there besides himself. Later, as he commenced to collect and dominate his faculties of thought he saw that the room was lighted by two immense candles that appeared to be fully three feet in diameter and, though evidently partially melted away, yet at least five feet tall. Each supported a wick fully as large as a man's wrist and though the manner of their burning was similar to the candles with which he was familiar, yet they gave off no smoke, nor were the beams and boards of the ceiling directly above them smoke-blackened.

The lights, being the most noticeable things in the room, had been the first to attract the ape-man's attention, but now his eyes wandered to the other occupants of the room. There were fifty or a hundred men of about his own height; but they were garbed and armed as had been the little men of Trohanadalmakus and Veltopismakus. Tarzan knit his brows and looked long and steadily at them. Who were they? Where was he?

As consciousness spread slowly throughout his body he realized that he was in pain and that his arms felt heavy and numb. He tried to move them, only to discover that he could not—they were securely bound behind his back. He moved his feet—they were not secured. At last, after considerable effort, for he found that he was very weak, he raised himself to a sitting posture and looked about him. The room was filled with warriors who looked precisely like the little Veltopismakusians, but they were as large as normal men, and the room itself was immense. There were a number of benches and tables standing about the floor and most of the men either were seated upon the benches or lay stretched upon the hard earth. A few men moved about among them and seemed to be working over them. Then it was that Tarzan saw that nearly all within the chamber were suffering from wounds, many of them severe ones. The men who moved about among them were evidently attending to the wounded, and those, who might have been the nurses, were garbed in white tunics like the high caste slaves of Trohanadalmakus. In addition to the wounded and the nurses there were a half dozen armed warriors who were uninjured. One of these was the first to espy Tarzan after he had raised himself to a sitting posture.

"Ho!" shouted he. "The giant has come into his senses," and crossing the room he approached the ape-man. Standing before him, his feet widespread, he eyed Tarzan with a broad grin upon his face. "Your great bulk availed you little," he taunted, "and now we are as large as you. We, too, are giants, eh?" and he turned to his fellows with a laugh in which they joined him.

Seeing that he was a prisoner, surrounded by enemies, the ape-man fell back upon that lifelong characteristic of the wild beast—sullen silence. He made no reply, but only sat there regarding them with the savage, level gaze of the brute at bay.

"He is dumb like the great beast-women of the caves," said the warrior to his fellows.

"Perhaps he is one of them," suggested another.

"Yes," seconded a third, "perhaps he is one of the Zertalacolols."

"But their men are all cowards," urged the first speaker; "and this one fought like a warrior born."

"Yes, with his bare hands he fought till he went down."

"You should have seen how he threw diadets and warriors as one might pick up tiny pebbles and hurl them afar."

"He would not give a step, or run; and always he smiled."

"He does not look like the men of the Zertalacolols; ask him if he is."

He who had first addressed him put the question to Tarzan, but the ape-man only continued to glare at them.

"He does not understand me," said the warrior. "I do not think that he is a Zertalacolol, though. What he is, however, I do not know."

He approached and examined Tarzan's wounds. "These will

soon be healed. In seven days, or less, he will be fit for the quarries."

They sprinkled a brown powder upon his wounds and brought him food and water and the milk of antelopes, and when they found that his arms were swelling badly and becoming discolored they brought an iron chain and, fastening one end about his waist with a clumsy padlock, secured him to a ring in the stone wall of the chamber, and cut the bonds from his wrists.

As they believed that he did not understand their language they spoke freely before him, but as their tongue was almost identical with that employed by the Trohanadalmakusians Tarzan understood everything that they said, and thus he learned that the battle before the city of Adendrohahkis had not gone as well for the Veltopismakusians as Elkomoelhago, their king, had desired. They had lost many in killed and prisoners and in return had not killed near so many of the enemy and had taken comparatively few prisoners, though Elkomoelhago, he learned, considered him worth the entire cost of the brief war.

How they had changed themselves into men of his own stature Tarzan could not comprehend, nor did any of the remarks he overheard shed any light upon this mystery of mysteries. But the climax of improbability was attained a few days later when he saw pass through the corridor, upon which the room of his incarceration was located, a file of warriors as large as he, each of whom was mounted upon a huge antelope fully as tall at the shoulder as the great eland, though obviously, from its contour and markings, a Royal Antelope, which is the smallest known. Tarzan ran his brown fingers through his thatch of black hair and gave up attempting to solve the enigmas that surrounded him.

His wounds healed quickly, as did those of the Veltopismakusians who were convalescing about him, and upon the seventh day a half-dozen warriors came for him and the chain was removed from about his waist that he might accompany them. His captors had long since ceased to address him, believing that he was ignorant of their language, which meant to them that he was as speechless as an Alalus, since they could conceive of no language other than their own; but from their conversation, as they led him from the chamber and along a circular corridor, he discovered that he was being taken before their king, Elkomoelhago, who had expressed a desire to see this remarkable captive after he had recovered from his wounds.

The long corridor, through which they were proceeding, was lighted partially by small candles set in niches and by the light from illuminated chambers the doors of which opened upon it. Slaves and warriors moved in two continuous and opposing lines through this corridor and every one that crossed it. There were high caste slaves in white tunics with the red emblems of their owners and their own occupation insignia upon them; there were green-tunicked slaves of the second generation with their master's insignia upon breast and back in black, and green-tunicked slaves of the first generation with a black emblem upon their breasts denoting the city of their nativity and their master's emblem upon their backs; there were warriors of every rank and position; there were the plain leather trappings of the young and poor, and the jewel-studded harness of the rich; and passing all these in both directions and often at high speed were other warriors mounted upon the mighty antelopes that were still the greatest wonder that had confronted Tarzan since his incarceration in the city of Veltopismakus.

At intervals along the corridor Tarzan saw ladders extending to a floor above, but as he never saw one descending to a lower level he assumed that they were then upon the lowest floor of the structure. From the construction that he noted he was convinced that the building was similar to the dome he had seen in the course of construction in the city of Adendrohahkis; but when he permitted his mind to dwell upon the tremendous proportions of such a dome capable of housing men of his own size he was staggered. Had Adendrohahkis' dome been dupli-cated in these greater dimensions, though in the same propor-tions, it would have been eight hundred eighty feet in diam-eter and four hundred forty feet high. It seemed preposterous to think that any race existed capable of accomplishing such an architectural feat with only the primitive means that these people might be able to command, yet here were the corridors with the arched roofs, the walls of neatly laid bowlders and the great chambers with their heavy ceiling beams and stout columns, all exactly as he had seen the dome in Trohanadal-makus, but on a vastly larger scale.

As his eyes and mind dwelt upon these enigmas which con-fronted them his escort led him from the circular corridor into one that ran at right angles to it where presently they stopped at the entrance to a chamber filled with row upon row of shelving packed full with all manner of manufactured articles. There were large candles and small candles, candles of every conceivable size and shape; there were helmets, belts, sandals, tunics, bowls, jars, vases and the thousand other articles of the daily life of the Minunians with which Tarzan had become more or less familiar during his sojourn among the Trohanadalmakusians.

As they halted before the entrance to this room a white-tunicked slave came forward in response to the summons of one of the warriors of the escort.

"A green tunic for this fellow from Trohanadalmakus," he ordered.

"Whose insignia upon his back?" inquired the slave.

"He belongs to Zoanthrohago," replied the warrior.

The slave ran quickly to one of the shelves from which he selected a green tunic. From another he took two large, wooden blocks upon the face of each of which was carved a different device. These he covered evenly with some sort of paint or ink, slipped a smooth board inside the tunic, placed one of the dies face downward upon the cloth, tapped it smartly with a wooden mallet several times and then repeated the operation with the other die upon the reverse side of the tunic. When he handed the garment to Tarzan with the instructions to don it the ape-man saw that it bore a device in black upon the breast and another upon the back, but he could not read them—his education had not progressed thus far.

The slave then gave him a pair of sandals and when he had strapped these to his feet the warriors motioned him on down the corridor, which, as they proceeded, he was aware changed rapidly in appearance. The rough bowlder walls were plastered now and decorated with colored paintings portraying, most often, battle scenes and happenings of the hunt, usually framed in panels bordered in intricate, formal designs. Vivid colorings predominated. Many-hued candles burned in frequent niches. Gorgeously trapped warriors were numerous. The green-tunicked slave almost disappeared, while the white tunics of the higher caste bondsmen were of richer material and the slaves themselves were often resplendently trapped with jewels and fine leather.

The splendor of the scene, the brilliancy of the lighting, increased until the corridor came to an abrupt end before two massive doors of hammered gold in front of which stood gorgeously trapped warriors who halted them and questioned the commander of the escort as to their business.

"By the king's command we bring the slave of Zoanthrohago," replied the commander; "the giant who was taken prisoner at Trohanadalmakus."

The warrior who had challenged them turned to one of his

fellows. "Go with this message and deliver it to the king!"
he said.

After the messenger had departed the warriors fell to examining Tarzan and asking many questions concerning him,
to few of which could his guard give more than speculative
answers, and then, presently, the messenger returned with word
that the party was immediately to be admitted to the king's
presence. The heavy doors were swung wide and Tarzan found
himself upon the threshold of an enormous chamber, the walls
of which converged toward the opposite end, where a throne
stood upon a dais. Massive wooden columns supported the
ceiling, which was plastered between its beams. The beams
as well as the columns were ornamented with carving, while
the plastered portions of the ceiling carried gorgeous arabesques in brilliant colors. The walls were paneled to half their
height, and above the paneling of wood were painted panels
which Tarzan assumed depicted historical events from the
history of Veltopismakus and her kings.

The room was vacant except for two warriors who stood
before doors that flanked the throne dais, and as the party
moved down the broad center aisle toward the throne one of
these warriors signaled the leader and motioned to the door
which he was guarding and which he now threw open before
them, revealing a small antechamber in which were half a
dozen handsomely trapped warriors seated on small, carved
benches, while a seventh lolled in a high-backed chair, his
fingers tapping upon its broad arms as he listened to the conversation of the others, into which he threw an occasional word
that always was received with deepest attention. If he scowled
when he spoke, the others scowled still more deeply; if he
smiled, they broke into laughter, and scarcely for an instant
did their eyes leave his face, lest they miss some fleeting index
of his changing moods.

Just inside the doorway the warriors who were conducting
Tarzan halted, where they remained in silence until the man
in the high-backed armchair deigned to notice them, then the
leader knelt upon one knee, raised his arms, palms forward,
high above his head, leaned as far back as he could and in a
monotonous dead level intoned his salutation.

"O, Elkomoelhago, King of Veltopismakus, Ruler of All
Men, Master of Created Things, All-Wise, All-Courageous,
All-Glorious! we bring these, as thou hast commanded, the
slave of Zoanthrohago."

"Arise and bring the slave closer," commanded the man in
the high-backed armchair, and then to his companions: "This

is the giant that Zoanthrohago brought back from Trohanadal-makus."

"We have heard of him, All-Glorious," they replied.

"And of Zoanthrohago's wager?" questioned the king.

"And of Zoanthrohago's wager, All-Wise!" replied one.

"What think you of it?" demanded Elkomoelhago.

"Even as you think, Ruler of All Men," quickly spoke another.

"And how is that?" asked the king.

The six looked quickly and uneasily, one at the others. "How *does* he think?" whispered he who was farthest from Elko-moelhago to his neighbor, who shrugged his shoulders hope-lessly and looked to another.

"What was that, Gofoloso?" demanded the king. "What was that you said?"

"I was about to remark that unless Zoanthrohago first con-sulted our august and all-wise ruler and is now acting upon his judgment he must, almost of necessity, lose the wager," replied Gofoloso glibly.

"Of course," said the king, "there is something in what you say, Gofoloso. Zoanthrohago did consult me. It was I who discovered the vibratory principle which made the thing pos-sible. It was I who decided just how the first experiments were to be carried out. Heretofore it has not been enduring; but we believe that the new formula will have a persistency of thirty-nine moons at least—it is upon this that Zoanthrohago has made his wager. If he is wrong he loses a thousand slaves to Dalfastomalo."

"Wonderful!" exclaimed Gofoloso. "Blessed indeed are we above all other peoples, with a king so learned and so wise as Elkomoelhago."

"You have much to be thankful for, Gofoloso," agreed the king; "but nothing compared to what will follow the success of my efforts to apply this principle of which we have been speaking, but with results diametrically opposite to those we have so far achieved; but we work upon it, we work upon it! Some day it will come and then I shall give to Zoanthrohago the formula that will revolutionize Minuni—then with a hun-dred men might we go forth and conquer the world!"

Elkomoelhago now turned his attention suddenly upon the green-tunicked slave standing a short distance before him. He scrutinized him closely and in silence for several minutes.

"From what city do you come?" demanded the king, at last.

"O, All-Glorious Elkomoelhago," spoke up the leader of the escort, "the poor ignorant creature is without speech."

"Utters he any sound?" inquired the king.

"None since he was captured, Master of Men," replied the warrior.

"He is a Zertalacolol," stated Elkomoelhago. "Why all this silly excitement over one of these low, speechless creatures?"

"See now!" exclaimed Gofoloso, "how quickly and surely the father of wisdom grasps all things, probing to the bottom of all mysteries, revealing their secrets. Is it not marvelous!"

"Now that the Sun of Science has shone upon him even the dullest may see that the creature is indeed a Zertalacolol," cried another of the king's companions. "How simple, how stupid of us all! Ah, what would become of us were it not for the glorious intelligence of the All-Wise."

Elkomoelhago was examining Tarzan closely. He seemed not to have heard the eulogies of his courtiers. Presently he spoke again.

"He has not the features of the Zertalacolols," he pondered musingly. "See his ears. They are not the ears of the speechless ones, nor his hair. His body is not formed as theirs and his head is shaped for the storing of knowledge and the functioning of reason. No, he cannot be a Zertalacolol."

"Marvelous!" cried Gofoloso. "Did I not tell you! Elkomoelhago, our king, is always right."

"The most stupid of us may easily see that he is not a Zertalacolol, now that the king's divine intelligence has made it so plain," exclaimed the second courtier.

At this juncture a door, opposite that through which Tarzan had been brought into the apartment, opened and a warrior appeared. "O, Elkomoelhago, King of Veltopismakus," he droned, "thy daughter, the Princess Janzara, has come. She would see the strange slave that Zoanthrohago brought from Trohanadalmakus and craves the royal permission to enter."

Elkomoelhago nodded his assent. "Conduct the princess to us!" he commanded.

The princess must have been waiting within earshot immediately outside the door, for scarcely had the king spoken when she appeared upon the threshold, followed by two other young women, behind whom were a half dozen warriors. At sight of her the courtiers rose, but not the king.

"Come in, Janzara," he said, "and behold the strange giant who is more discussed in Veltopismakus than Veltopismakus' king."

The princess crossed the room and stood directly in front of the ape-man, who remained standing, as he had since he had entered the chamber, with arms folded across his broad chest, an expression of absolute indifference upon his face. He glanced at the princess as she approached him and saw that she was a very beautiful young woman. Except for an occasional distant glimpse of some of the women of Trohanadalmakus she was the first Minunian female Tarzan had seen. Her features were faultlessly chiseled, her soft, dark hair becomingly arranged beneath a gorgeous, jeweled headdress, her clear skin shaming the down of the peach in its softness. She was dressed entirely in white, befitting a virgin princess in the palace of her sire; her gown, of a soft, clinging stuff, fell in straight and simple lines to her arched insteps. Tarzan looked into her eyes. They were gray, but the shadows of her heavy lashes made them appear much darker than they were. He sought there an index to her character, for here was the young woman whom his friend, Komodoflorensal, hoped some day to espouse and make queen of Trohanadalmakus, and for this reason was the ape-man interested. He saw the beautiful brows knit into a sudden frown.

"What is the matter with the beast?" cried the princess. "Is it made of wood?"

"It speaks no language, nor understands any," explained her father. "It has uttered no sound since it was captured."

"It is a sullen, ugly brute," said the princess. "I'll wager to make it utter a sound, and that quickly," with which she snatched a thin dagger from her belt and plunged it into Tarzan's arm. With such celerity had she moved that her act had taken all who witnessed it by surprise; but she had given the Lord of the Jungle an instant's warning in the few words she had spoken before she struck and these had been sufficient for him. He could not avoid the blow, but he could and did avoid giving her the satisfaction of seeing her cruel experiment succeed, for he uttered no sound. Perhaps she would have struck again, for she was very angry now, but the king spoke sharply to her.

"Enough, Janzara!" he cried. "We would have no harm befall this slave upon whom we are conducting an experiment that means much to the future of Veltopismakus."

"He has dared to stare into my eyes," cried the princess, "and he has refused to speak when he knew that it would give me pleasure. He should be killed!"

"He is not yours to kill," returned the king. "He belongs to Zoanthrohago."

"I will buy him," and turning to one of her warriors, "Fetch Zoanthrohago!"

10

WHEN Esteban Miranda regained consciousness, the fire before his rude shelter was but a heap of cold ashes and dawn had almost come. He felt weak and dizzy and his head ached. He put his hand to it and found his thick hair matted with coagulated blood. He found something else as well—a great wound in his scalp, that made him shudder and turn sick, so that he fainted. When again he opened his eyes it was quite daylight. He looked about him questioningly. Where was he? He called aloud in Spanish—called to a woman with a musical name. Not Flora Hawkes, but a soft, Spanish name that Flora never had heard.

He was sitting up now and presently he regarded his nakedness in evident surprise. He picked up the loincloth that had been cut from his body. Then he looked all about him on the ground—his eyes dull, stupid, wondering. He found his weapons and picking them up examined them. For a long time he sat fingering them and looking at them, his brows puckered in thought. The knife, the spear, the bow and arrows he went over time and time again.

He looked out upon the jungle scene before him and the expression of bewilderment on his face but increased. He half-rose, remaining upon his knees. A startled rodent scurried across the clearing. At sight of it the man seized his bow and fitted an arrow, but the animal was gone before he could loose his shaft. Still kneeling, the bewildered expression upon his countenance deepening, he gazed in mute astonishment upon the weapon he held so familiarly in his hand. He arose, gathered up his spear and knife and the balance of his arrows and started off into the jungle.

A hundred yards from his shelter he came upon a lion feeding upon the carcass of its kill that it had dragged into the bushes beside the wide elephant trail along which the man made his way. The lion growled ominously. The man halted, listening intently. He was still bewildered; but only for an instant did he remain motionless in the trail. With the spring of a panther he gained the low swinging limb of the nearest tree. There he squatted for a few minutes. He could see Numa the lion feeding upon the carcass of some animal—what the animal had been he could not determine. After a while the man dropped silently from the tree and went off into the jungle in the opposite direction from that he had at first chanced upon. He was naked, but he did not know it. His diamonds were gone, but he would not have known a diamond had he seen one. Uhha had left him, but he did not miss her, for he knew not that she ever had existed.

Blindly and yet well, his muscles reacted to every demand made upon them in the name of the first law of nature. He had not known why he leaped to a tree at the sound of Numa's growl, nor could he have told why he walked in the opposite direction when he saw where Numa lay up with his kill. He did not know that his hand leaped to a weapon at each new sound or movement in the jungle about him.

Uhha had defeated her own ends. Esteban Miranda was not being punished for his sins for the very excellent reason that he was conscious of no sins nor of any existence. Uhha had killed his objective mind. His brain was but a storehouse of memories that would never again be raised above the threshold of consciousness. When acted upon by the proper force they stimulated the nerves that controlled his muscles, with results seemingly identical with those that would have followed had he been able to reason. An emergency beyond his experience would, consequently, have found him helpless, though ignorant of his helplessness. It was almost as though a dead man walked through the jungle. Sometimes he moved along in silence, again he babbled childishly in Spanish, or, perhaps, quoted whole pages of Shakespeare in English.

Could Uhha have seen him now, even she, savage little cannibal, might have felt remorse at the horror of her handi-work, which was rendered even more horrible because its miserable object was totally unconscious of it; but Uhha was not there to see, nor any other mortal; and the poor clay that once had been a man moved on aimlessly through the jungle, killing and eating when the right nerves were excited, sleeping, talking, walking as though he lived as other men live; and thus, watching him from afar, we see him disappear amidst the riotous foliage of a jungle trail.

The Princess Janzara of Veltopismakus did not purchase the slave of Zoanthrohago. Her father, the king, would not permit it, and so, very angry, she walked from the apartment where she had come to examine the captive and when she had passed into the next room and was out of her royal sire's range of vision, she turned and made a face in his direction, at which all her warriors and the two hand-maidens laughed.

"Fool!" she whispered in the direction of her unconscious father. "I shall own the slave yet and kill him, too, if I mind."

The warriors and the hand-maidens nodded their heads approvingly.

King Elkomoelhago arose languidly from his chair. "Take it to the quarries," he said, indicating Tarzan with a motion of his thumb, "but tell the officer in charge that it is the king's wish that it be not overworked, nor injured," and as the ape-man was led away through one doorway, the king quitted the chamber by another, his six courtiers bowing in the strange, Minunian way until he was gone. Then one of them tiptoed quickly to the doorway through which Elkomoelhago had disappeared, flattened himself against the wall beside the door and listened for a moment. Apparently satisfied, he cautiously insinuated his head beyond the doorframe until he could view the chamber adjoining with one eye, then he turned back toward his fellows.

"The old half-wit has gone," he announced, though in a whisper that would have been inaudible beyond the chamber in which it was breathed, for even in Minuni they have learned that the walls have ears, though they express it differently, saying, instead: *Trust not too far the loyalty of even the stones of your chamber.*

"Saw you ever a creature endowed with such inordinate vanity!" exclaimed one.

"He believes that he is wiser than, not any man, but all men combined," said another. "Sometimes I feel that I can abide his arrogance no longer."

"But you will, Gefasto," said Gofoloso. "To be Chief of Warriors of Veltopismakus is too rich a berth to be lightly thrown aside."

"When one might simultaneously throw away one's life at the same time," added Torndali, Chief of Quarries.

"But the colossal effrontery of the man!" ejaculated another, Makahago, Chief of Buildings. "He has had no more to do with Zoanthrohago's success than have I and yet he claims the successes all for himself and blames the failures upon Zoanthrohago."

"The glory of Veltopismakus is threatened by his egotism," cried Throwaldo, Chief of Agriculture. "He has chosen us as his advisers, six princes, whose knowledge of their several departments should be greater than that of any other individuals and whose combined knowledge of the needs of Veltopismakus and the affairs of state should form a bulwark against the egregious errors that he is constantly committing; but never will he heed our advice. To offer it he considers a usurpation of his royal prerogatives, to urge it, little short of treason. To question his judgment spells ruin. Of what good are we to Veltopismakus? What must the people of the state think of us?"

"It is well known what they think of us," snapped Gofoloso. "They say that we were chosen, not for what we know, but for what we do not know. Nor can you blame them. I, a breeder of diadets, master of ten thousand slaves who till the soil and raise a half of all the food that the city consumes, am chosen Chief of Chiefs, filling an office for which I have no liking and no training, while Throwaldo, who scarce knows the top of a vegetable from its roots, is Chief of Agriculture. Makahago worked the quarry slaves for a hundred moons and is made Chief of Buildings, while Torndali, who is acclaimed the greatest builder of our time, is Chief of Quarries. Gefasto and Vestako, alone, are masters of their bureaus. Vestako the king chose wisely as Chief of the Royal Dome, that his royal comfort and security might be assured; but in Gefasto behold his greatest blunder! He elevated a gay young pleasure-seeker to the command of the army of Veltopismakus and discovered in his new Chief of Warriors as great a military genius as Veltopismakus has ever produced."

Gefasto bowed his acknowledgment of the compliment.

"Had it not been for Gefasto the Trohanadalmakusians would have trapped us fairly the other day," continued Gofoloso.

"I advised the king against pushing the assault," interjected Gefasto, "as soon as it became evident that we had failed to surprise them. We should have withdrawn. It was only after we had advanced and I was free from him that I could direct the affair without interference, and then, as you saw, I quickly extricated our troops and withdrew them with as little loss of men and prestige as possible."

"It was nobly done, Gefasto," said Torndali. "The troops worship you. They would like a king who led them in battle as you might lead them."

"And let them have their wine as of old," interjected Makahago.

"We would all rally around a king who permitted us the innocent pleasure of our wine," said Gofoloso: "What say you, Vestako?"

The Chief of the Royal Dome, the king's major-domo, who had remained silent throughout the arraignment of his master, shook his head.

"It is not wise to speak treason now," he said.

The three looked sharply at him and glanced quickly at one another.

"Who has spoken treason, Vestako?" demanded Gofoloso.

"You have all come too close to it for safety," said the oily Vestako. He spoke in a much louder voice than the others had spoken, as though, far from being fearful of being overheard, he rather hoped that he would be. "Elkomoelhago has been good to us. He has heaped honors and riches upon us. We are very powerful. He is a wise ruler. Who are we to question the wisdom of his acts?"

The others looked uneasily about. Gofoloso laughed nervously. "You were ever slow to appreciate a joke, my good Vestako," he said. "Could you not see that we were hoaxing you?"

"I could not," replied Vestako; "but the king has a fine sense of humor. I will repeat the joke to him and if he laughs then I shall laugh, too, for I shall know that it was indeed a joke. But I wonder upon whom it will be!"

"Oh, Vestako, do not repeat what we have said—not to the king. He might not understand. We are good friends and it was said only among friends." Gofoloso was evidently perturbed in spirit—he spoke rapidly. "By the way, my good Vestako, I just happened to recall that the other day you admired one of my slaves. I have intended giving him to you. If you will accept him he is yours."

"I admire a hundred of your slaves," said Vestako, softly.

"They are yours, Vestako," said Gofoloso. "Come with me now and select them. It is a pleasure to make my friend so trifling a present."

Vestako looked steadily at the other four. They shifted uneasily in momentary silence, which was broken by Throwaldo, Chief of Agriculture. "If Vestako would accept a hundred of my poor slaves I should be overwhelmed with delight," he said.

"I hope they will be slaves of the white tunic," said Vestako.

"They will," said Throwaldo.

"I cannot be outdone in generosity," said Torndali; "you must accept a hundred slaves from me."

"And from me!" cried Makahago, Chief of Buildings.

"If you will send them to my head slave at my quarters before the Sun enters the Warriors' Corridor I shall be overwhelmed with gratitude," said Vestako, rubbing his palms and smiling unctuously. Then he looked quickly and meaningly at Gefasto, Chief of Warriors of Veltopismakus.

"Best can I show my friendship for the noble Vestako," said Gefasto, unsmiling, "by assuring him that I shall, if possible, prevent my warriors from slipping a dagger between his ribs. Should aught of harm befall me, however, I fear that I cannot be responsible for the acts of these men, who, I am told, love me." For a moment longer he stood looking straight into the eyes of Vestako, then he turned upon his heel and strode from the room.

Of the six men who composed the Royal Council, Gefasto and Gofoloso were the most fearless, though even they flattered the vain and arrogant Elkomoelhago, whose despotic powers rendered him a most dangerous enemy. Custom and inherent loyalty to the royal family, in addition to that most potent of human instrumentalities—self-interest, held them to the service of their king, but so long had they been plotting against him, and so rife was discontent throughout the city, that each now felt that he might become bolder with impunity.

Torndali, Makahago and Throwaldo, having been chosen by the king for their supposed pliability and having, unlike Gefasto and Gofoloso, justified his expectations, counted for little one way or another. Like the majority of the Veltopismakusian nobles under the reign of Elkomoelhago they had become corrupt, and self-interest guided their every act and thought. Gefasto did not trust them, for he knew that they could be bought even while professing their virtue, and Gefasto had taken to the study of men since his success with the warriors of his city—a success that was fully as much a surprise to him as to others—and his knowledge of the mounting restlessness of the people had implanted in the fertile soil of a virile brain the idea that Veltopismakus was ripe for a new dynasty.

Vestako he knew for a self-acknowledged and shameless bribetaker. He did not believe that there was an honest hair in the man's head, but he had been surprised at the veiled threat of exposure he had used to mulct his fellows.

"Low indeed have fallen the fortunes of Veltopismakus," he said to Gofoloso as the two walked along the Warriors' Corridor after quitting the council chamber of the king.

"As exemplified by—?" queried the Chief of Chiefs.

"By Vestako's infamy. He cares neither for king nor for people. For slaves or gold he would betray either, and Vestako is typical of the majority of us. No longer is friendship sacred, for even from Throwaldo he exacted the toll of his silence, and Throwaldo has ever been accounted his best friend."

"What has brought us to such a pass, Gefasto?" asked

Gofoloso, thoughtfully. "Some attribute it to one cause and some to another, and though there should be no man in Velopismakus better able than myself to answer my own question, I confess that I am at a loss. There are many theories, but I doubt me the right one has yet been expounded."

"If one should ask me, Gofoloso, and you have asked me, I should say to him as I am about to say to you that the trouble with Veltopismakus is too much peace. Prosperity follows peace—prosperity and plenty of idle time. Time must be occupied. Who would occupy it in labor, even the labor of preparing one's self to defend one's peace and prosperity, when it may so easily be occupied in the pursuit of pleasure? The material prosperity that has followed peace has given us the means to gratify our every whim. We have become satiated with the things we looked upon in the days of yesterday as luxuries to be sparingly enjoyed upon rare occasion. Consequently we have been forced to invent new whims to be gratified and you may rest assured that these have become more and more extravagant and exaggerated in form and idea until even our wondrous prosperity has been taxed to meet the demands of our appetites.

"Extravagance reigns supreme. It rests, like a malign incubus, upon the king and his government. To mend its inroads upon the treasury, the burden of the incubus is shifted from the back of the government to the back of the people in the form of outrageous taxes which no man can meet honestly and have sufficient remaining wherewith to indulge his appetites, and so by one means or another, he passes the burden on to those less fortunate or less shrewd."

"But the heaviest taxation falls upon the rich," Gofoloso reminded him.

"In theory, but not in fact," replied Gefasto. "It is true that the rich pay the bulk of the taxes into the treasury of the king, but first they collect it from the poor in higher prices and other forms of extortion, in the proportion of two *jetaks* for every one that they pay to the tax collector. The cost of collecting this tax added to the loss in revenue to the government by the abolition of wine and the cost of preventing the unscrupulous from making and selling wine illicitly would, if turned back into the coffers of the government, reduce our taxes so materially that they would fall as a burden upon none."

"And that, you think, would solve our problems and restore happiness to Veltopismakus?" asked Gofoloso.

"No," replied his fellow prince. "We must have war. As we

have found that there is no enduring happiness in peace or virtue, let us have a little war and a little sin. A pudding that is all of one ingredient is nauseating—it must be seasoned, it must be spiced, and before we can enjoy the eating of it to the fullest we must be forced to strive for it. War and work, the two most distasteful things in the world, are, nevertheless, the most essential to the happiness and the existence of a people. Peace reduces the necessity for labor, and induces slothfulness. War compels labor, that her ravages may be effaced. Peace turns us into fat worms. War makes men of us."

"War and wine, then, would restore Veltopismakus to her former pride and happiness, you think?" laughed Gofoloso. "What a firebrand you have become since you came to the command of all the warriors of our city!"

"You misunderstand me, Gofoloso," said Gefasto, patiently. "War and wine alone will accomplish nothing but our ruin. I have no quarrel with peace or virtue or temperance. My quarrel is with the misguided theorists who think that peace alone, or virtue alone, or temperance alone will make a strong, a virile, a contented nation. They must be mixed with war and wine and sin and a great measure of hard work—especially hard work—and with nothing but peace and prosperity there is little necessity for hard work, and only the exceptional man works hard when he does not have to.

"But come, you must hasten to deliver the hundred slaves to Vestako before the Sun enters the Warriors' Corridor, or he will tell your little joke to Elkomoelhago."

Gofoloso smiled ruefully. "Some day he shall pay for these hundred slaves," he said, "and the price will be very high."

"If his master falls," said Gefasto.

"*When* his master falls!" Gofoloso corrected.

The Chief of Warriors shrugged his shoulders, but he smiled contentedly, and he was still smiling after his friend had turned into an intersecting corridor and gone his way.

11

TARZAN of the Apes was led directly from the Royal Dome to the quarries of Veltopismakus, which lie a quarter of a mile from the nearer of the eight domes which constitute the city. A ninth dome was in course of construction and it was toward this that the line of burdened slaves wound from the entrance to the quarry to which the ape-man was conducted. Just below the surface, in a well-lighted chamber, he was turned over to the officer in charge of the quarry guard, to whom the king's instructions concerning him were communicated.

"Your name?" demanded the officer, opening a large book that lay upon the table at which he was seated.

"He is as dumb as the Zertalacolols," explained the commander of the escort that had brought him to the quarry. "Therefore he has no name."

"We will call him The Giant, then," said the officer, "for as such has he been known since his capture," and he wrote in his book, *Zuanthrol,* with Zoanthrohago as the owner, and Trohanadalmakus as the city of his origin, and then he turned to one of the warriors lolling upon a nearby bench. "Take him to the timbering crew in the extension of tunnel thirteen at the thirty-sixth level and tell the Vental in charge to give him light work and see that no harm befalls him, for such are the commands of the thagosto—go! But wait! here is his number. Fasten it upon his shoulder."

The warrior took the circular piece of fabric with black hieroglyphics stamped upon it and affixed it with a metal clasp to the left shoulder of Tarzan's green tunic and then, motioning the ape-man to precede him, quit the chamber.

Tarzan now found himself in a short, dark corridor which presently opened into a wider and lighter one along which innumerable, unladen slaves were moving in the same direction that his guard now escorted him. He noticed that the floor of the corridor had a constant downward gradient and that it turned ever to the right, forming a great spiral leading downward into the earth. The walls and ceiling were timbered and the floor paved with flat stones, worn smooth by the millions of sandaled feet that had passed over them. At sufficiently frequent intervals candles were set in niches in the left-hand wall, and, also at regular intervals, other corridors opened out of it. Over each of these openings were more of the strange hieroglyphics of Minuni. As Tarzan was to learn later, these designated the levels at which the tunnels lay and led to circular corridors which surrounded the main spiral runway. From these circular corridors ran the numerous horizontal tunnels leading to the workings at each level. Shafts for ventilation and emergency exit pierced these tunnels at varying distances, running from the surface to the lowest levels of the quarry.

At almost every level a few slaves turned off into these

lateral tunnels which were well lighted, though not quite as
brilliantly as the spiral. Shortly after they had commenced the
descent, Tarzan, accustomed from infancy to keen observation, had taken note of the numbers of tunnel entrances they
passed, but he could only conjecture at the difference in the
depths of the levels into which they opened. A rough guess
placed them at fifteen feet, but before they reached the thirty-
sixth, into which they turned, Tarzan felt that there must be
an error in his calculations, for he was sure that they could
not be five hundred and forty feet below the earth's surface
with open flames and no forced ventilation.

The horizontal corridor they now entered after leaving the
spiral curved sharply to the right and then back to the left.
Shortly afterward it crossed a wide, circular corridor in which
were both laden and unladen slaves, beyond which were two
lines, those laden with rock moving back in the direction from
which Tarzan had come, while others, bearing lumber moved
in the same direction that he did. With both lines there were
unladen slaves.

After traversing the horizontal tunnel for a considerable
distance they came at last upon the working party, and here
Tarzan was turned over to the Vental, a warrior who, in the
military organizations of the Minunians, commands ten men.

"So this is The Giant!" exclaimed the Vental. "And we are
not to work him too hard." His tone was sneering and dis-
agreeable. "Such a giant!" he cried. "Why, he is no larger than
I and they are afraid to let him do any work into the bargain.
Mark you, he will work here or get the lash. Kalfastoban per-
mits no sluggards," and the fellow struck his chest vauntingly.

He who had brought Tarzan appeared disgusted. "You will
do well, Kalfastoban," he said, as he turned away to retrace
his steps to the guard room, "to heed the king's commands. I
should hate to be wearing your harness if aught befell this
speechless slave that has set every tongue in Veltopismakus
going and made Elkomoelhago so jealous of Zoanthrohago
that he would slip steel between his ribs were it not that he
could then no longer steal the great wizard's applause."

"Kalfastoban fears no king," blustered the Vental, "least of
all the sorry specimen that befouls the throne of Veltopishago.
"He fools no one but himself. We all know that Zoanthrohago
is his brain and Gefasto his sword."

"However," warned the other, "be careful of Zuanthrol,"
and he departed.

Kalfastoban Vental set the new slave to work upon the timbering of the tunnel as it was excavated from the great mo-

raine that formed the quarry, the line of slaves coming from the surface empty-handed passed down one side of the tunnel to the end, loosened each a rock, or if heavy a rock to two men, and turned back up the tunnel's opposite side, carrying their burdens back to the spiral runway used by those leaving the workings and so up and out to the new dome. The earth, a light clay, that filled the interstices between the rocks in the moraine was tamped into the opening behind the wall timbers, the tunnel being purposely made sufficiently large to permit of this. Certain slaves were detailed for this work, others carried timbers cut to the right dimensions down to the timbering crew, of which Tarzan was one. It was only necessary for this crew of three to scoop a narrow, shallow trench in which to place the foot of each wall board, set them in place and slip the ceiling board on top of them. At each end of the ceiling boards was a cleat, previously attached at the surface, which kept the wall boards from falling in after being set in place. The dirt tamped behind them fastened them solidly in their places, the whole making a quickly erected and substantial shoring.

The work was light for the ape-man, though he still was weak from the effects of his wounds, and he had opportunities constantly to observe all that went on around him and to gather new information relative to the people in whose power he found himself. Kalfastoban he soon set down as a loud-mouthed braggart, from whom one need have nothing to fear during the routine of their everyday work, but who would bear watching if ever opportunity came for him to make a show of authority or physical prowess before the eyes of his superiors.

The slaves about him worked steadily, but seemed not to be overtaxed, while the guards, which accompanied them constantly, in the ratio of about one warrior to every fifty slaves, gave no indications of brutality in the treatment they accorded their charges, insofar as Tarzan was able to observe.

The fact that puzzled him most now as it had since the moment of his first return to consciousness, was the stature of these people. They were no pygmies, but men fully as large as the usual run of Europeans. There was none quite as tall as the ape-man, but there were many who missed it by but the scantiest fraction of an inch. He knew that they were Veltopismakusians, the same people he had seen battling with the Trohanadalmakusians; they spoke of having captured him in the battle that he had seen waged; and they called him Zuanthrol, The Giant, yet they were as large as he, and as he had passed from the Royal Dome to the quarry he had seen their gigantic dome dwellings rising fully four hundred feet above his head. It was all preposterous and impossible, yet he had the testimony of all his faculties that it was true. Contemplation of it but tended to confuse him more and so he gave over all attempts to solve the mystery and set himself to the gathering of information concerning his captors and his prison against that time which he well knew must some day come when the means of escape should offer itself to the alert and cunning instincts of the wild beast that, at heart, he always considered himself.

Wherever he had been in Veltopismakus, whoever he had heard refer to the subject, he had had it borne in upon him that the people were generally dissatisfied with their king and his government, and he knew that among a discontented people efficiency would be at low ebb and discipline demoralized to such an extent that, should he watch carefully, he must eventually discover the opportunity he sought, through the laxity of those responsible for his safekeeping. He did not expect it today or tomorrow, but today and tomorrow were the days upon which to lay the foundation of observation that would eventually reveal an avenue of escape.

When the long working day at last drew to a close the slaves were conducted to their quarters, which, as Tarzan discovered, were always on levels near to those in which they labored. He, with several other slaves, was conducted to the thirty-fifth level and into a tunnel the far end of which had been widened to the proportions of a large chamber, the narrow entrance to which had been walled up with stone except for a small aperture through which the slaves were forced to pass in and out of their chamber upon all fours, and when the last of them was within, this was closed and secured by a heavy door outside which two warriors watched throughout the night.

Once inside and standing upon his feet the ape-man looked about him to discover himself within a chamber so large that it seemed easy to accommodate the great throng of slaves that must have numbered fully five thousand souls of both sexes. The women were preparing food over small fires the smoke of which found its way from the chamber through openings in the ceiling. For the great number of fires the amount of smoke was noticeably little, a fact which was, however, accounted for by the nature of the fuel, a clean, hard charcoal; but why the liberated gases did not asphyxiate them all was quite beyond the ape-man, as was still the riddle of the open flames and the pure air at the depth where the workings lay. Candles burned in niches all about the walls and there were at least half-a-dozen large ones standing upon the floor.

The slaves were of all ages from infancy to middle age, but there were no aged venerables among them. The skins of the women and children were the whitest Tarzan had ever seen and he marveled at them until he came to know that some of the former and all of the latter had never seen daylight since birth. The children who were born here would go up into the daylight some time, when they were of an age that warranted beginning the training for the vocations their masters had chosen for them, but the women who had been captured from other cities would remain here until death claimed them, unless that rarest of miracles occurred—they should be chosen by a Veltopismakusian warrior as his mate; but that was scarce even a remote possibility, since the warriors almost invariably chose their mates from the slaves of the white tunic with whom they came in daily contact in the domes above ground.

The faces of the women bore the imprint of a sadness that brought a spontaneous surge of sympathy to the breast of the savage ape-man. Never in his life had he seen such abject hopelessness depicted upon any face.

As he crossed the room many were the glances that were cast upon him, for it was obvious from his deep tan that he was a newcomer, and, too, there was that about him that marked him of different clay from them, and soon there were whispers running through the throng, for the slaves who had entered with him had passed the word of his identity to the others, and who, even in the bowels of the earth, had not heard of the wondrous giant captured by Zoanthrohago during the battle with the Trohanadalmakusians?

Presently a young girl, kneeling above a brazier over which she was grilling a cut of flesh, caught his eye and motioned him to her. As he came he saw that she was very beautiful, with a pale, translucent skin the whiteness of which was accentuated by the blue-black of a wealth of lustrous hair.

"You are The Giant?" she asked.

"I am Zuanthrol," he replied.

"He has told me about you," said the girl. "I will cook for you, too. I cook for him. Unless," she added with a trace of embarrassment, "there is another you would rather have cook for you."

"There is no one I would rather have cook for me," Tarzan told her; "but who are you and who is *he?*"

"I am Talaskar," she replied; "but I know him only by his

number. He says that while he remains a slave he has no name, but will go always by his number, which is Eight Hundred Cubed, Plus Nineteen. I see that you are Eight Hundred Cubed, Plus Twenty-one." She was looking at the hieroglyphics that had been fastened upon his shoulder. "Have you a name?"

"They call me Zuanthrol."

"Ah," she said, "you are a large man, but I should scarcely call you a giant. He, too, is from Trohanadalmakus and he is about your height. I never heard that there were any giants in Minuni except the people they call Zertalacolols."

"I thought you were a Zertalacolol," said a man's voice at Tarzan's ear.

The ape-man turned to see one of the slaves with whom he had been working eyeing him quizzically, and smiled.

"I am a Zertalacolol to my masters," he replied.

The other raised his brows. "I see," he said. "Perhaps you are wise. I shall not be the one to betray you," and passed on about his business.

"What did he mean?" asked the girl.

"I have never spoken, until now, since they took me prisoner," he explained, "and they think I am speechless, though I am sure that I do not look like a Zertalacolol, yet some of them insist that I am one."

"I have never seen one," said the girl.

"You are fortunate," Tarzan told her. "They are neither pleasant to see nor to meet."

"But I should like to see them," she insisted. "I should like to see anything that was different from these slaves whom I see all day and every day."

"Do not lose hope," he encouraged her, "for who knows but that it may be very soon that you will return to the surface."

" 'Return,' " she repeated. "I have never been there."

"Never been to the surface! You mean since you were captured."

"I was born in this chamber," she told him, "and never have I been out of it."

"You are a slave of the second generation and are still confined to the quarries—I do not understand it. In all Minunian cities, I have been told, slaves of the second generation are given the white tunic and comparative freedom above ground."

"It was not for me. My mother would not permit it. She would rather I had died than mated with a Veltopismakusian or another slave, as I must do if I go into the city above."

"But how do you avoid it? Your masters certainly do not leave such things to the discretion of their slaves."

"Where there are so many one or two may go unaccounted for indefinitely, and women, if they be ill-favored, cause no comment upon the part of our masters. My birth was never reported and so they have no record of me. My mother took a number for me from the tunic of one who died, and in this way I attract no attention upon the few occasions that our masters or the warriors enter our chamber."

"But you are not ill-favored—your face would surely attract attention anywhere," Tarzan reminded her.

For just an instant she turned her back upon him, putting her hands to her face and to her hair, and then she faced him again and the ape-man saw before him a hideous and wrinkled hag upon whose crooked features no man would look a second time.

"God!" ejaculated Tarzan.

Slowly the girl's face relaxed, assuming its normal lines of beauty, and with quick, deft touches she arranged her disheveled hair. An expression that was almost a smile haunted her lips.

"My mother taught me this," she said, "so that when they came and looked upon me they would not want me."

"But would it not be better to be mated with one of them and live a life of comfort above ground than to eke out a terrible existence below ground?" he demanded. "The warriors of Veltopismakus are, doubtless, but little different from those of your own country."

She shook her head. "It cannot be, for me," she said. "My father is of far Mandalamakus. My mother was stolen from him but a couple of moons before I was born in this horrid chamber, far from the air and sunlight that my mother never tired of telling me about."

"And your mother?" asked Tarzan. "Is she here?"

The girl shook her head sadly. "They came for her over twenty moons since and took her away. I do not know what became of her."

"And these others, they never betray you?" he inquired.

"Never! Whatever slave betrayed another would be torn to pieces by his fellows. But come, you must be hungry," and she offered him of the flesh she had been cooking.

Tarzan would have preferred his meat raw, but he did not wish to offend her and so he thanked her and ate that which she offered him, squatting on his haunches across the brazier from her.

"It is strange that Aoponato does not come," she remarked, using the Minunian form of Eight Hundred Cubed, Plus Nineteen. "Never before has he been so late."

A brawny slave, who had approached from behind her, had halted and was looking scowlingly at Tarzan.

"Perhaps this is he," said Tarzan to the girl, indicating the man with a gesture.

Talaskar turned quickly, an almost happy light in her eyes, but when she saw who it was that stood behind her she rose quickly and stepped back, her expression altered to one of disgust.

"No," she said, "it is not he."

"You are cooking for him?" demanded the fellow, pointing at Tarzan. "But you would not cook for me," he accused, not waiting for a reply to his question, the answer to which was all too obvious. "Who is he that you should cook for him? Is he better than I? You will cook for me, also."

"There are plenty to cook for you, Caraftap," replied Talaskar, "and I do not wish to. Go to some other woman. Until there are too many men we are permitted to choose those whom we shall cook for. I do not choose to cook for you."

"If you know what is well for you, you will cook for me," growled the man. "You will be my mate, too. I have a right to you, because I have asked you many times before these others came. Rather than let them have you I will tell the Vental tomorrow the truth about you and he will take you away. Have you ever seen Kalfastoban?"

The girl shuddered.

"I will see that Kalfastoban gets you," continued Caraftap. "They will not permit you to remain here when they find that you refuse to produce more slaves."

"I should prefer Kalfastoban to you," sneered the girl, "but neither one nor the other shall have me."

"Do not be too sure of that," he cried, and stepping forward, quickly, seized her by the arm before she could elude him. Dragging her toward him the man attempted to kiss her—but he did not succeed. Steel fingers closed upon his shoulder, he was torn roughly from his prey and hurled ruthlessly a dozen paces, stumbling and falling to the floor. Between him and the girl stood the gray-eyed stranger with the shock of black hair.

Almost roaring in his rage, Caraftap scrambled to his feet and charged Tarzan—charged as a mad bull charges, with lowered head and bloodshot eyes.

"For this you shall die," he screamed.

12

THE Son of The First Woman strode proudly through the forest. He carried a spear, jauntily, and there were a bow and arrows slung to his back. Behind him came ten other males of his species, similarly armed, and each walked as though he owned the earth he trod. Toward them along the trail, though still beyond their sight, or hearing, or smell, came a woman of their kind. She, too, walked with fearless step. Presently her eyes narrowed and she paused, up-pricking her great, flat ears to listen; sniffing the air. Men! She increased her gait to a trot, bearing down upon them. There was more than one—there were several. If she came upon them suddenly they would be startled, filled with confusion, and no doubt she could seize one of them before they took to flight. If not—the feathered pebbles at her girdle would seek one out.

For some time men had been scarce. Many women of her tribe who had gone out into the forest to capture mates had never returned. She had seen the corpses of several of these herself, lying in the forest. She had wondered what had killed them. But here were men at last, the first she had discovered in two moons, and this time she would not return empty-handed to her cave.

At a sudden turning of the forest trail she came within sight of them, but saw, to her dismay, that they were still a long way off. They would be sure to escape if they saw her, and she was upon the point of hiding when she realized that already it was too late. One of them was pointing at her. Loosing a missile from her girdle and grasping her cudgel more firmly she started toward them at a rapid, lumbering run. She was both surprised and pleased when she saw that they made no attempt to escape. How terrified they must be to stand thus docilely while she approached them. But what was this? They were advancing to meet her! And now she saw the expressions upon their faces. No fear there—only rage and menace. What were the strange things they carried in their hands? One who was running toward her, the nearest, paused and hurled a long pointed stick at her. It was sharp and when it grazed her shoulder it brought blood. Another paused and holding a little stick across a longer stick, the ends of which were bent back with a piece of gut, suddenly released the smaller stick, which leaped through the air and pierced the flesh beneath one of her arms. And behind these two the others were rushing upon her with similar weapons. She recalled the corpses of women she had seen in the forest and the dearth of men for the past several moons, and though she was dull of wit yet she was not without reasoning faculties and so she compared these facts with the occurrences of the past few seconds with a resultant judgment that sent her lumbering away, in the direction from which she had come, as fast as her hairy legs could carry her, nor did she once pause in her mad flight until she sank exhausted at the mouth of her own cave.

The men did not pursue her. As yet they had not reached that stage in their emancipation that was to give them sufficient courage and confidence in themselves to entirely overcome their hereditary fear of women. To chase one away was sufficient. To pursue her would have been tempting Providence.

When the other women of the tribe saw their fellow stagger to her cave and sensed that her condition was the result of terror and the physical strain of long flight they seized their cudgels and ran forth, prepared to meet and vanquish her pursuer, which they immediately assumed to be a lion. But no lion appeared and then some of them wandered to the side of the woman who lay panting on her threshold.

"From what did you run?" they asked her in their simple sign language.

"Men," she replied.

Disgust showed plainly upon every face, and one of them kicked her and another spat upon her.

"There were many," she told them, "and they would have killed me with flying sticks. Look!" and she showed them the spear wound, and the arrow still embedded in the flesh beneath her arm. "They did not run from me, but came forward to attack me. Thus have all the women been killed whose corpses we have seen in the forest during the past few moons."

This troubled them. They ceased to annoy the prostrate woman. Their leader, the fiercest of them, paced to and fro, making hideous faces. Suddenly she halted.

"Come!" she signaled. "We shall go forth together and find these men, and bring them back and punish them." She shook her cudgel above her head and grimaced horribly.

The others danced about her, imitating her expression and her actions, and when she started off toward the forest they trooped behind her, a savage, bloodthirsty company—all but the woman who still lay panting where she had fallen. She had had enough of man—she was through with him forever.

"For this you shall die!" screamed Caraftap, as he rushed upon Tarzan of the Apes in the long gallery of the slaves' quarters in the quarry of Elkomeolhago, king of Veltopismakus.

The ape-man stepped quickly aside, avoiding the other, and tripped him with a foot, sending him sprawling, face downward, upon the floor. Caraftap, before he arose, looked about as though in search of a weapon and, his eyes alighting upon the hot brazier, he reached forth to seize it. A murmur of disapproval rose from the slaves who, having been occupied nearby, had seen the inception of the quarrel.

"No weapons!" cried one. "It is not permitted among us. Fight with your bare hands or not at all."

But Caraftap was too drunk with hate and jealousy to hear them or to heed, and so he grasped the brazier and, rising, rushed at Tarzan to hurl it in his face. Now it was another who tripped him and this time two slaves leaped upon him and wrenched the brazier from his hand. "Fight fair!" they admonished him, and dragged him to his feet.

Tarzan had stood smiling and indifferent, for the rage of others amused him where it was greater than circumstances warranted, and now he waited for Caraftap and when his adversary saw the smile upon his face it but increased his spleen, so that he fairly leaped upon the ape-man in his madness to destroy him, and Tarzan met him with the most surprising defense that Caraftap, who for long had been a bully among the slaves, ever had encountered. It was a doubled fist at the end of a straight arm and it caught Caraftap upon the point of his chin, stretching him upon his back. The slaves, who had by this time gathered in considerable numbers to watch the quarrel, voiced their approval in the shrill, "Ee-ah-ee-ah," that constituted one form of applause.

Dazed and groggy, Caraftap staggered to his feet once more and with lowered head looked about him as though in search of his enemy. The girl, Talaskar, had come to Tarzan's side and was standing there looking up into his face.

"You are very strong," she said, but the expression in her eyes said more, or at least it seemed to Caraftap to say more. It seemed to speak of love, whereas it was only the admiration that a normal woman always feels for strength exercised in a worthy cause.

Caraftap made a noise in his throat that sounded much like the squeal of an angry pig and once again he rushed upon the ape-man. Behind them some slaves were being let into the corridor and as the aperture was open one of the warriors beyond it, who chanced to be stooping down at the time, could see within. He saw but little, though what he saw was enough —a large slave with a shock of black hair raising another large slave high above his head and dashing him to the hard floor. The warrior, pushing the slaves aside, scrambled through into the corridor and ran forward toward the center. Before they were aware of his presence he stood facing Tarzan and Talaskar. It was Kalfastoban.

"What is the meaning of this?" he cried in a loud voice, and then: "Ah, ha! I see. It is The Giant. He would show the other slaves how strong he is, would he?" He glanced at Caraftap, struggling to rise from the floor, and his face grew very dark —Caraftap was a favorite of his. "Such things are not permitted here, fellow!" he cried, shaking his fist in the ape-man's face, and forgetting in his anger that the new slave neither spoke nor understood. But presently he recollected and motioned Tarzan to follow him. "A hundred lashes will explain to him that he must not quarrel," he said aloud to no one in particular, but he was looking at Talaskar.

"Do not punish him," cried the girl, still forgetful of herself. "It was all Caraftap's fault, Zuanthrol but acted in self-defense."

Kalfastoban could not take his eyes from the girl's face and presently she sensed her danger and flushed, but still she stood her ground, interceding for the ape-man. A crooked smile twisted Kalfastoban's mouth as he laid a familiar hand upon her shoulder.

"How old are you?" he asked.

She told him, shuddering.

"I shall see your master and purchase you," he announced. "Take no mate."

Tarzan was looking at Talaskar and it seemed that he could see her wilt, as a flower wilts in noxious air, and then Kalfastoban turned upon him.

"You cannot understand me, you stupid beast," he said; "but I can tell you, and those around you may listen and, perhaps, guide you from danger. This time I shall let you off, but let it happen again and you shall have a hundred lashes, or worse, maybe; and if I hear that you have had aught to do with this girl, whom I intend to purchase and take to the surface, it will go still harder with you," with which he strode to the entrance and passed through into the corridor beyond.

After the Vental had departed and the door of the chamber

had been closed a hand was laid upon Tarzan's shoulder from behind and a man's voice called him by name: "Tarzan!" It sounded strange in his ears, far down in this buried chamber beneath the ground, in an alien city and among an alien people, not one of whom ever had heard his name, but as he turned to face the man who had greeted him a look of recognition and a smile of pleasure overspread his features.

"Kom—!" he started to ejaculate, but the other placed a finger to his lips. "Not here," he said. "Here I am Aoponato."

"But your stature! You are as large as I. It is beyond me. What has happened to swell the race of Minunians to such relatively gigantic proportions?"

Komodoflorensal smiled. "Human egotism would not permit you to attribute this change to an opposite cause from that to which you have ascribed it," he said.

Tarzan knit his brows and gazed long and thoughtfully at his royal friend. An expression that was of mingled incredulity and amusement crept gradually over his countenance.

"You mean," he asked slowly, "that I have been reduced in size to the stature of a Minunian?"

Komodoflorensal nodded. "Is it not easier to believe that than to think that an entire race of people and all their belongings, even their dwellings and the stones that they were built of, and all their weapons and their diadets, had been increased in size to your own stature?"

"But I tell you it is impossible!" cried the ape-man.

"I should have said the same thing a few moons ago," replied the prince. "Even when I heard the rumor here that they had reduced you I did not believe it, not for a long time, and I was still a bit skeptical until I entered this chamber and saw you with my own eyes."

"How was it accomplished?" demanded Tarzan.

"The greatest mind in Veltopismakus, and perhaps in all Minuni, is Zoanthrohago," explained Komodoflorensal. "We have recognized this for many moons, for, during the occasional intervals that we are at peace with Veltopismakus, there is some exchange of ideas as well as goods between the two cities, and thus we heard of many marvels attributed to this greatest of walmaks."

"I have never heard a wizard spoken of in Minuni until now," said Tarzan, for he thought that that was the meaning of the word *walmak*, and perhaps it is, as nearly as it can be translated into English. A scientist who works miracles would be, perhaps, a truer definition.

"It was Zoanthrohago who captured you," continued Aoponato, "encompassing your fall by means at once scientific and miraculous. After you had fallen he caused you to lose consciousness and while you were in that condition you were dragged hither by a score of diadets hitched to a hastily improvised litter built of small trees tied securely one to the other, after their branches had been removed. It was after they had you safely within Veltopismakus that Zoanthrohago set to work upon you to reduce your stature, using apparatus that he has built himself. I have heard them discussing it and they say that it did not take him long."

"I hope that Zoanthrohago has the power to undo that which he has done," said the ape-man.

"They say that that is doubtful. He has never been able to make a creature larger than it formerly was, though in his numerous experiments he has reduced the size of many of the lower animals. The fact of the matter is," continued Aoponato, "that he has been searching for a means to enlarge the Veltopismakusians so that they may overcome all the other peoples of Minuni, but he has only succeeded in developing a method that gives precisely opposite results from that which they seek, so, if he cannot make others larger, I doubt if he can make you any larger than you now are."

"I would be rather helpless among the enemies of my own world," said Tarzan, ruefully.

"You need not worry about that, my friend," said the prince gently.

"Why?" asked the ape-man.

"Because you have very little chance of reaching your own world again," said Komodoflorensal a trifle sadly. "I have no hope of ever seeing Trohanadalmakus again. Only by the utter overthrow of Veltopismakus by my father's warriors could I hope for rescue, since nothing less could overcome the guard in the quarry mouth. While we often capture slaves of the white tunic from the enemies' cities, it is seldom that we gather in any of the green tunic. Only in the rare cases of utter surprise attacks by daylight do any of us catch an enemies' green slaves above ground, and surprise day attacks may occur once in the lifetime of a man, or never."

"You believe that we will spend the rest of our lives in this underground hole?" demanded Tarzan.

"Unless we chance to be used for labor above ground during the daytime, occasionally," replied the prince of Trohanadalmakus, with a wry smile.

The ape-man shrugged. "We shall see," he said.

After Kalfastoban had left, Caraftap had limped away to

the far end of the chamber, muttering to himself, his ugly face black and scowling.

"I am afraid that he will make you trouble," Talaskar said to Tarzan, indicating the disgruntled slave with a nod of her shapely head, "and I am sorry, for it is all my fault."

"Your fault?" demanded Komodoflorensal.

"Yes," said the girl. "Caraftap was threatening me when Aopontando interfered and punished him."

"Aopontando?" queried Komodoflorensal.

"That is my number," explained Tarzan.

"And it was on account of Talaskar that you were fighting? I thank you, my friend. I am sorry that I was not here to protect her. Talaskar cooks for me. She is a good girl." Komodoflorensal was looking at the girl as he spoke and Tarzan saw how her eyes lowered beneath his gaze and the delicate flush that mounted her cheeks, and he realized that he was downwind from an idea, and smiled.

"So this is the Aoponato of whom you told me?" he said to Talaskar.

"Yes, this is he."

"I am sorry that he was captured, but it is good to find a friend here," said the ape-man. "We three should be able to hit upon some plan of escape," but they shook their heads, smiling sadly.

For a while, after they had eaten, they sat talking together, being joined occasionally by other slaves, for Tarzan had many friends here now since he had chastized Caraftap and they would have talked all night had not the ape-man questioned Komodoflorensal as to the sleeping arrangements of the slaves.

Komodoflorensal laughed, and pointed here and there about the chamber at recumbent figures lying upon the hard earthen floor; men, women and children sleeping, for the most part, where they had eaten their evening meal.

"The green slaves are not pampered," he remarked laconically.

"I can sleep anywhere," said Tarzan, "but more easily when it is dark. I shall wait until the lights are extinguished."

"You will wait forever, then," Komodoflorensal told him.

"The lights are never extinguished?" demanded the ape-man.

"Were they, we should all be soon dead," replied the prince. "These flames serve two purposes—they dissipate the darkness and consume the foul gases that would otherwise quickly asphyxiate us. Unlike the ordinary flame, that consumes oxygen, these candles, perfected from the discoveries and inventions of an ancient Minunian scientist, consume the deadly gases and liberate oxygen. It is because of this even more than for the light they give that they are used exclusively throughout Minuni. Even our domes would be dark, ill-smelling, noxious places were it not for them, while the quarries would be absolutely unworkable."

"Then I shall not wait for them to be extinguished," said Tarzan, stretching himself at full length upon the dirt floor, with a nod and a "Tuano!"—a Minunian "Good night!"—to Talaskar and Komodoflorensal.

13

As Talaskar was preparing their breakfast the following morning Komodoflorensal remarked to Tarzan that he wished they two could be employed upon the same work, that they might be always together.

"If there is ever the chance for escape that you seem to think will some day present itself," he said, "then it will be well if we are together."

"When we go," replied Tarzan, "we must take Talaskar with us."

Komodoflorensal shot a swift glance at the ape-man, but made no comment upon his suggestion.

"You would take me with you!" exclaimed Talaskar. "Ah, if such a dream could but be realized! I would go with you to Trohanadalmakus and be your slave, for I know that you would not harm me; but, alas, it can be nothing more than a pleasant daydream, enduring for a brief time, for Kalfastoban has spoken for me and doubtless my master will be glad to sell me to him, for I have heard it said among the slaves that he sells many of his each year to raise the money to pay his taxes."

"We will do what we can, Talaskar," said Tarzan, "and if Aoponato and I find a means of escape we will take you with us; but first he and I must find a way to be together more."

"I have a plan," said Komodoflorensal, "that might prove successful. They believe that you neither speak nor understand our language. To work a slave with whom they cannot communicate is, to say the least, annoying. I shall tell them that

I can communicate with you, when it is quite probable that they will assign us to the same crew."

"But how will you communicate with me without using the Minunian language?" demanded the ape-man.

"Leave that to me," replied Komodoflorensal. "Until they discover in some other way that you speak Minunian I can continue to deceive them."

It was not long before the fruits of Komodoflorensal's plan ripened. The guards had come for the slaves and the various parties had gone forth from the sleeping chamber, joining in the corridors without the thousands of others wending their way to the scene of their daily labor. The ape-man joined the timbering crew at the extension of the thirteenth tunnel at the thirty-sixth level where he once more attacked the monotonous work of shoring the sides and roof of the shaft with an enthusiasm that elicited commendation from even the surly Kalfastoban, though Caraftap, who was removing rocks just ahead of Tarzan, often shot venomous looks at the ape-man.

The work had been progressing for perhaps two or three hours when two warriors descended the tunnel and halted beside Kalfastoban. They were escorting a green-tunicked slave, to whom Tarzan paid no more attention than he did to the warriors until a scrap of the conversation between the warriors and Kalfastoban reached his ears, then he shot a quick glance in the direction of the four and saw that the slave was Komodoflorensal, Prince of Trohanadalmakus, known in the quarries of Vetlopismakus as Slave Aoponato, or $800^3 + 19$,

which is written in Minunian hieroglyphics ⊙ .

Tarzan's number Aopontando, $800^3 + 21$, appeared thus,

upon the shoulder of his green tunic: ⊙ . Although the

Minunian form occupies less space than would our English equivalent of Tarzan's number, which is 512,000,021, it would be more difficult to read if expressed in English words, for it then would be, ten times ten times eight, cubed, plus seven times three; but the Minunians translate it in no such way. To them it is a whole number, Aopontando, which represents at first glance a single quantity as surely as do the digits 37 represent to our minds an invariable amount, a certain, definite measure of quantity which we never think of as three times ten plus seven, which, in reality, it is. The Minunian system of numerals, while unthinkably cumbersome and awkward from the European point of view, is, however, not without its merits.

As Tarzan looked up Komodoflorensal caught his eye and winked and then Kalfastoban beckoned to the ape-man, who crossed the corridor and stood in silence before the Vental.

"Let us hear you talk to him," cried Kalfastoban to Komodoflorensal. "I don't believe that he will understand you. How could he when he cannot understand us?" The fellow could not conceive of another language than his own.

"I will ask him in his own language," said Komodoflorensal, "if he understands me, and you will see that he nods his head affirmatively."

"Very good," cried Kalfastoban; "ask him."

Komodoflorensal turned toward Tarzan and voiced a dozen syllables of incomprehensible gibberish and when he was done the ape-man nodded his head.

"You see," demanded Komodoflorensal.

Kalfastoban scratched his head. "It is even as he says," he admitted, ruefully, "the Zertalacolol has a language."

Tarzan did not smile, though he should have liked to, at the clever manner in which Komodoflorensal had deceived the Veltopismakusians into believing that he had communicated with Tarzan in a strange language. As long as he could contrive to put all his communications into questions that could be answered by yes or no, the deception would be easily maintained; but under circumstances that made this impossible some embarrassments might be expected to arise, and he wondered how the resourceful Trohanadalmakusian would handle these.

"Tell him," said one of the warriors to Komodoflorensal, "that his master, Zoanthrohago, has sent for him, and ask him if he fully understands that he is a slave and that upon his good behavior depends his comfort; yes, even his life, for Zoanthrohago has the power of life and death over him; as much so as have the royal family. If he comes docilely to his master and is obedient he will not fare ill, but if he be lazy, impudent, or threatening he may expect to taste the point of a freeman's sword."

Komodoflorensal strung out, this time, a much longer series of senseless syllables, until he could scarce compose his features to comport with the seriousness of his mien.

"Tell them," said Tarzan, in English, which, of course, not one of them understood, "that at the first opportunity I shall break the neck of my master; that it would require but little incentive to cause me to seize one of these timbers and crack the skull of Kalfastoban and the rest of the warriors about us;

and I shall run away at the first opportunity and take you and Talaskar with me."

Komodoflorensal listened intently until Tarzan had ceased speaking and then turned to the two warriors who had come with him to find the ape-man.

"Zuanthrol says that he fully understands his position and that he is glad to serve the noble and illustrious Zoanthrohago, from whom he claims but a single boon," translated the Trohanadalmakusian prince, rather freely.

"And what boon is that?" demanded one of the warriors.

"That I be permitted to accompany him that he may thus better fulfil the wishes of his master, since without me he could not even know what was desired of him," explained Aoponato.

Tarzan understood now how Komodoflorensal would surmount whatever difficulties of communication might arise and he felt that he would be safe in the hands of his quick-witted friend for as long a time as he cared to pretend ignorance of the Minunian tongue.

"The thought was even in our minds, slave, when we heard that you could communicate with this fellow," said the warrior to whom Komodoflorensal had addressed the suggestion. "You shall both be taken to Zoanthrohago, who will doubtless decide his wishes without consulting you or any other slave. Come! Kalfastoban Vental, we assume responsibility for the Slave Zuanthrol," and they handed the Vental a slip of paper upon which they had marked some curious hieroglyphics.

Then, with swords drawn, they motioned Komodoflorensal and Tarzan to precede them along the corridor, for the story of Tarzan's handling of Caraftap had reached even to the guard room of the quarry, and these warriors were taking no chances.

The way led through a straight corridor and up a winding spiral runway to the surface, where Tarzan greeted the sunlight and the fresh air almost with a sob of gratitude, for to be shut away from them for even a brief day was to the ape-man cruel punishment, indeed. Here he saw again the vast, endless multitude of slaves bearing their heavy burdens to and fro, the trim warriors who paced haughtily upon either flank of the long lines of toiling serfs, the richly trapped nobles of the higher castes and the innumerable white-tunicked slaves who darted hither and thither upon the errands of their masters, or upon their own business or pleasure, for many of these had a certain freedom and independence that gave them almost the standing of freemen. Always were these slaves of the white tunic owned by a master, but, especially in the case of skilled artisans, about the only allegiance they owed to this master was to pay to him a certain percentage of their incomes. They constituted the bourgeoisie of Minuni and also the higher caste serving class. Unlike the green-tunicked slaves, no guard was placed over them to prevent their escape, since there was no danger that they would attempt to escape, there being no city in Minuni where their estate would be improved, for any other city than that of their birth would treat them as alien prisoners, reducing them immediately to the green tunic and lifelong hard labor.

The domes of Veltopismakus were as imposing as those of Trohanadalmakus. In fact, to Tarzan, they appeared infinitely larger since he now was one-fourth the size he had been when he had left Trohanadalmakus. There were eight of them fully occupied and another in course of construction, for the surface population of Veltopismakus was already four hundred and eighty thousand souls, and as overcrowding was not permitted in the king's dome the remaining seven were packed densely with humanity.

It was to the royal dome that Tarzan and Komodoflorensal were conducted, but they did not enter by way of the King's Corridor, before the gates of which fluttered the white and gold of the royal standards. Instead they were escorted to the Warrior's Corridor, which opens toward the west. Unlike the city of Trohanadalmakus, Veltopismakus was beautiful in the areas between the domes with flowers and shrubbery and trees, among which wound graveled walks and broad roadways. The royal dome faced upon a large parade where a body of mounted warriors was at drill. There were a thousand of them, forming an amak, consisting of four novands of two hundred fifty men each, the larger body being commanded by a kamak and the smaller by a novand. Five entex of fifty men each compose a novand, there being five entals of ten men each to an entex; these latter units commanded by a Vental and a Ventex, respectively. The evolutions of the amak were performed with kaleidoscopic rapidity, so quick upon their feet and so well trained were the tiny diadets. There was one evolution in particular, performed while he was passing, that greatly interested the ape-man. Two novands formed line at one end of the parade and two at the other and at the command of the kamak the thousand men charged swiftly down the field in two solid ranks that approached one another with the speed of an express train. Just when it seemed impossible that a serious accident could be averted, when it seemed that in another instant diadets and riders must crash together in a bloody jumble of broken bones, the warriors rushing so swiftly toward the east raised their agile mounts, which fairly flew above the heads of the opposing force and alighting upon the other side in an unbroken line continued to the far end of the field.

Tarzan was commenting on this maneuver and upon the beauties of the landscaping of the city of Veltopismakus to Komodoflorensal as they proceeded along the Warrior's Corridor, sufficiently ahead of their escort that Tarzan might speak in a low tone without the guard being cognizant of the fact that he was using the language of Minuni.

"It is a beautiful evolution," replied Komodoflorensal, "and it was performed with a precision seldom attained. I have heard that Elkomoelhago's troops are famous for the perfection of their drill, and as justly so as is Veltopismakus for the beauty of her walks and gardens; but, my friend, these very things constitute the weakness of the city. While Elkomoelhago's warriors are practicing to perfect their appearance upon parade, the warriors of my father, Adendrohahkis, are far afield, out of sight of admiring women and spying slaves, practicing the art of war under the rough conditions of the field and camp. The amaks of Elkomoelhago might easily defeat those of Adendrohahkis in a contest for the most beautiful; but it was not long since you saw less than fifteen thousand Trohanadalmakusians repulse fully thirty thousand warriors of Veltopismakus, for they never passed the infantry line that day. Yes, they can drill beautifully upon parade and they are courageous, all Minunians are that, but they have not been trained in the sterner arts of war—it is not the way of Elkomoelhago. He is soft and effeminate. He cares not for war. He listens to the advice he likes best—the advice of the weaklings and the women who urge him to refrain from war entirely, which would be not altogether bad if he could persuade the other fellow to refrain, also.

"The beautiful trees and shrubs that almost make a forest of Veltopismakus, and which you so admire! I, too, admire them—especially do I admire them in the city of an enemy. How easy it would be for a Trohanadalmakusian army to creep through the night, hidden by the beautiful trees and shrubs, to the very gateways of the domes of Veltopismakus! Do you understand now, my friend, why you saw less perfect maneuvers upon the parade grounds of my city than you have seen here, and why, though we love trees and shrubbery, we have none planted within the city of Trohanadalmakus?"

One of the guards who had approached him quickly from the rear touched Komodoflorensal upon the shoulder. "You said that Zuanthrol does not understand our language. Why then do you speak to him in this tongue which he cannot understand," the fellow demanded.

Komodoflorensal did not know how much the warrior had overheard. If he had heard Tarzan speak in Minuni it might be difficult to persuade the fellow that The Giant did not understand the language; but he must act on the assumption that he, alone, had been overheard.

"He wishes to learn it and I am trying to teach him," replied Komodoflorensal quickly.

"Has he learned anything of it?" asked the warrior.

"No," said Komodoflorensal, "he is very stupid."

And after this they went in silence, winding up long, gentle inclines, or again scaling the primitive ladders that the Minunians use to reach the upper levels of their dome-houses between the occasional levels that are not connected by the inclined runways, which are thus frequently broken for purposes of defense, the ladders being easily withdrawn upward behind hard-pressed defenders and the advance of the enemy thus more easily checked.

The royal dome of Elkomoelhago was of vast proportions, its summit rising to an equivalent of over four hundred feet, had it been built upon a scale corresponding to the relatively larger size of ordinary mankind. Tarzan ascended until he was almost as far above ground as he had been below ground in the quarry. Where the corridors on lower levels had been crowded with humanity, those which they now traversed were almost devoid of life. Occasionally they passed a tenanted chamber, but far more generally the rooms were utilized for storage purposes, especially for food, great quantities of which, cured, dried neatly wrapped, was packed ceiling-high in many large chambers.

The decorations of the walls were less ornate and the corridors narrower, on the whole, than those at lower levels. However, they passed through many large chambers, or halls, which were gorgeously decorated, and in several of which were many people of both sexes and all ages variously occupied, either with domestic activities or with the handiwork of one art or another.

Here was a man working in silver, perhaps fashioning a bracelet of delicate filigree, or another carving beautiful arabesques upon leather. There were makers of pottery, weavers of cloth, metal-stampers, painters, makers of candles, and these appeared to predominate, for the candle was in truth life to these people.

And then, at last, they reached the highest level, far above the ground, where the rooms were much closer to daylight because of the diminished thickness of the walls near the summit of the dome, but even here were the ever-present candles. Suddenly the walls of the corridor became gorgeously decorated, the number of candles increased, and Tarzan sensed that they were approaching the quarters of a rich or powerful noble. They halted, now, before a doorway where stood a sentinel, with whom one of the warriors conducting them communicated.

"Tell Zoanthrohago Zertol that we have brought Zuanthrol and another slave who can communicate with him in a strange tongue."

The sentinel struck a heavy gong with his lance and presently, from the interior of the chamber, a man appeared to whom the sentinel repeated the warrior's message.

"Let them enter," said the newcomer, who was a white-tunicked slave; "my glorious master, Zoanthrohago Zertol, expects his slave Zuanthrol. Follow me!"

They followed him through several chambers until at last he led them into the presence of a gorgeously garbed warrior who was seated behind a large table, or desk, upon which were numerous strange instruments, large, cumbersome looking volumes, pads of heavy Minunian writing paper and the necessary implements for writing. The man looked up as they entered the room.

"It is your slave, Zuanthrol, Zertol," announced the fellow who had led them hither.

"But the other?" Prince Zoanthrohago pointed at Komodoflorensal.

"He speaks the strange language that Zuanthrol speaks, and he was brought along that you might communicate with Zuanthrol if you so wished." Zoanthrohago nodded.

He turned to Komodoflorensal. "Ask him," he ordered, "if he feels any differently since I reduced his size."

When the question was put to Tarzan by Komodoflorensal in the imaginary language with which they were supposed to communicate the ape-man shook his head, at the same time speaking a few words in English.

"He says no, illustrious prince," translated Komodoflorensal out of his imagination, "and he asks when you will restore him to his normal size and permit him to return to his own country, which is far from Minuni."

"As a Minunian he should know," replied the Zertol, "that

he never will be permitted to return to his own country—Trohandadalmakus never will see him again."

"But he is not of Trohanadalmakus, nor is he a Minunian," explained Komodoflorensal. "He came to us and we did not make a slave of him, but treated him as a friend, because he is from a far country with which we have never made war."

"What country is that?" demanded Zoanthrohago.

"That we do not know, but he says that there is a great country beyond the thorns where dwell many millions as large as was he. He says that his people would not be unfriendly to ours and for this reason we should not enslave him, but treat him as a guest."

Zoanthrohago smiled. "If you believe this you must be a simple fellow, Trohanadalmakusian," he said. "We all know that there is naught beyond Minuni but impenetrable forests of thorn to the very uttermost wall of the blue dome within which we all dwell. I can well believe that the fellow is no Trohanadalmakusian, but he most certainly is a Minunian, since all creatures of whatever kind dwell in Minuni. Doubtless he is a strange form of Zertalacolol, a member of a tribe inhabiting some remote mountain fastness, which we have never previously discovered; but be that as it may, he will never—"

At this juncture the prince was interrupted by the clanging of the great gong at the outer entrance to his apartments. He paused to count the strokes and when they reached five and ceased he turned to the warriors who had conducted Tarzan and Komodoflorensal to his presence.

"Take the slaves into that chamber," he instructed, pointing to a doorway in the rear of the apartment in which he had received them. "When the king has gone I will send for them."

As they were crossing toward the doorway Zoanthrohago had indicated a warrior halted in the main entrance to the chamber. "Elkomoelhago," he announced, "Thagosto of Veltopismakus, Ruler of All Men, Master of Created Things, All-Wise, All-Courageous, All-Glorious! Down before the thagosto!"

Tarzan glanced back as he was quitting the chamber to see Zoanthrohago and the others in the room kneel and lean far back with arms raised high above their heads as Elkomoelhago entered with a guard of a dozen gorgeous warriors, and he could not but compare this ruler with the simple and dignified soldier who ruled Trohanadalmakus and who went about his city without show or pomp, and oftentimes with no other escort than a single slave; a ruler to whom no man bent his knee, yet to whom was accorded the maximum of veneration and respect.

And Elkomoelhago had seen the slaves and the warriors leave the chamber as he had entered it. He acknowledged the salutes of Zoanthrohago and his people with a curt wave of the hand and commanded them to arise.

"Who quitted the apartment as I entered?" he demanded, looking suspiciously at Zoanthrohago.

"The slave Zuanthrol and another who interprets his strange language for me," explained the Zertol.

"Have them back," commanded the thagosto; "I would speak with you concerning Zuanthrol."

Zoanthrohago instructed one of his slaves to fetch them and, in the few moments that it required, Elkomoelhago took a chair behind the desk at which his host had been sitting. When Tarzan and Komodoflorensal entered the chamber the guard who accompanied them brought them to within a few paces of the desk behind which the king sat, and here he bade them kneel and make their obeisance to the thagosto.

Familiar since childhood, was every tradition of slavery to Komodoflorensal the Trohanadamakusian. Almost in a spirit of fatalism had he accepted the conditions of this servitude that the fortunes of war had thrust him into and so it was that, without question or hesitation, he dropped to one knee in servile salute to this alien king; but not so Tarzan of the Apes. He was thinking of Adendrohahkis. He had bent no knee to him and he did not propose to do greater honor to Elkomoelhago, whose very courtiers and slaves despised him, than he had done to the really great king of Veltopismakus.

Elkomoelhago glared at him. "The fellow is not kneeling," he whispered to Zoanthrohago, who had been leaning back so far that he had not noticed the new slave's act of disrespect.

The Zertol glanced toward Tarzan. "Down, fellow!" he cried, and then recalling that he understood no Minunian, he commanded Komodoflorensal to order him to kneel, but when the Trohanadalmakusian Zertolosto pretended to do so Tarzan but shook his head.

Elkomoelhago signaled the others to rise. "We will let it pass this time," he said, for something in the attitude of the slave told him that Zuanthrol never would kneel to him and as he was valuable because of the experiment of which he was the subject, the king preferred to swallow his pride rather than risk having the slave killed in an effort to compel him to kneel. "He is but an ignorant Zertalacolol. See that he is properly instructed before we see him again."

14

T HE Alali women, fifty strong, sallied forth into the forest to chastise their recalcitrant males. They carried their heavy bludgeons and many-feathered pebbles, but most formidable of all was their terrific rage. Never in the memory of one of them had man dared question their authority, never had he presumed to show aught but fear of them; but now, instead of slinking away at their approach, he had dared defy them, to attack them, to slay them! But such a condition was too preposterous, too unnatural, to exist, nor would it exist much longer. Had they had speech they would have said that and a number of other things. It was looking black for the men; the women were in an ugly mood—but what else could be expected of women who were denied the power of speech?

And in this temper they came upon the men in a large clearing where the renegades had built a fire and were cooking the flesh of a number of antelope. Never had the women seen their men so sleek and trim. Always before had they appeared skinny to the verge of cadaverousness, for in the past they had never fared so well as since the day that Tarzan of the Apes had given weapons to the son of The First Woman. Where before they had spent their lives fleeing in terror from their terrible women, with scarce time to hunt for decent food, now they had leisure and peace of mind and their weapons brought them flesh that otherwise they might not have tasted once in a year. From caterpillars and grubworms they had graduated to an almost steady diet of antelope meat.

But the women gave very little heed at the moment to the physical appearance of the men. They had found them. That was enough. They were creeping nearer when one of the men looked up and discovered them, and so insistent are the demands of habit that he forget his new-found independence and leaping to his feet, bolted for the trees. The others, scarce waiting to know the cause of his precipitancy, followed close upon his heels. The women raced across the clearing as the men disappeared among the trees upon the opposite side. The former knew what the men would do. Once in the forest they would stop behind the nearest trees and look back to see if their pursuers were coming in their direction. It was this silly habit of the males that permitted their being easily caught by the less agile females.

But all the men had not disappeared. One had taken a few steps in the mad race for safety and had then halted and wheeled about, facing the oncoming women. He was the son of The First Woman, and to him Tarzan had imparted something more than knowledge of new weapons, for from the Lord of the Jungle, whom he worshipped with doglike devotion, he had acquired the first rudiments of courage, and so it now happened that when his more timorous fellows paused behind the trees and looked back they saw this one standing alone facing the charge of fifty infuriated shes. They saw him fit arrow to bow, and the women saw, too, but they did not understand—not immediately—and then the bow string twanged and the foremost woman collapsed with an arrow in her heart; but the others did not pause, because the thing had been done so quickly that the full purport of it had not as yet penetrated their thick skulls. The son of The First Woman fitted a second arrow and sped it. Another woman fell, rolling over and over, and now the others hesitated—hesitated and were lost, for that momentary pause gave courage to the other men peering from behind the trees. If one of their number could face fifty women and bring them to halt what might not eleven men accomplish? They rushed forth then with spears and arrows just as the women renewed their assault. The feathered pebbles flew thick and fast, but faster and more accurately flew the feathered arrows of the men. The leading women rushed courageously forward to close quarters where they might use their bludgeons and lay hold of the men with their mighty hands, but they learned then that spears were more formidable weapons than bludgeons, with the result that those who did not fall wounded, turned and fled.

It was then that the son of The First Woman revealed possession of a spark of generalship that decided the issue for that day, and, perhaps, for all time. His action was epochal in the existence of the Zertalacolols. Instead of being satisfied with repulsing the women, instead of resting upon laurels gloriously won, he turned the tables upon the hereditary foe and charged the women, signaling his fellows to accompany him, and when they saw the women running from them, so enthused were they by this reversal of a custom ages old, they leaped swiftly in pursuit.

They thought that the son of The First Woman intended that they should slay all of the enemy and so they were surprised when they saw him overhaul a comely, young female and, seizing her by the hair, disarm her. So remarkable did it seem to them that one of their number, having a woman in his power, did not immediately slay her, they were constrained to pause and gather around him, asking questions in their strange sign language.

"Why do you hold her?" "Why do you not kill her?" "Are you not afraid that she will kill you?" were some of the many that were launched at him.

"I am going to keep her," replied the son of The First Woman. "I do not like to cook. She shall cook for me. If she refuses I shall stick her with this," and he made a jab toward the young woman's ribs with his spear, a gesture that caused her to cower and drop fearfully upon one knee.

The men jumped up and down in excitement as the value of this plan and the evident terror of the woman for the man sank into their dull souls.

"Where are the women?" they signed to one another; but the women had disappeared.

One of the men started off in the direction they had gone. "I go!" he signaled. "I come back with a woman of my own, to cook for me!" In a mad rush the others followed him, leaving the son of The First Woman alone with his she. He turned upon her.

"You will cook for me?" he demanded.

To his signs she but returned a sullen, snarling visage. The son of The First Woman raised his spear and with the heavy shaft struck the girl upon the head, knocking her down, and he stood over her, himself snarling and scowling, menacing her with further punishment, while she cowered where she had fallen. He kicked her in the side.

"Get up!" he commanded.

Slowly she crawled to her knees and embracing his legs gazed up into his face with an expression of doglike adulation and devotion.

"You will cook for me!" he demanded again.

"Forever!" she replied in the sign language of their people.

Tarzan had remained but a short time in the little room adjoining that in which Zuanthrohago had received Elkomoelhago, when he was summoned to appear before them alone, and as he entered the room his master motioned him to approach the desk behind which the two men sat. There was no other person in the room, even the warriors having been dismissed.

"You are quite positive that he understands nothing of our language?" demanded the king.

"He has not spoken a word since he was captured," replied Zoanthrohago. "We had supposed him some new form of Zertalalcolol until it was discovered that he possessed a language through which he was able to communicate with the other Trohanadalmakusian slave. It is perfectly safe to speak freely before him, All-Wise."

Elkomoelhago cast a quick, suspicious glance at his companion. He would have preferred that Zoanthrohago of all men address him as All-Glorious—it was less definite in its implication. He might deceive others, even himself, as to his wisdom, but he was perfectly aware that he could not fool Zoanthrohago.

"We have never discussed fully," said the king, "the details of this experiment. It was for this purpose that I came to the labortatory today. Now that we have the subject here let us go into the matter fully and determine what next step we should take."

"Yes, All-Wise," replied Zoanthrohago.

"Call me Thagosoto," snapped Elkomoelhago.

"Yes, Thagosoto," said the prince, using the Minunian word for Chief-Royal, or King, as Elkomolehago had commanded. "Let us discuss the matter, by all means. It presents possibilities of great importance to your throne." He knew that what Elkomoelhago meant by *discussing* the matter consisted only in receiving from Zoanthrohago a detailed explanation of how he had reduced the stature of the slave Zuanthrol to one quarter its original proportions; but he proposed, if possible, to obtain value received for the information, which he knew the king would use for his own aggrandizement, giving Zoanthrohago no credit whatever for his discoveries or all the long moons he had devoted to accomplishing this marvelous, scientific miracle.

"Before we enter into this discussion, O, Thagosoto," he said, "I beg that you will grant me one boon, which I have long desired and have hitherto hesitated to request, knowing that I did not deserve the recognition I crave for my poor talents and my mean service to thy illustrious and justly renowned rule."

"What boon do you wish?" demanded Elkomoelhago, crustily. At heart he feared this wisest of men, and, like the coward that he was, with him to fear was to hate. If he could have destroyed Zoanthrohago he would gladly have done so; but he could not afford to do this, since from this greatest of walmaks came whatever show of scientific ability the king could make, as well as all the many notable inventions for the safeguarding of the royal person.

"I would sit at the royal council," said Zoanthrohago, simply.

The king fidgeted. Of all the nobles of Veltopismakus here was the very last he would wish to see numbered among the royal councilors, whom he had chosen with especial reference to the obtuseness of their minds.

"There are no vacancies," he said, at last.

"The ruler of all men might easily make a vacancy," suggested Zoanthrohago, "or create a new post—Assistant Chief of Chiefs, for example, so that when Gofoloso was absent there would be one to take his place. Otherwise I should not have to attend upon your council meetings, but devote my time to the perfection of our discoveries and inventions."

Here was a way out and Elkomoelhago seized it. He had no objection to Zoanthrohago being a royal councilor and thus escaping the burdensome income tax, which the makers of the tax had been careful to see proved no burden to themselves, and he knew that probably that was the only reason that Zoanthrohago wished to be a councilor. No, the king had no objection to the appointment, provided it could be arranged that the new minister was present at no council meetings, for even Elkomoelhago would have shrunk a bit from claiming as his own all the great discoveries of Zoanthrohago had Zoanthrohago been present.

"Very well," said the king, "you shall be appointed this very day—and when I want you at the council meetings I will send for you."

Zoanthrohago bowed. "And now," he said, "to the discussion of our experiments, which we hope will reveal a method for increasing the stature of our warriors when they go forth to battle with our enemies, and of reducing them to normal size once more when they return."

"I hate the mention of battles," cried the king, with a shudder.

"But we must be prepared to win them when they are forced upon us," suggested Zoanthrohago.

"I suppose so," assented the king; "but once we perfect this method of ours we shall need but a few warriors and the rest may be turned to peaceful and useful occupations. However, go on with the discussion."

Zoanthrohago concealed a smile, and rising, walked around the end of the table and stopped beside the ape-man. "Here," he said, placing a finger at the base of Tarzan's skull, "there lies, as you know, a small, oval, reddish gray body containing a liquid which influences the growth of tissues and organs. It long ago occurred to me that interference with the normal functioning of this gland would alter the growth of the subject to which it belonged. I experimented with small rodents and achieved remarkable results; but the thing I wished to accomplish, the increase of man's stature I have been unable to achieve. I have tried many methods and some day I shall discover the right one. I think I am on the right track, and that it is merely now a matter of experimentation. You know that stroking your face lightly with a smooth bit of stone produces a pleasurable sensation. Apply the same stone to the same face in the same manner, but with greatly increased force and you produce a diametrically opposite sensation. Rub the stone slowly across the face and back again many times, and then repeat the same motion rapidly for the same number of times and you will discover that the results are quite different. I am that close to a solution; I have the correct method but not quite, as yet, the correct application. I can reduce creatures in size, but I cannot enlarge them; and although I can reduce them with great ease, I cannot determine the period or endurance of their reduction. In some cases, subjects have not regained their normal size under thirty-nine moons, and in others, they have done so in as sort a period as three moons. There have been cases where normal stature was regained gradually during a period of seven suns, and others where the subject passed suddenly from a reduced size to normal size in less than a hundred heartbeats; this latter phenomenon being always accompanied by fainting and unconsciousness when it occurred during waking hours."

"Of course," commented Elkomoelhago. "Now, let us see. I believe the thing is simpler than you imagine. You say that to reduce the size of this subject you struck him with a rock upon the base of the skull. Therefore, to enlarge his size, the most natural and scientific thing to do would be to strike him a similar blow upon the forehead. Fetch the rock and we will prove the correctness of my theory."

For a moment Zoanthrohago was at a loss as to how best to circumvent the stupid intention of the king without humiliating his pride and arousing his resentment; but the courtiers of Elkomoelhago were accustomed to think quickly in similar emergencies and Zoanthrohago speedily found an avenue of escape from his dilemma.

"You sagacity is the pride of your people, Thagosoto," he said, "and your brilliant hyperbole the despair of your courtiers. In a clever figure of speech you suggest the way to achievement. By reversing the manner in which we reduced the stature of Zuanthrol we should be able to increase it; but, alas, I have tried this and failed. But wait, let us repeat the experiment precisely as it was originally carried out and then, by reversing it, we shall, perhaps, be enabled to determine why I have failed in the past."

He stepped quickly across the room to one of a series of large cupboards that lined the wall and opening the door of it revealed a cage in which were a number of rodents. Selecting one of these he returned to the table, where, with wooden pegs and bits of cord he fastened the rodent securely to a smooth board, its legs spread out and its body flattened, the under side of the lower jaw resting firmly upon a small metal plate set flush with the surface of the board. He then brought forth a small wooden box and a large metal disc, the latter mounted vertically between supports that permitted it to be revolved rapidly by means of a hand crank. Mounted rigidly upon the same axis as the revolving disc was another which remained stationary. The latter disc appeared to have been constructed of seven segments, each of a different material from all the others, and from each of these segments a pad, or brush, protruded sufficiently to press lightly against the revolving disc.

To the reverse side of each of the seven segments of the stationary disc a wire was attached, and these wires Zoanthrohago now connected to seven posts projecting from the upper surface of the wooden box. A single wire attached to a post upon the side of the box had at its other extremity a small, curved metal plate attached to the inside of a leather collar. This collar Zoanthrohago adjusted about the neck of the rodent so that the metal plate came in contact with its skin at the base of the skull and as close to the hypophysis gland as possible.

He then turned his attention once more to the wooden box, upon the top of which, in addition to the seven binding posts, was a circular instrument consisting of a dial about the periphery of which were a series of hieroglyphics. From the center of this dial projected seven tubular, concentric shafts, each of which supported a needle, which was shaped or painted in some distinguishing manner, while beneath the dial seven small metal discs were set in the cover of the box so that they lay in the arc of a circle from the center of which a revolving metal shaft was so arranged that its free end might be moved to any of the seven metal discs at the will of the operator.

The connections having all been made, Zoanthrohago moved the free end of the shaft from one of the metal discs to another, keeping his eyes at all times intently upon the dial, the seven needles of which moved variously as he shifted the shaft from point to point.

Elkomoelhago was an intent, if somewhat bewildered, observer, and the slave, Zuanthrol, unobserved, had moved nearer the table that he might better watch this experiment which might mean so much to him.

Zoanthrohago continued to manipulate the revolving shaft and the needles moved hither and thither from one series of hieroglyphics to another, until at last the walmak appeared satisfied.

"It is not always easy," he said, "to attune the instrument to the frequency of the organ upon which we are working. From all matter and even from such incorporeal a thing as thought there emanate identical particles, so infinitesimal as to be scarce noted by the most delicate of my instruments. These particles constitute the basic structure of all things whether animate or inanimate, corporeal or incorporeal. The frequency, quantity and rhythm of the emanations determine the nature of the substance. Having located upon this dial the coefficient of the gland under discussion it now becomes necessary, in order to so interfere with its proper functioning that the growth of the creature involved will be not only stopped but actually reversed, that we decrease the frequency, increase the quantity and compound the rhythm of these emanations. This I shall now proceed to do," and he forthwith manipulated several small buttons upon one side of the box, and grasping the crank handle of the free disc revolved it rapidly.

The result was instantaneous and startling. Before their eyes Elkomoelhago, the king, and Zuanthrol, the slave, saw the rodent shrink rapidly in size, while retaining its proportions unchanged. Tarzan, who had followed every move and every word of the walmak, leaned far over that he might impress indelibly upon his memory the position of the seven needles. Elkomoelhago glanced up and discovered his interest.

"We do not need this fellow now," he said, addressing Zoanthrohago. "Have him sent away."

"Yes, Thagosoto," replied Zoanthrohago, summoning a warrior whom he directed to remove Tarzan and Komodoflorensal to a chamber where they could be secured until their presence was again required.

15

T HROUGH several chambers and corridors they were conducted toward the center of the dome on the same level
as the chamber in which they had left the king and the
walmak until finally they were thrust into a small chamber
and a heavy door was slammed and barred behind them.

There was no candle in the chamber. A faint light, however, relieved the darkness so that the interior of the room
was discernible. The chamber contained two benches and a
table—that was all. The light which faintly illuminated it entered through a narrow embrasure which was heavily barred,
but it was evidently daylight.

"We are alone," whispered Komodoflorensal, "and at last
we can converse; but we must be cautious," he added. " 'Trust
not too far the loyalty of even the stones of your chamber!' "
he quoted.

"Where are we?" asked Tarzan. "You are more familiar
with Minunian dwellings than I."

"We are upon the highest level of the Royal Dome of Elkomoelhago," replied the prince. "With no such informality does
a king visit the other domes of his city. You may rest assured
that this is Elkomoelhago's. We are in one of the innermost
chambers, next the central shaft that pierces the dome from
its lowest level to its roof. For this reason we do not need a
candle to support life—we will obtain sufficient air through
this embrasure. And now, tell me what happened within the
room with Elkomoelhago and Zoanthrohago."

"I discovered how they reduced my stature," replied Tarzan, "and, furthermore, that at almost any time I may regain
my full size—an occurrence that may eventuate from three
to thirty-nine moons after the date of my reduction. Even
Zoanthrohago cannot determine when this thing will happen."

"Let us hope that it does not occur while you are in this
small chamber," exclaimed Komodoflorensal.

"I would have a devil of a time getting out," agreed Tarzan.

"You would never get out," his friend assured him. "While
you might, before your reduction, have crawled through some
of the larger corridors upon the first level, or even upon many
of the lower levels, you could not squeeze into the smaller

corridors of the upper levels, which are reduced in size as the necessity for direct supports for the roof increase as we approach the apex of the dome."

"Then it behooves me to get out of here as quickly as possible," said Tarzan.

Komodoflorensal shook his head. "Hope is a beautiful thing, my friend," he said, "but if you were a Minunian you would know that under such circumstances as we find ourselves it is a waste of mental energy. Look at these bars," and he walked to the window and shook the heavy irons that spanned the embrasure. "Think you that you could negotiate these?"

"I haven't examined them," replied the ape-man, "but I shall never give up hope of escaping; that your people do is doubtless the principal reason that they remain forever in bondage. You are too much a fatalist, Komodoflorensal."

As he spoke Tarzan crossed the room and standing at the prince's side took hold of the bars at the window. "They do not seem overheavy," he remarked, and at the same time exerted pressure upon them. They bent! Tarzan was interested now and Komodoflorensal, as well. The ape-man threw all his strength and weight into the succeeding effort with the result that two bars, bent almost double, were torn from their setting.

Komodoflorensal gazed at him in astonishment. "Zoanthrohago reduced your size, but left you with your former physical prowess," he cried.

"In no other way can it be accounted for," replied Tarzan, who now, one by one, was removing the remaining bars from the window embrasure. He straightened one of the shorter ones and handed it to Komodoflorensal. "This will make a good weapon," he said, "if we are forced to fight for our liberty," and then he straightened another for himself.

The Trohandalmakusian gazed at him in wonder. "And you intend," he demanded, "to defy a city of four hundred and eighty thousand people, armed only with a bit of iron rod?"

"And my wits," added Tarzan.

"You will need them," said the prince.

"And I shall use them," Tarzan assured him.

"When shall you start?" asked Komodoflorensal, chaffingly.

"Tonight, tomorrow, next moon—who knows?" replied the ape-man. "Conditions must be ripe. All the time I shall be watching and planning. In that sense I started to escape the instant I regained consciousness and knew that I was a prisoner."

Komodoflorensal shook his head.

"You have no faith in me?" demanded Tarzan.

"That is precisely what I have—faith," replied Komodoflorensal. "My judgment tells me that you cannot succeed and yet I shall cast my lot with you, hoping for success, yes, believing in success. If that is not faith I do not know what it might be called."

The ape-man smiled. He seldom, if ever, laughed aloud. "Let us commence," he said. "First we will arrange these rods so that they will have the appearance, from the doorway, of not having been disturbed, for I take it we shall have an occasional visitor. Some one will bring us food, at least, and whoever comes must suspect nothing."

Together they arranged the rods so that they might be quickly removed and as quickly replaced. By that time it was getting quite dark within the chamber. Shortly after they had finished with the rods their door opened and two warriors, lighting their way with candles, appeared escorting a slave who bore food in bucketlike receptacles and water in bottles made of glazed pottery.

As they were going away again, after depositing the food and drink just inside the doorway, taking their candles with them, Komodoflorensal addressed them.

"We are without candles, warrior," he said to the nearer. "Will you not leave us one of yours?"

"You need no candle in this chamber," replied the man. "One night in darkness will do you good, and tomorrow you return to the quarry. Zoanthrohago is done with you. In the quarry you will have plenty of candles," and he passed out of the chamber, closing the door behind him.

The two slaves heard the heavy bolt shot into place upon the opposite side of the door. It was very dark now. With difficulty they found the receptacles containing the food and water.

"Well?" inquired Komodoflorensal, dipping into one of the food jars. "Do you think it is going to be so easy now, when tomorrow you will be back in the quarry, perhaps five hundred huals below ground?"

"But I shall not be," replied Tarzan, "and neither shall you."

"Why not?" asked the prince.

"Because, since they expect to remove us to the quarries tomorrow, it follows that we must escape tonight," explained Tarzan.

Komodoflorensal only laughed.

When Tarzan had eaten his fill he arose and walked to the window, where he removed the bars and, taking the one that he had selected for himself, crawled through the passage that led to the opposite end of the embrasure, for even so close to the apex of the dome the wall was quite thick, perhaps ten huals. The hual, which is about three inches in length by our standards, constitutes the Minunian basic unit of measure, corresponding most closely to our foot. At this high level the embrasure was much smaller than those opening at lower levels, practically all of which were of sufficient size to permit a warrior to walk erect within them; but here Tarzan was forced to crawl upon all fours.

At the far end he found himself looking out into a black void above which the stars were shining and about the sides of which were dotted vague reflections of inner lights, marking the lighted chambers within the dome. Above him it was but a short distance to the apex of the dome, below was a sheer drop of four hundred huals.

Tarzan, having seen all that could be seen from the mouth of the embrasure, returned to the chamber. "How far is it, Komodoflorensal," he asked, "from the floor of this embrasure to the roof of the dome?"

"Twelve huals, perhaps," replied the Trohanadalmakusian.

Tarzan took the longest of the bars from the embrasure and measured it as best he could. "Too far," he said.

"What is too far?" demanded Komodoflorensal.

"The roof," explained Tarzan.

"What difference does it make where the roof is—you did not expect to escape by way of the roof of the dome, did you?"

"Most certainly—had it been accessible," replied the apeman; "but now we shall have to go by way of the shaft, which will mean crossing entirely through the dome from the interior shaft to the outer periphery. The other route would have entailed less danger of detection."

Komodoflorensal laughed aloud. "You seem to think that to escape a Minunian city it is only necessary to walk out and away. It cannot be done. What of the sentries? What of the outer patrols? You would be discovered before you were halfway down the outside of the dome, provided that you could get that far without falling to your death."

"Then perhaps the shaft would be safer," said Tarzan. "There would be less likelihood of discovery before we reached the bottom, for from what I could see it is as dark as pitch in the shaft."

"Clamber down the inside of the shaft!" exclaimed Komodoflorensal. "You are mad! You could not clamber from this level to the next without falling, and it must be a full four hundred huals to the bottom."

"Wait!" Tarzan admonished him.

Komodoflorensal could hear his companion moving around in the dark chamber. He heard the scraping of metal on stone and presently he heard a pounding, not loud, yet heavy.

"What are you doing?" he asked.

"Wait!" said Tarzan.

And Komodoflorensal waited, wondering. It was Tarzan who spoke next.

"Could you find the chamber in which Talaskar is confined in the quarry?" he asked.

"Why?" demanded the prince.

"We are going after her," explained Tarzan. "We promised that we would not leave without her."

"I can find it," said Komodoflorensal, rather sullenly Tarzan thought.

For some time the ape-man worked on in silence, except for the muffled pounding and the scraping of iron on stone, or of iron on iron.

"Do you know every one in Trohanadalmakus?" Tarzan asked, suddenly.

"Why, no," replied Komodoflorensal. "There are a million souls, including all the slaves. I could not know them all."

"Did you know by sight all those that dwelt in the royal dome?" continued the ape-man.

"No, not even those who lived in the royal dome," replied the Trohanadalmakusian; "though doubtless I knew practically all of the nobles, and the warrior class by sight if not by name."

"Did any one?" asked Tarzan.

"I doubt it," was the reply.

"Good!" exclaimed Tarzan.

Again there was a silence, broken again by the Englishman.

"Can a warrior go anywhere without question in any dome of his own city?" he inquired.

"Anywhere, under ordinary circumstances, except into the king's dome, in daytime."

"One could not go about at night, then?" asked Tarzan.

"No," replied his companion.

"By day, might a warrior go and come in the quarries as he pleased?"

"If he appeared to be employed he would not be questioned, ordinarily."

Tarzan worked a little longer in silence. "Come!" he said presently; "we are ready to go."

"I shall go with you," said Komodoflorensal, "because I like you and because I think it would be better to be dead than a slave. At least we shall have some pleasure out of what remains to us of life, even though it be not a long life."

"I think we shall have some pleasure, my friend," replied Zuanthrol. "We may not escape; but, like you, I should rather die now than remain a slave for life. I have chosen tonight for our first step toward freedom, because I realize that once returned to the quarry our chances for a successful break for liberty will be reduced to almost nothing, and tonight is our only night above ground."

"How do you propose that we escape from this chamber?"

"By way of the central shaft," replied Tarzan; "but first tell me, may a white-tunicked slave enter the quarries freely by day?"

Komodoflorensal wondered what bearing all these seemingly immaterial questions had upon the problem of their escape; but he answered patiently:

"No, white tunics are never seen in the quarries."

"Have you the iron bar I straightened for you?"

"Yes."

"Then follow me through the embrasure. Bring the other rods that I shall leave in the opening. I will carry the bulk of them. Come!"

Komodoflorensal heard Tarzan crawling into the embrasure, the iron rods that he carried breaking the silence of the little chamber. Then he followed. In the mouth of the embrasure he found the rods that Tarzan had left for him to carry. There were four rods, the ends of each bent into hooks. It had been upon this work that Tarzan had been engaged in the darkness —Komodoflorensal wondered to what purpose. Presently his further advance was halted by Tarzan's body.

"Just a moment," said the ape-man. "I am making a hole in the window ledge. When that is done we shall be ready." A moment later he turned his head back toward his companion. "Pass along the rods," he said.

After Komodoflorensal had handed the hooked rods to Tarzan he heard the latter working with them, very quietly, for several minutes, and then he heard him moving his body about in the narrow confines of the embrasure and presently when the ape-man spoke again the Trohanadalmakusian realized that he had turned around and that his head was close to that of his companion.

"I shall go first, Komodoflorensal," he said. "Come to the edge of the embrasure and when you hear me whistle once, follow me."

"Where?" asked the prince.

"Down the shaft to the first embrasure that will give us foot-hold, and let us pray that there is one directly below this within the next eighteen huals. I have hooked the rods together, the upper end hooked into the hole I made in the ledge, the lower end dangling down a distance of eighteen huals."

"Good-bye, my friend," said Komodoflorensal.

Tarzan smiled and slipped over the edge of the embrasure. In one hand he carried the rod that he had retained as a weapon, with the other he clung to the window ledge. Below him for eighteen huals dangled the slender ladder of iron hooks, and below this, four hundred huals of pitchy darkness hid the stone flagging of the inner courtyard. Perhaps it roofed the great central throne room of the king, as was true in the royal dome of Adendrohahkis; perhaps it was but an open court. The truth was immaterial if the frail support slipped from the shallow hole in the ledge above, or if one of the hooks straightened under the weight of the ape-man.

Now he grasped the upper section of his ladder with the hand that held his improvised weapon, removed the hand from the ledge and grasped the rod again, still lower down. In this way he lowered his body a few inches at a time. He moved very slowly for two reasons, the more important of which was that he feared that any sudden strains upon his series of hooks might straighten one of them and precipitate him into the abyss below; the other was the necessity for silence. It was very dark even this close to the summit of the dome, but that was rather an advantage than otherwise, for it hid his presence from any chance observer who might glance through one of the embrasures in the opposite wall of the shaft. As he descended he felt in both directions for an embrasure, but he was almost at the end of his ladder before he felt himself swing slightly into one. When he had lowered himself still farther and could look into the opening he saw that it was dark, an indication that it did not lead into an inhabited chamber, a fact for which he was thankful. He hoped, too, that the inner end of the embrasure was not barred, nor the door beyond bolted upon the outside.

He whistled once, very low, for Komodoflorensal, and an instant later he felt the movement of the iron ladder that told him his companion had commenced the descent. The embrasure in which he stood was higher than the one they had just quitted, permitting him to stand erect. There he waited for the Trohanadalmakusian who was soon standing upon the ledge beside him.

"Whew!" exclaimed the prince, in a whisper. "I should hate to have had to do that in the daytime when I could have seen all the way to the bottom. What next? We have come farther already than ever I dreamed would be possible. Now I am commencing to believe that escape may lie within the realm of possibilities."

"We haven't started yet," Tarzan assured him; "but we are going to now. Come!"

Grasping their rude weapons the two walked stealthily the length of the embrasure. There were no bars to impede their progress and they stepped to the floor of the chamber beyond. Very carefully, feeling each step before he planted a foot and with his weapon extended before him, Tarzan groped his way about the chamber, which he found was fairly well filled with casks and bottles, the latter in wooden and wicker cases. Komodoflorensal was directly behind him.

"We are in one of the rooms where the nobles charged with enforcing the laws against wine have hidden confiscated liquor," whispered the Trohanadalmakusian. "I have heard much talk concerning the matter since I was made prisoner—the warriors and the slaves, too, seem to talk of nothing else but this and the high taxes. The chances are that the door is heavily barred—they guard these forbidden beverages as never they guarded their gold or jewels."

"I have found the passageway leading to the door," whispered Tarzan, "and I can see a light beneath it."

They crept stealthily the length of the passage. Each grasped his weapon more firmly as Tarzan gently tried the latch. It gave! Slowly the ape-man pushed the door ajar. Through the tiny aperture thus opened he could see a portion of the room. Its floor was strewn with gorgeous carpets, thick and soft. That portion of the wall that was revealed to him was hung with heavy fabrics woven in many colors and strange patterns —splended, barbaric. Directly in the line of his vision the body of a man lay sprawled, face down, upon the floor—a pool of red stained a white rug beneath his head.

Tarzan opened the door a little farther, revealing the bodies of three other men. Two lay upon the floor, the third upon a low divan. The scene, gorgeous in its coloring, tragic in its suggestion of mystery and violent death, held the eyes of the ape-man yet a moment longer before he opened the door still wider and leaped quickly to the center of the room, his weapon raised and ready, giving no possible skulking foe behind the door the opportunity to fell him that would have offered had he edged into the room slowly.

A quick glance about the apartment showed the bodies of six men that had not been visible from the partially opened door. These were lying in a pile in one corner of the room.

16

KOMODOFLORENSAL stood at Tarzan's side, his weapon ready to take issue with any who might question their presence here; but presently the end of his iron rod dropped to the floor and a broad smile overspread his features.

Tarzan looked at him. "Who are they?" he demanded, "and why have they been killed?"

"They are not dead, my friend," replied Komodoflorensal. "They are the nobles whose duty it is to prevent the use of wine. They are not dead—they are drunk."

"But the blood beneath the head of this one at my feet!" demanded the ape-man.

"It is red wine, not blood," his companion assured him. Then Tarzan smiled.

"They could not have chosen a better night for their orgy," he said. "Had they remained sober the door through which we entered from the storeroom would have been securely fastened, I imagine."

"Assuredly, and we would have had a sober guard of warriors to deal with in this chamber, instead of ten drunken nobles. We are very fortunate, Zuanthrol."

He had scarcely ceased speaking when a door in the opposite side of the room swung open, revealing two warriors, who stepped immediately into the chamber. They eyed the two who faced them and then glanced about the room at the inert forms of its other occupants.

"What do you here, slaves?" demanded one of the newcomers.

"Sh-sh-sh!" cautioned Tarzan, placing a finger to his lips. "Enter and close the door, lest others hear."

"There is no one near to hear," snapped one of them, but they entered and he closed the door. "What is the meaning of this?"

"That you are our prisoners," cried the ape-man, leaping past them and placing himself before the door, his iron rod in readiness.

A sneer twisted the mouth of each of the two Veltopismakusians as they whipped out their rapiers and leaped toward the ape-man, ignoring for the moment the Trohanadalmakusian, who, seizing upon the opportunity thus afforded him, threw aside his iron rod and snatched a rapier from the side of one of the drunken nobles—a substitution of weapons that would render Komodoflorensal a dangerous opponent anywhere in Minuni, for there was no better swordsman among all the warlike clans of Trohanadalmakus, whose blades were famed throughout Minuni.

Facing, with only an iron rod, two skilled swordsmen placed Tarzan of the Apes at a disadvantage that might have proved his undoing had it not been for the presence of Komodoflorensal, who, no sooner than he had appropriated a weapon, leaped forward and engaged one of the warriors. The other pressed Tarzan fiercely.

"Your prisoner, eh, slave?" he sneered as he lunged for his opponent; but though less skilled, perhaps, in swordplay than his antagonist, the Lord of the Jungle had not faced Bolgani and Numa for nothing. His movements were as lightning, his strength as great as before Zoanthrohago had reduced his stature. At the first onslaught of the warriors he had leaped to one side to avoid the thrust of a blade, and as much to his own astonishment as to theirs, what he had intended for a nimble sidestep had carried him the length of the room, and then the man had been at him again, while the other was having his time well occupied with the Zertolosto of Trohanadalmakus.

Twice Tarzan parried cuts with his cumbersome bar and then a thrust but missed him by a hairbreadth, his sidestep coming but in the nick of time. It was a close call, for the man had lunged at his abdomen—a close call for Tarzan and death for his opponent, for as the point slipped harmlessly by him the ape-man swung his rod upon the unguarded head of the Veltopismakusian, and with a grunt the fellow slumped to the floor, his skull crushed to the bridge of his nose.

Then Tarzan turned to aid Komodoflorensal, but the son of Adendrohahkis needed no aid. He had his man against the wall and was running him through the heart as Tarzan turned in their direction. As the man fell, Komodoflorensal swung toward the center of the room and as his eye fell upon the ape-man a smile crossed his face.

"With an iron bar you bested a swordsman of Minuni!" he cried. "I would not have believed it possible and so I hastened to dispatch my man that I might come to your rescue before it was too late."

Tarzan laughed. "I had the same thought in mind concerning you," he said.

"And you could have well held it had I not been able to secure this rapier," Komodoflorensal assured him. "But what now? We have again come much farther than it seems possible we can have. Naught will surprise me hereafter."

"We are going to trade apparel with these two unfortunate gentlemen," said Tarzan, divesting himself of the green tunic as he spoke.

Komodoflorensal chuckled as he followed the example of his companion.

"There are other peoples as great as the Minunians," he declared, "though until I met you, my friend, I should never have believed it."

A few moments later the two stood garbed in the habiliments of Veltopismakusian warriors and Tarzan was slipping his green tunic upon the corpse of him whom he had slain.

"But why are you doing that?" asked the prince.

"Do likewise with yours and you will see, presently," Tarzan replied.

Komodoflorensal did as the other bid him and when the change had been completed the ape-man threw one of the corpses across his shoulder and carried it into the storeroom, followed closely by Komodoflorensal with the other. Walking through the window embrasure to the edge of the shaft Tarzan hurled his burden out into space, and reaching back took Komodoflorensal's from him and pitched it after the first.

"If they do not examine them too closely," he said, "the ruse may serve to convince them that we died attempting to escape." As he spoke he detached two of the hooks from the ladder down which they had clambered from the window of their dungeon and dropped them after the corpses. "These will lend color to the suggestion," he added, in explanation.

Together they returned to the room where the drunken nobles lay, where Komodoflorensal began to rifle the fat money pouches of the unconscious men.

"We shall need all of this that we can get if we are to pose as Veltopismakusian warriors for any length of time," he said. "I know these people by reputation and that gold will buy many of the things that we may require—the blindness of guards and the complaisance of officials, if they do not guess too close to the truth concerning us."

"That part of it you must attend to, Komodoflorensal," said Tarzan, "for I am unfamiliar with the ways of your people; but we may not remain here. These gentlemen have served us well, and themselves, too, for their faithlessness and debauchery saved their lives, while the two who followed in sobriety the path of duty were destroyed."

"Matters are strangely ordered," commented Komodoflorensal.

"In Minuni as elsewhere," agreed Tarzan, leading the way to the door of the chamber which they found opened into a corridor instead of into another chamber as they had rather expected would be the fact at a point thus close to the central shaft.

In silence they proceeded along the passageway, which, at this hour of the morning, was deserted. They passed lighted chambers, where men and women were sleeping peacefully in the glare of many candles. They saw a sentry asleep before the door of a noble's quarters. No one discovered them and thus they passed down a series of inclined runways and along interminable corridors until they were far from that portion of the royal dome in which they had been incarcerated and where it would be most natural for the search for them to commence in the event that the bodies they had hurled into the shaft were not immediately discovered, or were identified for what they really were, rather than for what the two fugitives had tried to make them appear.

And now a white-tunicked slave was approaching them along the corridor. He passed without paying them any heed, and presently another and another appeared until the two realized that morning was approaching and the corridors would soon be filled with the inhabitants of the dome.

"It will be best," said Komodoflorensal, "to find a hiding place until there are more people abroad. We shall be safer in a crowd than among just a few where we shall be the more noticeable."

Nearly all the chambers they passed now were occupied by families, while those that were untenanted were without candles and therefore unsafe as hiding places for any length of time; but presently Komodoflorensal touched Tarzan's arm and pointed to a hieroglyphic beside a door they were approaching.

"Just the place," he said.

"What is it?" asked Tarzan, and as they came opposite the open door; "Why, it is filled with men! When they awake we shall be discovered."

"But not recognized," returned the Trohanadalmakusian; "or at least the chances are slight that we shall be. This is a common chamber where any man may purchase lodgings over night. Doubtless there are visitors from other domes and strangers will not be particularly remarked on this account."

He entered the room, followed by Tarzan. A white-tunicked slave approached them. "Candles for two," demanded Komodoflorensal, handing the slave one of the smaller golden coins he had filched from the sleeping nobles.

The fellow led them to a far corner of the room where there was plenty of space upon the floor, lit two candles and left them. A moment later they were stretched at full length, their faces toward the wall as a further protection against recognition, and were soon asleep.

When Tarzan awoke he saw that he and Komodoflorensal were the only remaining occupants of the chamber, other than the slave who had admitted them, and he awoke his companion, believing that they should do nothing that might even in a slight degree call more than ordinary attention to them. A bucket of water was brought them and they performed their ablutions at a gutter which encircled the chamber, passing along the foot of each wall, as was the custom throughout Minuni, the waste water being carried away in pipes to the fields beyond the cities, where it was used for irrigating the crops. As all the water had to be carried into the domes and to the different levels in buckets, the amount used for ablutions was reduced to the minimum, the warrior and noble class getting the bulk of it, while the white-tunicked slaves depended principally upon the rivers, near which domes are always erected, for their baths. The green slaves fare the worst, and suffer a real hardship through lack of bathing facilities, for the Minunians are a cleanly people; but they manage to alleviate their plight to some extent, where the quarry masters are more kindly disposed, by the use of stagnant seepage water that accumulates in every quarry at the lower levels and which, not being fit for drinking purposes, may be used by the slaves for bathing when they are permitted the time to obtain it.

Having washed, Tarzan and Komodoflorensal passed out into the corridor, a broad thoroughfare of the dome city, where there were now passing two solid lines of humanity moving in opposite directions, the very numbers of the people proving their greatest safeguard against detection. Candles at frequent intervals diffused a brilliant light and purified the air. Open doorways revealed shops of various descriptions within which men and women were bartering for goods, and now Tarzan had his first real glimpse of Veltopismakusian life. The shops were all conducted by white-tunicked slaves, but slaves and warriors intermingled as customers, both sexes of each class being represented. It was Tarzan's first opportunity, also, to see the women of the warrior class outside their own homes. He had seen the Princess Janzara in the palace quarters and, through the doorways in various portions of the dome, he had seen other women of varying stations in life; but these were the first that he had seen abroad at close hand. Their faces were painted deep vermilion, their ears blue, and their apparel so arranged that the left leg and left arm were bare, though if even so much as the right ankle or wrist became uncovered they hastily readjusted their garments to hide them, giving every evidence of confusion and embarrassment. As the ape-man watched them he was reminded of fat dowagers he had seen at home whose evening gowns left them naked to their kidneys, yet who would rather have died than to have exposed a knee.

The front of the shops were covered with brilliant paintings, usually depicting the goods that were on sale, together with hieroglyphics describing the wares and advertising the name of the proprietor. One of these finally held the attention of the Trohanadalmakusian, and he touched Tarzan's arm and pointed toward it.

"A place where food is served," he said. "Let us eat."

"Nothing would suit me better. I am famished," Tarzan assured him, and so the two entered the little shop where several customers were already sitting upon the floor with small benches pulled close to them, upon which food was being served in wooden dishes. Komodoflorensal found a space near the rear of the shop, not far from a doorway leading into another chamber, which was also a shop of a different character, not all the places of business being fortunately located upon a corridor, but having their entrances, like this one, through another place of business.

Having seated themselves and dragged a bench before them they looked about while waiting to be served. It was evidently a poor shop, Komodoflorensal told Tarzan, catering to the slave caste and the poorer warriors, of which there were several sitting at benches in different parts of the room. By their harness and apparel, which was worn and shabby, one might easily guess at their poverty. In the adjoining shop were several more of the same class of unfortunate warriors mending their own clothes with materials purchased from the poor shopkeeper.

The meal was served by a slave in a white tunic of very cheap material, who was much surprised when payment for the meal and the service was offered in gold.

"It is seldom," he said, "that warriors rich enough to possess gold come to our poor shop. Pieces of iron and bits of lead, with much wooden money, pass into my coffers; but rarely do I see gold. Once I did, and many of my customers were formerly of the richest of the city. Yonder see that tall man with the heavily wrinkled face. Once he was rich—the richest warrior in his dome. Look at him now! And see them in the next room performing menial services, men who once owned slaves so prosperous that they, in turn, hired other slaves to do the meaner duties for them. Victims, all of them, of the tax that Elkomoelhago has placed upon industry.

"To be poor," he continued, "assures one an easier life than being rich, for the poor have no tax to pay, while those who work hard and accumulate property have only their labor for their effort, since the government takes all from them in taxes.

"Over there is a man who was very rich. He worked hard all his life and accumulated a vast fortune. For several years after Elkomoelhago's new tax law was enforced, he struggled to earn enough to insure that his income would be at least equal to his taxes and the cost of his living; but he found that it was impossible. He had one enemy, a man who had wronged him grievously. This man was very poor, and to him he gave all of what remained of his great fortune and his property. It was a terrible revenge. From being a contented man, this victim of another's spleen is now a haggard wreck, laboring unceasingly eighteen hours each day in a futile attempt to insure himself an income that will defray his taxes."

Having finished their meal the two fugitives returned to the corridor and continued their way downward through the dome toward the first level, keeping always to the more crowded corridors, where detection seemed least likely. Now, mounted men were more frequently encountered and so rapidly and recklessly did the warriors ride along the narrow corridors that it was with difficulty that the pedestrians avoided being ridden down and trampled, and it seemed to Tarzan but little less than a miracle that any of them arrived at their destinations

uninjured. Having at last come to the lowest level, they were
engaged in searching for one of the four corridors that would
lead them from the dome, when their way was completely
blocked by a great throng that had congregated at the inter-
section of two corridors. Those in the rear were stretching
their necks to observe what was going on in the center of the
gathering. Everyone was asking questions of his neighbor, but
as yet no one upon the outskirts of the mob appeared to know
what had occurred, until at last fragments of rumors filtered
back to the farthermost. Tarzan and Komodoflorensal dared
ask no questions, but they kept their ears open and presently
they were rewarded by overhearing repeated what seemed to be
an authoritative account of what had transpired to cause this
congestion. In answer to a question put by one of the throng
a fellow who was elbowing his way out from the center of the
jam explained that those in front had halted to view the remains of two slaves who had been killed while trying to
escape.

"They were locked in one of Zoanthrohago's slave cells at
the very highest level," he told his questioner, "and they tried
to escape by climbing down an improvised ladder into the
central shaft. Their ladder broke and they were precipitated
to the roof of the throne room, where their bodies, terribly
mangled, were but just found. They are being carried out
to the beasts, now. One of them was a great loss to Zoanthrohago as it was the slave Zuanthrol, upon whom he was experi-
menting."

"Ah," exclaimed a listener, "I saw them but yesterday."

"You would not know them today," vouchsafed the in-
former, "so terribly are their faces disfigured."

When the press of humanity had been relieved Tarzan and
Komodoflorensal continued their way, finding that the Slaves'
Corridor lay just before them, and that it was down this avenue
that the bodies of their victims of the previous night were
being carried.

"What," asked the ape-man, "did he mean by saying that
they were being carried to the beasts?"

"It is the way in which we dispose of the bodies of slaves,"
replied the Trohanadalmakusian. "They are carried to the edge
of the jungle, where they are devoured by wild beasts. There
are old and toothless lions near Trohanadalmakus that subsist
entirely upon slave meat. They are our scavengers and so accustomed are they to being fed that they often come to meet
the parties who bring out the corpses, pacing beside them,

roaring and growling, until the spot is reached where the bodies are to be deposited."

"You dispose of all your dead in this manner?"

"Only the slave dead. The bodies of warriors and nobles are burned."

"In a short time, then," continued Tarzan, "there will be no danger of there ever being a correct identification of those two," he jerked his thumb along the corridor ahead, where the bodies of the two dead warriors were being bounced and jolted along upon the backs of diadets.

17

"WHERE now?" demanded Komodoflorensal as the two emerged from the mouth of the Slaves' Corridor and stood for a moment in the brilliant sunlight without.

"Lead the way to the quarry where we were confined and to the chamber in which we slept."

"You must be weary of your brief liberty," remarked the Trohanadalmakusian.

"We are returning for Talaskar, as I promised," Tarzan reminded him.

"I know," said the Zertolosto, "and I commend your loyalty and valor while deprecating your judgment. It will be impossible to rescue Talaskar. Were it otherwise I should be the first to her assistance; but I know, and she knows, that, for her, escape is beyond hope. We will but succeed in throwing ourselves again into the hands of our masters."

"Let us hope not," said Tarzan; "but, if you feel as you say, that our effort is foredoomed to failure and that we shall but be recaptured, do not accompany me. My only real need of you is to guide me to the apartment where Talaskar is confined. If you can direct me to it that is all I ask."

"Think you I was attempting to evade the danger?" demanded Komodoflorensal. "No! Where you go, I will go. If you are captured I shall be captured. We shall fail, but let us not separate. I am ready to go wherever you go."

"Good," commented Tarzan. "Now lead the way to the

quarry and use your knowledge of things Minunian and your best wits to gain us entrance without too much talking."

They passed, unchallenged, along the shaded walks between the domes of Veltopismakus and past the great parade where gorgeously caparisoned warriors were executing intricate evolutions with the nicest precision, and out beyond the domes along well-worn trails filled with toiling slaves and their haughty guards. Here they fell in beside the long column moving in the direction of the quarry in which they had been imprisoned, taking their places in the column of flanking guards, and thus they came to the entrance to the quarry.

Perfunctorily the numbers of the slaves were taken, as they passed in, and entered in a great book; but to Tarzan's relief he noted that no attention was paid to the guards, who moved along beside their charges and down into the interior without being checked or even counted, and with them went Komodoflorensal, Prince Royal of Trohanadalmakus, and Tarzan of the Apes.

Once inside the quarry and past the guard room the two fell gradually to the rear of the column, so that when it turned into a level above that which they wished to reach they were enabled to detach themselves from it without being noticed. To leave one column was but to join another, for there was no break in them and often there were several moving abreast; but when they reached the thirty-fifth level and entered the tunnel leading to the chamber in which Talaskar was confined they found themselves alone, since there is little or no activity in these corridors leading to slave quarters except early in the morning when the men are led forth to their labors and again at night when they are brought back.

Before the door of the chamber they found a single warrior on guard. He was squatting on the floor of the tunnel leaning against the wall, but at their approach he rose and challenged them.

Komodoflorensal, who was in the lead, approached him and halted. "We have come for the slave girl, Talaskar," he said.

Tarzan, who was just behind Komodoflorensal, saw a sudden light leap to the eyes of the warrior. Was it recognition?

"Who sent you?" demanded the warrior.

"Her master, Zoanthrohago," replied the Trohanadalmakusian.

The expression upon the face of the warrior changed to one of cunning.

"Go in and fetch her," he said, and unbolted the door, swinging it open.

Komodoflorensal dropped upon his hands and knees and crawled through the low aperture, but Tarzan stood where he was.

"Go in!" said the guard to him.

"I will remain where I am," replied the ape-man. "It will not require two of us to find a single slave girl and fetch her to the corridor."

For an instant the warrior hesitated, then he closed the door hurriedly and shot the heavy bolts. When he turned toward Tarzan again, who was now alone with him in the corridor, he turned with a naked sword in his hands; but he found Zuanthrol facing him with drawn rapier.

"Surrender!" cried the warrior. "I recognized you both instantly."

"I thought as much," said Zuanthrol. "You are clever, with the exception of your eyes—they are fools, for they betray you."

"But my sword is no fool," snapped the fellow, as he thrust viciously at the ape-man's breast.

Lieutenant Paul D'Arnot of the French navy had been recognized as one of the cleverest swordsmen in the service and to his friend Greystoke he had imparted a great measure of his skill during the many hours that the two had whiled away with the foils, and today Tarzan of the Apes breathed a prayer of gratitude to the far-distant friend whose careful training was, after many long years, to serve the ape-man in such good stead, for he soon realized that, though his antagonist was a master at the art of fence, he was not wholly outclassed, and to his skill was added his great strength and his agility.

They had fought for but a minute or two when the Veltopis-makusian realized that he was facing no mean antagonist and that he was laboring at a disadvantage in being unable to fall back when Tarzan rushed him, while his foeman had at his back the whole length of the tunnel. He tried then to force Tarzan back, but in this he failed, receiving a thrust in the shoulder for his pains, and then he commenced to call for help and the ape-man realized that he must silence him and that quickly. Awaiting the opportunity that was presently afforded by a feint that evoked a wild lunge, Tarzan stepped quickly in and passed his sword through the heart of the Veltopismakusian and as he withdrew his blade from the body of his antagonist he released the bolts that held the door and swung it open. Beyond it, white of face, crouched Komodoflorensal, but as his eyes fell upon Tarzan and the body of the guard behind him, a smile curved his lips and an instant later he was in the corridor beside his friend.

"How did it happen?" he demanded.

"He recognized us; but what of Talaskar? Is she not coming?"

"She is not here. Kalfastoban took her away. He has purchased her from Zoanthrohago."

Tarzan wheeled. "Rebolt the door and let us get out of here," he said.

Komodoflorensal closed and fastened the door. "Where now?" he asked.

"To find Kalfastoban's quarters," replied the ape-man.

Komodoflorensal shrugged his shoulders and followed on behind his friend. They retraced their steps toward the surface without incident until they were opposite the sixteenth level, when a face was suddenly turned toward them from a column of slaves crossing the runway from one lateral to another. Just for an instant did the eyes of the slave meet those of Tarzan, and then the fellow had passed into the mouth of the lateral and disappeared.

"We must hurry," whispered Tarzan to his companion.

"Why now more than before?" demanded Komodoflorensal.

"Did you not see the fellow who just passed us and turned to look a second time at me?"

"No; who was it?"

"Garaftap," replied Tarzan.

"Did he recognize you?"

"As to that I cannot say; but he evidently found something familiar in my appearance. Let us hope that he did not place me, though I fear that he did."

"Then we must lose no time in getting out of here, and out of Veltopismakus, as well."

They hurried on. "Where are Kalfastoban's quarters?" asked Tarzan.

"I do not know. In Trohanadalmakus warriors are detailed to the quarries for but short periods and do not transfer their quarters or their slaves during the time that they are there. I do not know the custom here. Kalfastoban may have finished his tour of duty in the quarries. On the other hand it may be for a long period that they are detailed for that service and his quarters may lie on the upper level of the quarry. We shall have to inquire."

Soon after this Tarzan stepped up to a warrior moving in

the same direction as he and Komodoflorensal. "Where can I find Kalfastoban Vental?" he asked.

"They will tell you in the guard room, if it is any of your affair," he replied, shooting a quick glance at the two. "I do not know."

After that they passed the fellow and at the first turn that hid them from him they increased their speed, for both were becoming suspicious of every least untoward incident, and their one wish now was to escape the quarry in safety. Nearing the entrance they attached themselves to a column of slaves toiling upward with their heavy burdens of rocks for the new dome, and with them they came to the guard room where the slaves were checked out. The officer and the clerks labored in a mechanical manner, and it appeared that it was to be as easy to leave the quarry as it had been to enter it, when the officer suddenly drew his brow together and commenced to count.

"How many slaves in this crew?" he asked.

"One hundred," replied one of the warriors accompanying them.

"Then why four guards?" he demanded.

"There are but two of us," rejoined the warrior.

"We are not with them," Komodoflorensal spoke up quickly.

"What do you here?" demanded the officer.

"If we can see you alone we can explain that quickly," replied the Trohanadalmakusian.

The officer waved the crew of slaves upon their way and beckoned to Komodoflorensal and Tarzan to follow him into an adjoining chamber, where they found a small anteroom in which the commander of the guard slept.

"Now," he said, "let me see your passes."

"We have none," replied Komodoflorensal.

"No passes! That will be difficult to explain, will it not?"

"Not to one of your discrimination," replied the prince, accidentally jingling the golden coins in his pouch. "We are in search of Kalfastoban. We understand that he owns a slave we wish to purchase and not being able to obtain a pass to the quarry in the short time at our disposal we ventured to come, upon so simple an errand, without one. Could you direct us to Kalfastoban?" Again he jingled the coins.

"I shall be delighted," replied the officer. "His quarters are upon the fifth level of the Royal Dome upon the central corridor and about midway between the King's Corridor and the Warrior's Corridor. As he was relieved from duty in the quarry this very morning I have no doubt but that you will find him there."

"We thank you," said Komodoflorensal, leaning far back in the Minunian bow. "And now," he added, as though it was an afterthought, "if you will accept it we shall be filled with gratitude if you will permit us to leave this slight token of our appreciation," and he drew a large gold coin from the pouch and proffered it to the officer.

"Rather than seem ungrateful," replied the officer, "I must accept your gracious gift, with which I may alleviate the sufferings of the poor. May the shadow of disaster never fall upon you!"

The three then bowed and Tarzan and Komodoflorensal quitted the guard room and a moment later were in the free, fresh air of the surface.

"Even in Minuni!" breathed Tarzan.

"What was that?" asked his friend.

"I was just thinking of my simple, honest jungle and God's creatures that men call beasts."

"What should they call them?" demanded Komodoflorensal.

"If judged by the standards that men themselves make, and fail to observe, they should be called demigods," replied the ape-man.

"I believe I get your point," laughed the other; "but think! had a lion guarded the entrance to this quarry no gold piece would have let us pass. The frailties of man are not without their virtues; because of them right has just triumphed over wrong and bribery has worn the vestments of virtue."

Returning to the Royal Dome they passed around the east side of the structure to the north front, where lies the Slaves' Corridor in every dome. In quitting the dome they had come from the Warriors' Corridor on the west and they felt that it would be but increasing the chances of detection were they to pass too often along the same route where someone, half-recognizing them in one instance, might do so fully after a second or third inspection.

To reach the fifth level required but a few minutes after they had gained entrance to the dome. With every appearance of boldness they made their way toward the point in the central corridor at which the officer of the guard had told them they would find Kalfastoban's quarters, and perhaps Kalfastoban himself; but they were constantly on the alert, for both recognized that the greatest danger of detection lay through the chance that Kalfastoban might recall their features, as he of all Veltopismakusians would be most apt to do so, since he had seen the most of them, or at least the most of Tarzan since he had donned the slave's green.

They had reached a point about midway between the Slaves' Corridor and the Warriors' Corridor when Komodoflorensal halted a young, female slave and asked her where the quarters of Kalfastoban were located.

"It is necessary to pass through the quarters of Hamadalban to reach those of Kalfastoban," replied the girl. "Go to the third entrance," and she pointed along the corridor in the direction they had been going.

After they had left her Tarzan asked Komodoflorensal if he thought there would be any difficulty in gaining entrance to Kalfastoban's quarters.

"No," he replied; "the trouble will arise in knowing what to do after we get there."

"We know what we have come for," replied the ape-man. "It is only necessary to carry out our design, removing all obstacles as they intervene."

"Quite simple," laughed the prince.

Tarzan was forced to smile. "To be candid," he admitted, "I haven't the remotest idea what we are going to do after we get in there, or after we get out either, if we are successful in finding Talaskar and bringing her away with us, but that is not strange, since I know nothing, or practicaly nothing, of what conditions I may expect to confront me from moment to moment in this strange city of a strange world. All that we can do is to do our best. We have come thus far much more easily than I expected—perhaps we will go the whole distance with no greater friction—or we may stop within the next dozen steps, forever."

Pausing before the third entrance they glanced in, discovering several women squatting upon the floor. Two of them were of the warrior class, the others slaves of the white tunic. Komodoflorensal entered boldly.

"These are the quarters of Hamadalban?" he asked.

"They are," replied one of the women.

"And Kalfastoban's are beyond?"

"Yes."

"And beyond Kalfastoban's?" inquired the Trohanadalma-kusian.

"A long gallery leads to the outer corridor. Upon the gallery open many chambers where live hundreds of people. I do not know them all. Whom do you seek?"

"Palastokar," replied Komodoflorensal quickly, choosing the first name that presented itself to his memory.

"I do not recall the name," said the woman, knitting her brows in thought.

"But I shall find him now, thanks to you," said Komodoflorensal, "for my directions were to pass through the quarters of Hamadalban and Kalfastoban, when I should come upon a gallery into which opened the quarters of Palastokar; but perhaps if Kalfastoban is in, he will be able to direct me more exactly."

"Kalfastoban has gone out with Hamadalban," replied the woman; "but I expect them back momentarily. If you will wait, they will soon be here."

"Thank you," said Komodoflorensal, hastily; "but I am sure that we shall have no trouble finding the quarters of Palastokar. May your candles burn long and brilliantly!" and without waiting on further ceremony he crossed the room and entered the quarters of Kalfastoban, into which Tarzan of the Apes followed at his heels.

"I think, my friend," said the prince, "that we shall have to work rapidly."

Tarzan glanced quickly around the first chamber that they entered. It was vacant. Several doors opened from it. They were all closed either with wooden doors or with hangings. The ape-man stepped quickly to the nearer and tried the latch. It gave and he pushed the door ajar. All was darkness within.

"Bring a candle, Komodoflorensal," he said.

The prince brought two from their niches in the wall. "A storeroom," he said, as the rays of the candles illuminated the interior of the room. "Food and candles and raiment. Kalfastoban is no pauper. The tax collector has not ruined him yet."

Tarzan, standing in the doorway of the storeroom, just behind Komodoflorensal, turned suddenly and looked out across the other chamber. He had heard voices in the quarters of Hamadalban beyond—men's voices. One of them he recognized an instant later—it was the voice of Kalfastoban Vental.

"Come!" roared the bull voice of the Vental. "Come to my quarters, Hamadalban, and I will show you this new slave of mine."

Tarzan pushed Komodoflorensal into the storeroom and following him, closed the door. "Did you hear?" he whispered.

"Yes, it was Kalfastoban!"

The storeroom door was ornamented with a small, open grill covered with a hanging of some heavy stuff upon the inside. By drawing the hanging aside the two could obtain a view of most of the interior of the outer chamber, and they could hear all that was said by the two men who now entered from Hamadalban's quarters.

"I tell you she is the greatest bargain I have ever seen," cried Kalfastoban; "but wait, I'll fetch her," and he stepped to another door, which he unlocked with a key. "Come out!" he roared, flinging the door wide.

With the haughty bearing of a queen a girl stepped slowly into the larger room—no cowering servility of the slave here. Her chin was high, her gaze level. She glanced almost with contempt upon the Vental. And she was beautiful. It was Talaskar. Komodoflorensal realized that he had never before appreciated how really beautiful was the little slave girl, who had cooked for him. Kalfastoban had given her a white tunic of good quality, which set off the olive of her skin and the rich blackness of her hair to better effect than had the cheap green thing that he had always seen her in.

"She belonged to Zoanthrohago," Kalfastoban explained to his friend, "but I doubt that he ever saw her, else he never would have parted with her for the paltry sum I paid."

"You will take her for your own woman and raise her to our class?" asked Hamadalban.

"No," replied Kalfastoban, "for then she would no longer be a slave and I could not sell her. Women are too expensive. I shall keep her for a time and then sell her while her value is still high. I should make a pretty profit from her."

Tarzan's fingers closed tightly, as though upon the throat of an enemy, and the right hand of Komodoflorensal crept to the hilt of his rapier.

A woman came from the quarters of Hamadalban and stood in the doorway.

"Two of the guards from the quarry are here with a green slave inquiring for Kalfastoban," she said.

"Send them in," directed the Vental.

A moment later the three entered—the slave was Caraftap.

"Ah!" exclaimed Kalfastoban, "my good slave, Caraftap; the best in the quarry. Why is he brought here?"

"He says that he has information of great value," replied one of the guard; "but he will divulge it to none but you. He has staked his life against the worth of his information and the Novand of the guard ordered him brought hither."

"What information have you?" demanded Kalfastoban.

"It is of great moment," cried Caraftap. "Noble Zoanthrohago, and even the king, will be grateful for it; but were I to give it and have to return to the quarries the other slaves would kill me. You were always good to me, Kalfastoban Vental, and so I asked to be brought to you, for I know that if you promise that I shall be rewarded with the white tunic, if my service is considered worthy of it, I shall be safe."

"You know that I cannot do that," replied Kalfastoban.

"But the king can, and if you intercede with him he will not refuse."

"I can promise to intercede with the king in your behalf if the information you bring is of value; but that is all I can do."

"That is enough—if you promise," said Caraftap.

"Very well, I promise. What do you know that the king would like to know?"

"News travels fast in Veltopismakus," said Caraftap, "and so it was that we in the quarry heard of the death of the two slaves, Aoponato and Zuanthrol, within a short time after their bodies were discovered. As both had been slaves of Zoanthro-hago we were all confined together in one chamber and thus I knew them both well. Imagine then my surprise when, while crossing one of the main spirals with a crew of other slaves, I beheld both Zuanthrol and Aoponato, in the habiliments of warriors, ascending toward the surface."

"What is the appearance of these two?" suddenly demanded one of the warriors who had accompanied Caraftap from the quarry.

The slave described them as fully as he could.

"The same!" cried the warrior. "These very two stopped me upon the spiral and inquired the whereabouts of Kalfastoban."

A crowd of women and men had gathered in the doorway of Kalfastoban's chamber, having been attracted by the presence of a green slave accompanied by members of the quarry guard. One of them was a young slave girl.

"I, too, was questioned by these very men," she exclaimed, "only a short time since, and they asked me the same question."

One of Hamadalban's women voiced a little scream. "They passed through our quarters but a moment since," she cried, "and entered Kalfastoban's, but they asked not where lay the quarters of Kalfastoban, the name they mentioned was unknown to me—a strange name."

"Palastokar," one of her companions reminded her.

"Yes, Palastokar, and they said he had his quarters upon the gallery leading from Kalfastoban's to the outer corridor."

"There is no one of such a name in the Royal Dome," said Kalfastoban. "It was but a ruse to enter my quarters."

"Or to pass through them," suggested one of the quarry guard.

"We must hurry after them," said the other.

"Keep Caraftap here until we return, Kalfastoban," said the first guard, "and also search your own quarters and those adjoining carefully. Come!" and motioning to the other guard he crossed the chamber and departed along the gallery that led to the outer corridor, followed not alone by his fellow but by Hamadalban and all the other men who had congregated in the chamber, leaving Kalfastoban and Caraftap, with the women, in the Vental's quarters.

18

KALFASTOBAN turned immediately to a search of the various chambers of his quarters, but Caraftap laid a restraining hand upon his arm.

"Wait, Vental," he begged. "If they be here would it not be best to insure their capture by fastening the doors leading from your quarters?"

"A good thought, Caraftap," replied Kalfastoban, "and then we may take our time searching for them. Out of here, all you women!" he cried, waving the females back into Hamadalban's quarters. A moment later the two doors leading from the chamber to Hamadalban's quarters and the gallery were closed and locked.

"And now, master," suggested Caraftap, "as there be two of them would it not be well to supply me with a weapon."

Kalfastoban smote his chest. "A dozen such could Kalfastoban overcome alone," he cried; "but for your own protection get you a sword from yonder room while I lock this proud she-cat in her cell again."

As Kalfastoban followed Talaskar to the room in which she had been confined, Caraftap crossed to the door of the storeroom where the Vental had told him he would find a weapon.

The Vental reached the door of the room just behind the girl and reaching out caught her by the arm.

"Not so fast, my pretty!" he cried. "A kiss before you leave me; but fret not! The moment we are sure that those villainous slaves are not within these rooms I shall join you, so do not pine for your Kalfastoban."

Talaskar wheeled and struck the Vental in the face. "Lay not your filthy hands upon me, beast!" she cried, and struggled to free herself from his grasp.

"So-ho! a cat, indeed!" exclaimed the man, but he did not release her, and so they struggled until they disappeared from sight within the cell, and at the same moment Caraftap, the slave, laid his hand upon the latch of the storeroom door, and opening it stepped within.

As he did so steel fingers reached forth out of the darkness and closed upon his throat. He would have screamed in terror, but no sound could he force through his tight-closed throat. He struggled and struck at the thing that held him—a thing so powerful that he knew it could not be human, and then a low voice, cold and terrifying, whispered in his ear.

"Die, Caraftap!" it said. "Meet the fate that you deserve and that you well knew you deserved when you said that you dared not return to the quarters of the slaves of Zoanthrohago after betraying two of your number. Die, Caraftap! and know before you die that he whom you would have betrayed is your slayer. You searched for Zuanthrol and—you have found him!" With the last word the terrible fingers closed upon the man's neck. Spasmodically the slave struggled, fighting for air. Then the two hands that gripped him turned slowly in opposite directions and the head of the traitor was twisted from his body.

Throwing the corpse aside Tarzan sprang into the main chamber of the Vental's quarters and ran quickly toward the door of Talaskar's cell, Komodoflorensal but half a pace behind him. The door of the little room had been pushed to by the struggles of the couple within, and as Tarzan pushed it open he saw the girl in the clutches of the huge Vental, who, evidently maddened by her resistance, had lost his temper completely and was attempting to rain blows upon her face, which she sought to ward off, clutching at his arms and hands.

A heavy hand fell upon the shoulder of the Vental. "You seek us!" a low voice whispered in his ear. "Here we are!"

Kalfastoban released the girl and swung around, at the same time reaching for his sword. Facing him were the two slaves and both were armed, though only Aoponato had drawn his weapon. Zuanthrol, who held him, had not yet drawn.

" 'A dozen such could Kalfastoban overcome alone,' " quoted Tarzan. "Here we are, braggart, and we are only two; but we cannot wait while you show us how mighty you be. We are sorry. Had you not molested this girl I should merely have locked you in your quarters, from which you would soon have

been released; but your brutality deserves but one punishment
—death."

"Caraftap!" screamed Kalfastoban. No longer was he a
blusterer, deep-toned and swaggering. His voice was shrill with
terror and he shook in the hands of the ape-man. "Caraftap!
Help!" he cried.

"Caraftap is dead," said Tarzan. "He died because he betrayed his fellows. You shall die because you were brutal to a
defenseless slave girl. Run him through, Komodoflorensal! We
have not time to waste here."

As the Trohanadalmakusian withdrew his sword from the
heart of Kalfastoban Vental and the corpse slid to the floor
of the cell Talaskar ran forward and fell at the feet of the
ape-man.

"Zuanthrol and Aopontato!" she cried. "Never did I think
to see you again. What has happened? Why are you here? You
have saved me, but now you will be lost. Fly—I know not
where to you may fly—but go from here! Do not let them find
you here. I cannot understand why you are here, anyway."

"We are trying to escape," explained Komodoflorensal, "and
Zuanthrol would not go without you. He searched the quarry
for you and now the Royal Dome. He has performed the impossible, but he has found you."

"Why did you do this for me?" asked Talaskar, looking wonderingly at Tarzan.

"Because you were kind to me when I was brought to the
chamber of Zoanthrohago's slaves," replied the ape-man, "and
because I promised that when the time for escape came we
three should be together."

He had lifted her to her feet and led her into the main
chamber. Komodoflorensal stood a little aside, his eyes upon
the floor. Tarzan glanced at him and an expression of puzzlement came into the eyes of the ape-man, but whatever thought
had caused it he must have put quickly aside for the consideration of more pressing matters.

"Komodoflorensal, you know best what avenues of escape
should be the least beset by the dangers of discovery. Whether
to go by way of Hamadalban's quarters or through the gallery they mentioned? These are questions I cannot answer to
my own satisfaction; and look!" his eyes had been roving about
the chamber, "there is an opening in the ceiling. Where might
that lead?"

"It might lead almost anywhere, or nowhere at all!" replied
the Trohanadalmakusian. "Many chambers have such openings. Sometimes they lead into small lofts that are not con-

nected with any other chamber; again they lead into secret chambers, or even into corridors upon another level."

There came a pounding upon the door leading into Hamadalban's quarters and a woman's voice called aloud: "Kalfastoban, open!" she cried. "There has come an ental from the quarry guard in search of Caraftap. The sentry at the entrance to the quarters of the slaves of Zoanthrohago has been found slain and they wish to question Caraftap, believing that there is a conspiracy among the slaves."

"We must go by the gallery," whispered Komodoflorensal, stepping quickly to the door leading thereto.

As he reached it someone laid a hand upon the latch from the opposite side and attempted to open the door, which was locked.

"Kalfastoban!" cried a voice from the gallery beyond. "Let us in! The slaves went not this way. Come, open quickly!"

Tarzan of the Apes glanced quickly about. Upon his face was a half-snarl, for once again was he the cornered beast. He measured the distance from the floor to the trap in the ceiling, and then with a little run he sprang lightly upward. He had forgotten to what extent the reduction of his weight affected his agility. He had hoped to reach a handhold upon the upper edge of the opening, but instead he shot entirely through it, alighting upon his feet in a dark chamber. Turning he looked down at his friends below. Consternation was writ large upon the countenance of each; but at that he could not wonder. He was almost as much surprised himself.

"Is it too far for you to jump?" he asked.

"Too far!" they replied.

He swung, then, head downward through the opening, catching the edge of the trap in the hollow of his knees. At the gallery door the knocking was becoming insistent and now at that leading into the quarters of Hamadalban a man's voice had supplanted that of the woman. The fellow was demanding entrance, angrily.

"Open!" he shouted. "In the name of the king, open!"

"Open yourself!" shouted the fellow who had been hammering at the opposite door, thinking that the demand to open came from the interior of the chamber to which he sought admission.

"How can I open?" screamed back the other. "The door is locked upon your side!"

"It is not locked upon my side. It is locked upon yours," cried the other, angrily.

"You lie!" shouted he who sought entrance from Hamadalban's quarters, "and you will pay well when this is reported to the king."

Tarzan swung, head downward, into the chamber, his hands extended toward his companions. "Lift Talaskar to me," he directed Komodolflorensal, and as the other did so he grasped the girl's wrists and raised her as far as he could until she could seize upon a part of his leather harness and support herself alone without falling. Then he took another hold upon her, lower down, and lifted still higher, and in this way she managed to clamber into the chamber above.

The angry warriors at the two doors were now evidently engaged in an attempt to batter their way into the chamber. Heavy blows were falling upon the substantial panels that threatened to splinter them at any moment.

"Fill your pouch with candles, Komodoflorensal," said Tarzan, "and then jump for my hands."

"I took all the candles I could carry while we were in the storeroom," replied the other. "Brace yourself! I am going to jump."

A panel splintered and bits of wood flew to the center of the floor from the door at the gallery just as Tarzan seized the outstretched hands of Komodoflorensal and an instant later, as both men kneeled in the darkness of the loft and looked down into the chamber below the opposite door flew open and the ten warriors who composed the ental burst in at the heels of their Vental.

For an instant they looked about in blank surprise and then their attention was attracted by the pounding upon the other door. A smile crossed the face of the Vental as he stepped quickly to the gallery door and unlocked it. Angry warriors rushed in upon him, but when he had explained the misapprehension under which both parties had been striving for entrance to the chamber they all joined in the laughter, albeit a trifle shamefacedly.

"But who was in here?" demanded the Vental who had brought the soldiers from the quarry.

"Kalfastoban and the green slave Caraftap," proffered a woman belonging to Hamadalban.

"They must be hiding!" said a warrior.

"Search the quarters!" commanded the Vental.

"It will not take long to find one," said another warrior, pointing at the floor just inside the storeroom doorway.

The others looked and there they saw a human hand resting upon the floor. The fingers seemed frozen into the semblance of clutching claws. Mutely they proclaimed death. One of the warriors stepped quickly to the storeroom, opened the door and dragged forth the body of Caraftap, to which the head was clinging by a shred of flesh. Even the warriors stepped back, aghast. They looked quickly around the chamber.

"Both doors were barred upon the inside," said the Vental. "Whatever did this must still be here."

"It could have been nothing human," whispered a woman who had followed them from the adjoining quarters.

"Search carefully," said the Vental, and as he was a brave man, he went first into one chamber and then another. In the last one they found Kalfastoban, run through the heart.

"It is time we got out of here if there is any way out," whispered Tarzan to Komodofloresal. "One of them will espy this hole directly."

Very cautiously the two men felt their way in opposite direction around the walls of the dark, stuffy loft. Deep dust, the dust of ages, rose about them, chokingly, evidencing the fact that the room had not been used for years, perhaps for ages. Presently Komodofloresal heard a "H-s-s-t!" from the ape-man who called them to him. "Come here, both of you. I have found something."

"What have you found?" asked Talaskar, coming close.

"An opening near the bottom of the wall," replied Tarzan. "It is large enough for a man to crawl through. Think you, Komodofloresal, that it would be safe to light a candle?"

"No, not now," replied the prince.

"I will go without it, then," announced the ape-man, "for we must see where this tunnel leads, if anywhere."

He dropped upon his hands and knees, then, and Talaskar, who had been standing next him, felt him move away. She could not see him—it was too dark in the gloomy loft.

The two waited, but Zuanthrol did not return. They heard voices in the room below. They wondered if the searchers would soon investigate the loft, but really there was no need for apprehension. The searchers had determined to invest the place—it would be safer than crawling into that dark hole after an unknown thing that could tear the head from a man's body. When it came down, as come down it would have to, they would be prepared to destroy or capture it; but in the meantime they were content to wait.

"What has become of him?" whispered Talaskar, anxiously.

"You care very much for him, do you not?" asked Komodofloresal.

"Why should I not?" asked the girl. "You do, too, do you not?"

"Yes," replied Komodoflorensal.

"He is very wonderful," said the girl.

"Yes," said Komodoflorensal.

As though in answer to their wish they heard a low whistle from the depths of the tunnel into which Tarzan had crawled. "Come!" whispered the ape-man.

Talaskar first, they followed him, crawling upon hands and knees through a winding tunnel, feeling their way through the darkness, until at last a light flared before them and they saw Zuanthrol lighting a candle in a small chamber, that was only just high enough to permit a tall man to sit erect within it.

"I got this far," he said to them, "and as it offered a fair hiding place where we might have light without fear of discovery I came back after you. Here we can stop a while in comparative comfort and safety until I can explore the tunnel further. From what I have been able to judge it has never been used during the lifetime of any living Veltopismakusian, so there is little likelihood that anyone will think of looking here for us."

"Do you think they will follow us?" asked Talaskar.

"I think they will," replied Komodoflorensal, "and as we cannot go back it will be better if we push on at once, as it is reasonable to assume that the opposite end of this tunnel opens into another chamber. Possibly there we shall find an avenue of escape."

"You are right, Komodoflorensal," agreed Tarzan. "Nothing can be gained by remaining here. I will go ahead. Let Talaskar follow me, and you bring up the rear. If the place proves a blind alley we shall be no worse off for having investigated it."

Lighting their way this time with candles the three crawled laboriously and painfully over the uneven, rock floor of the tunnel, which turned often, this way and that, as though passing around chambers, until, to their relief, the passageway abruptly enlarged, both in width and height, so that now they could proceed in an erect position. The tunnel now dropped in a steep declivity to a lower level and a moment later the three emerged into a small chamber, where Talaskar suddenly placed a hand upon Tarzan's arm, with a little intaking of her breath in a half gasp.

'What is that, Zuanthrol!" she whispered, pointing into the darkness ahead.

Upon the floor at one side of the room a crouching figure was barely discernible close to the wall.

"And that!" exclaimed the girl, pointing to another portion of the room.

The ape-man shook her hand from his arm and stepped quickly forward, his candle held high in his left hand, his right upon his sword. He came close to the crouching figure and bent to examine it. He laid his hand upon it and it fell into a heap of dust.

"What is it?" demanded the girl.

"It *was* a man," replied Tarzan; "but it has been dead many years. It was chained to this wall. Even the chain has rusted away."

"And the other, too?" asked Talaskar.

"There are several of them," said Komodoflorensal. "See? There and there."

"At least they cannot detain us," said Tarzan, and moved on again across the chamber toward a doorway on the opposite side.

"But they tell us something, possibly," ventured Komodoflorensal.

"What do they say?" asked the ape-man.

"That this corridor connected with the quarters of a very powerful Vetlopismakusian," replied the prince. "So powerful was he that he might dispose of his enemies thus, without question; and it also tells us that all this happened long years ago."

"The condition of the bodies told us that," said Tarzan.

"Not entirely," replied Komodoflorensal. "The ants would have reduced them to that state in a short time. In past ages the dead were left within the domes, and the ants, who were then our scavengers, soon disposed of them, but the ants sometimes attacked the living. They grew from a nuisance to a menace, and then every precaution had to be taken to keep from attracting them. Also we fought them. There were great battles waged in Trohanadalmakus between the Minunians and the ants and thousands of our warriors were devoured alive, and though we slew billions of ants their queens could propagate faster than we could kill the sexless workers who attacked us with their soldiers. But at last we turned our attention to their nests. Here the carnage was terrific, but we succeeded in slaying their queens and since then no ants have come into our domes. They live about us, but they fear us. However, we do not risk attracting them again by leaving our dead within the domes."

"Then you believe that this corridor leads to the quarters of some great noble?" inquired Tarzan.

"I believe that it once did. The ages bring change. Its end may now be walled up. The chamber to which it leads may have housed a king's son when these bones were quick; today it may be a barrack-room for soldiers, or a stable for diadets. About all that we know definitely about it," concluded Komodoflorensal, "is that it has not been used by man for a long time, and probably, therefore, is unknown to present-day Veltopismakusians."

Beyond the chamber of death the tunnel dropped rapidly to lower levels, entering, at last, a third chamber larger than either of the others. Upon the floor lay the bodies of many men.

"These were not chained to the walls," remarked Tarzan.

"No, they died fighting, as one may see by their naked swords and the position of their bones."

As the three paused a moment to look about the chamber there fell upon their ears the sound of a human voice.

19

A S THE days passed and Tarzan did not return to his home his son became more and more apprehensive. Runners were sent to nearby villages, but each returned with the same report. No one had seen The Big Bwana. Korak dispatched messages, then, to the nearest telegraph inquiring from all the principal points in Africa, where the ape-man might have made a landing, if aught had been seen or heard of him; but always again were the answers in the negative.

And at last, stripped to G string and carrying naught but his primitive weapons, Korak the Killer took the trail with a score of the swiftest and bravest of the Waziri in search of his father. Long and diligently they searched the jungle and the forest, often enlisting the friendly services of the villages near which they chanced to be carrying on their quest, until they had covered as with a fine-toothed comb a vast area of country, covered it as could have no other body of men; but for all their care and all their diligence they uncovered no single clew as to the fate or whereabouts of Tarzan of the Apes, and so, disheartened yet indefatigable, they searched on and on

through tangled miles of steaming jungle or across rocky up-
lands as inhospitable as the stunted thorns that dotted them.

And in the Royal Dome of Elkomoelhago, Thagosto of
Veltopismakus, three people halted in a rock-walled, hidden
chamber and listened to a human voice that appeared to come
to them out of the very rock of the walls surrounding them.
Upon the floor about them lay the bones of long-dead men.
About them rose the impalpable dust of ages.

The girl pressed closer to Tarzan. "Who is it?" she whispered.
Tarzan shook his head.

"It is a woman's voice," said Komodoflorensal.

The ape-man raised his candle high above his head and took
a step closer to the left-hand wall; then he stopped and
pointed. The others looked in the direction indicated by Tarzan's finger and saw an opening in the wall a hual or two above
his head. Tarzan handed his candle to Komodoflorensal, removed his sword and laid it on the floor, and then sprang
lightly for the opening. For a moment he clung to its edge,
listening, and then he dropped back into the chamber.

"It is pitch-black beyond," he said. "Whoever owns that
voice is in another chamber beyond that into which I was just
looking. There was no human being in the next apartment."

"If it was absolutely dark, how could you know that?" demanded Komodoflorensal.

"Had there been anyone there I should have smelled him,"
replied the ape-man.

The others looked at him in astonishment. "I am sure of it,"
said Tarzan, "because I could plainly feel a draught sucking up
from the chamber, through the aperture, and into this chamber. Had there been a human being there his effluvium would
have been carried directly to my nostrils."

"And you could have detected it?" demanded Komodoflorensal. "My friend, I can believe much of you, but not that."

Tarzan smiled. "I at least have the courage of my convic-
tions," he said, "for I am going over there and investigate.
From the clearness with which the voice comes to us I am
certain that it comes through no solid wall. There must be an
opening into the chamber where the woman is and as we should
investigate every possible avenue of escape, I shall investigate
this." He stepped again toward the wall below the aperture.

"Oh, let us not separate," cried the girl. "Where one goes,
let us all go!"

"Two swords are better than one," said Komodoflorensal,
though his tone was only halfhearted.

"Very well," replied Tarzan. "I will go first, and then you can pass Talaskar up to me."

Komodoflorensal nodded. A minute or two later the three stood upon the opposite side of the wall. Their candle revealed a narrow passage that showed indications of much more recent use than those through which they had passed from the quarters of Kalfastoban. The wall they had passed through to reach it was of stone, but that upon the opposite side was of studding and rough boards.

"This is a passage built along the side of a paneled room," whispered Komodoflorensal.

"The other side of these rough boards supports beautifully polished panels of brilliant woods or burnished metals."

"Then there should be a door, you think, opening from this passage into the adjoining chamber?" asked Tarzan.

"A secret panel, more likely," he replied.

They walked along the passage, listening intently. At first they had just been able to distinguish that the voice they heard was that of a woman; but now they heard the words.

"—had they let me have him," were the first that they distinguished.

"Most glorious mistress, this would not have happened then," replied another female voice.

"Zoanthrohago is a fool and deserves to die; but my illustrious father, the king, is a bigger fool," spoke the first voice. "He will kill Zoanthrohago and with him the chance of discovering the secret of making our warriors giants. Had they let me buy this Zuanthrol he would not have escaped. They thought that I would have killed him, but that was farthest from my intentions."

"What would you have done with him, wondrous Princess?"

"That is not for a slave to ask or know," snapped the mistress.

For a time there was silence.

"That is the Princess Janzara speaking," whispered Tarzan to Komodoflorensal. "It is the daughter of Elkomoelhago whom you would have captured and made your princess; but you would have had a handful."

"Is she as beautiful as they say?" asked Komodoflorsensal.

"She is very beautiful, but she is a devil."

"It would have been my duty to take her," said Komodoflorensal.

Tarzan was silent. A plan was unfolding itself within his mind. The voice from beyond the partition spoke again.

"He was very wonderful," it said. "Much more wonderful than our warriors," and then, after a silence, "You may go, slave, and see to it that I am not disturbed before the sun stands midway between the Women's Corridor and the King's Corridor."

"May your candles burn as deathlessly as your beauty, Princess," said the slave, as she backed across the apartment.

An instant later the three behind the paneling heard a door close.

Tarzan crept stealthily along the passage, seeking the secret panel that connected the apartment where the Princess Janzara lay composed for the night; but it was Talaskar who found it.

"Here!" she whispered and together the three examined the fastening. It was simple and could evidently be opened from the opposite side by pressure upon a certain spot in the panel.

"Wait here!" said Tarzan to his companions. "I am going to fetch the Princess Janzara. If we cannot escape with her we should be able to buy our liberty with such a hostage."

Without waiting to discuss the advisability of his action with the others, Tarzan gently slid back the catch that held the panel and pushed it slightly ajar. Before him was the apartment of Janzara—a creation of gorgeous barbarity in the center of which, upon a marble slab, the princess lay upon her back, a gigantic candle burning at her head and another at her feet.

Regardless of the luxuriousness of their surroundings, of their wealth, or their positions in life, the Minunians never sleep upon a substance softer than a single thickness of fabric, which they throw upon the ground, or upon wooden, stone, or marble sleeping slabs, depending upon their caste and their wealth.

Leaving the panel open the ape-man stepped quietly into the apartment and moved directly toward the princess, who lay with closed eyes, either already asleep, or assiduously wooing Morpheus. He had crossed halfway to her cold couch when a sudden draught closed the panel with a noise that might well have awakened the dead.

Instantly the princess was on her feet and facing him. For a moment she stood in silence gazing at him and then she moved slowly toward him, the sinuous undulations of her graceful carriage suggesting to the Lord of the Jungle a similarity to the savage majesty of Sabor, the lioness.

"It is you, Zuanthrol!" breathed the princess. "You have come for me?"

"I have come for you, Princess," replied the ape-man. "Make no outcry and no harm will befall you."

"I will make no outcry," whispered Janzara as with half-closed lids she glided to him and threw her arms about his neck.

Tarzan drew back and gently disengaged himself. "You do not understand, Princess," he told her. "You are my prisoner. You are coming with me."

"Yes," she breathed, "I am your prisoner, but it is you who do not understand. I love you. It is my right to choose whatever slave I will to be my prince. I have chosen you."

Tarzan shook his head impatiently. "You do not love me," he said. "I am sorry that you think you do, for I do not love you. I have no time to waste. Come!" and he stepped closer to take her by the wrist.

Her eyes narrowed. "Are you mad?" she demanded. "Or can it be that you do not know who I am?"

"You are Janzara, daughter of Elkomoelhago," replied Tarzan. "I know well who you are."

"And you dare to spurn my love!" She was breathing heavily, her breasts rising and falling to the tumultuous urge of her emotions.

"It is no question of love between us," replied the ape-man. "To me it is only a question of liberty and life for myself and my companions."

"You love another?" questioned Janzara.

"Yes," Tarzan told her.

"Who is she?" demanded the princess.

"Will you come quietly, or shall I be compelled to carry you away by force?" asked the ape-man, ignoring her question.

For a moment the woman stood silently before him, her every muscle tensed, her dark eyes two blazing wells of fire, and then slowly her expression changed. Her face softened and she stretched one hand toward him.

"I will help you, Zuanthrol," she said. "I will help you to escape. Because I love you I shall do this. Come! Follow me!" She turned and moved softly across the apartment.

"But my companions," said the ape-man. "I cannot go without them."

"Where are they?"

He did not tell her, for as yet he was none too sure of her motives.

"Show me the way," he said, "and I can return for them."

"Yes," she replied, "I will show you and then perhaps you will love me better than you love the other."

In the passage behind the paneling Talaskar and Komodoflorensal awaited the outcome of Tarzan's venture. Distinctly to their ears came every word of the conversation between the ape-man and the princess.

"He loves you," said Komodoflorensal. "You see, he loves you."

"I see nothing of the kind," returned Talaskar. "Because he does not love the Princess Janzara is no proof that he loves me."

"But he does love you—and you love him! I have seen it since first he came. Would that he were not my friend, for then I might run him through."

"Why would you run him through because he loves me—if he does?" demanded the girl. "Am I so low that you would rather see your friend dead than mated with me?"

"I—" he hesitated. "I cannot tell you what I mean."

The girl laughed, and then suddenly sobered. "She is leading him from her apartment. We had better follow."

As Talaskar laid her fingers upon the spring that actuated the lock holding the panel in place, Janzara led Tarzan across her chamber toward a doorway in one of the side walls—not the doorway through which her slave had departed.

"Follow me," whispered the princess, "and you will see what the love of Janzara means."

Tarzan, not entirely assured of her intentions, followed her warily.

"You are afraid," she said. "You do not trust me! Well, come here then and look, yourself, into this chamber before you enter."

Komodoflorensal and Talaskar had but just stepped into the apartment when Tarzan approached the door to one side of which Janzara stood. They saw the floor give suddenly beneath his feet and an instant later Zuanthrol had disappeared. As he shot down a polished chute he heard a wild laugh from Janzara following him into the darkness of the unknown.

Komodoflorensal and Talaskar leaped quickly across the chamber, but too late. The floor that had given beneath Tarzan's feet had slipped quietly back into place. Janzara stood above the spot trembling with anger and staring down at the place where the ape-man had disappeared. She shook as an aspen shakes in the breeze—shook in the mad tempest of her own passions.

"If you will not come to me you shall never go to another!" she screamed, and then she turned and saw Komodoflorensal and Talaskar running toward her. What followed occurred so quickly that it would be impossible to record the facts in the brief time that they actually consumed. It was over almost before Tarzan reached the bottom of the chute and picked himself from the earthen floor upon which he had been deposited.

The room in which he found himself was lighted by several candles burning in iron-barred niches. Opposite him was a heavy gate of iron bars through which he could see another lighted apartment in which a man, his chin sagging dejectedly upon his breast, was seated upon a low bench. At the sound of Tarzan's precipitate entrance into the adjoining chamber the man looked up and at sight of Zuanthrol, leaped to his feet.

"Quick! To your left!" he cried, and Tarzan, turning, saw two huge, green-eyed beasts crouching to spring.

His first impulse was to rub his eyes as one might to erase the phantom figures of a disquieting dream, for what he saw were two ordinary African wildcats—ordinary in contour and markings, but in size gigantic. For an instant the ape-man forgot that he was but one-fourth his normal size, and that the cats, that appeared to him as large as full-grown lions, were in reality but average specimens of their kind.

As they came toward him he whipped out his sword, prepared to battle for his life with these great felines as he had so often before with their mighty cousins of his own jungle.

"If you can hold them off until you reach this gate," cried the man in the next chamber, "I can let you through. The bolt is upon this side," but even as he spoke one of the cats charged.

Komodoflorensal, brushing past Janzara, leaped for the spot upon the floor at which Tarzan had disappeared and as it gave beneath him he heard a savage cry break from the lips of the Princess of Veltopismakus.

"So it is you he loves?" she screamed. "But he shall not have you—no! not even in death!" and that was all that Komodoflorensal heard as the black chute swallowed him.

Talaskar, confronted by the infuriated Janzara, halted, and then stepped back, for the princess was rushing upon her with drawn dagger.

"Die, slave!" she screamed, as she lunged for the white breast of Talaskar, but the slave girl caught the other's wrist and a moment later they went down, locked in one another's embrace. Together they rolled about the floor, the daughter of Elkomoelhago seeking to drive her slim blade into the breast of the slave girl, while Talaskar fought to hold off the menacing steel and to close with her fingers upon the throat of her antagonist.

As the first cat charged the other followed, not to be robbed of its share of the flesh of the kill, for both were half-starved and ravenous, and as the ape-man met the charge of the first, sidestepping its rush and springing in again to thrust at its side, Komodoflorensal, who had drawn his sword as he entered the apartment of Janzara, shot into the subterranean den almost into the teeth of the second beast, which was so disconcerted by the sudden appearance of this second human that it wheeled and sprang to the far end of the den before it could gather its courage for another attack.

In the chamber above, Talaskar and Janzara fought savagely, two she-tigers in human form. They rolled to and fro about the room, straining and striking; Janzara screaming: "Die, slave! You shall not have him!" But Talaskar held her peace and saved her breath, so that slowly she was overcoming the other when they chanced to roll upon the very spot that had let Tarzan and Komodoflorensal to the pit beneath.

As Janzara realized what had happened she uttered a scream of terror. "The cats! The cats!" she cried, and then the two disappeared into the black shaft.

Komodoflorensal did not follow the cat that had retreated to the far end of the pit; but sprang at once to Tarzan's aid, and together they drove off the first beast as they backed toward the gate where the man in the adjoining chamber stood ready to admit them to the safety of his own apartment.

The two cats charged and then retreated, springing in quickly and away again as quickly, for they had learned the taste of the sharp steel with which the humans were defending themselves. The two men were almost at the gate, another instant and they could spring through. The cats charged again and again were driven to the far corner of the pit. The man in the next chamber swung open the gate.

"Quick!" he cried, and at the same instant two figures shot from the mouth of the shaft and, locked tightly in one another's embrace, rolled to the floor of the pit directly in the path of the charging carnivores.

20

A S TARZAN and Komodoflorensal realized that Talaskar and Janzara lay exposed to the savage assault of the hungry beasts they both sprang quickly toward the two girls. As had been the case when Komodoflorensal had shot into the pit, the cats were startled by the sudden appearance of these two new humans, and in the first instant of their surprise had leaped again to the far end of the chamber.

Janzara had lost her dagger as the two girls had fallen into the shaft and now Talaskar saw it lying on the floor beside her. Releasing her hold upon the princess she seized the weapon and leaped to her feet. Already Tarzan and Komodoflorensal were at her side and the cats were returning to the attack.

Janzara arose slowly and half-bewildered. She looked about, terror disfiguring her marvelous beauty, and as she did so the man in the adjoining chamber saw her.

"Janzara!" he cried. "My Princess, I come!" and seizing the bench upon which he had been sitting, and the only thing within the chamber that might be converted into a weapon, he swung wide the gate and leaped into the chamber where the four were now facing the thoroughly infuriated beasts.

Both animals, bleeding from many wounds, were mad with pain, rage and hunger. Screaming and growling they threw themselves upon the swords of the two men, who had pushed the girls behind them and were backing slowly toward the gate, and then the man with the bench joined Tarzan and Komodoflorensal and the three fought back the charges of the infuriated carnivores.

The bench proved fully as good a weapon of defense as the swords and so together the five drew slowly back, until, quite suddenly and without the slightest warning both cats leaped quickly to one side and darted behind the party as though sensing that the women would prove easier prey. One of them came near to closing upon Janzara had not the man with the bench, imbued apparently with demoniacal fury, leaped upon it with his strange weapon and beaten it back so desperately that it was forced to abandon the princess.

Even then the man did not cease to follow it but, brandishing the bench, pursued it and its fellow with such terrifying cries and prodigious blows that, to escape him, both cats sud-

167

denly dodged into the chamber that the man had occupied, and before they could return to the attack he with the bench had slammed the gate and fastened them upon its opposite side. Then he wheeled and faced the four.

"Zoanthrohago!" cried the princess.

"Your slave!" replied the noble, dropping to one knee and leaning far back, with outstretched arms.

"You have saved my life, Zoanthrohago," said Janzara, "and after all the indignities that I have heaped upon you! How can I reward you?"

"I love you, Princess, as you have long known," replied the man; "but now it is too late; for tomorrow I die by the king's will. Elkomoelhago has spoken, and, even though you be his daughter, I do not hesitate to say his very ignorance prevents him ever changing a decision once reached."

"I know," said Janzara. "He is my sire but I love him not. He killed my mother in a fit of unreasoning jealousy. He is a fool—the fool of fools."

Suddenly she turned upon the others. "These slaves would escape, Zoanthrohago," she cried. "With my aid they might accomplish it. With their company we might succeed in escaping, too, and in finding an asylum in their own land."

"If any one of them is of sufficient power in his native city," replied Zoanthrohago.

"This one," said Tarzan, seeing a miraculous opportunity for freedom, "is the son of Adendrohahkis, King of Trohanadalmakus—the oldest son, and Zertolosto."

Janzara looked at Tarzan a moment after he had done speaking. "I was wicked, Zuanthrol," she said; "but I thought that I wanted you and being the daughter of a king I have seldom been denied aught that I craved," and then to Talaskar: "Take your man, my girl, and may you be happy with him," and she pushed Talaskar gently toward the ape-man; but Talaskar drew back.

"You are mistaken, Janzara," she said, "I do not love Zuanthrol, nor does he love me."

Komodoflorensa looked quickly at Tarzan as though expecting that he would quickly deny the truth of Talaskar's statement, but the ape-man only nodded his head in assent.

"Do you mean," demanded Komodoflorensal, "that you do not love Talaskar?" and he looked straight into the eyes of his friend.

"On the contrary, I love her very much," replied Tarzan; "but not in the way that you have believed, or should I say feared? I love her because she is a good girl and a kind girl and a loyal friend, and also because she was in trouble and needed the love and protection which you and I alone could give her; but as a man loves his mate, I do not love her, for I have a mate of my own in my country beyond the thorns."

Komodoflorensal said no more, but he thought a great deal. He thought of what it would mean to return to his own city where he was the Zertolosto, and where, by all the customs of ages, he would be supposed to marry a princess from another city. But he did not want a princess—he wanted Talaskar, the little slave girl of Veltopimakus, who scarcely knew her own mother and most probably had never heard that of her father, if her mother knew it.

He wanted Talaskar, but he could only have her in Trohanadalmakus as a slave. His love for her was real and so he would not insult her by thinking such a thing as that. If he could not make her his princess he would not have her at all, and so Komodoflorensal, the son of Adendrohahkis, was sad.

But he had none too much time to dwell upon his sorrow now, for the others were planning the best means for escape.

"The keepers come down to feed the cats upon this side," said Zoanthrohago, indicating a small door in the wall of the pit opposite that which led into the chamber in which he had been incarcerated.

"Doubtless it is not locked, either," said Janzara, "for a prisoner could not reach it without crossing through this chamber where the cats were kept."

"We will see," said Tarzan, and crossed to the door.

A moment sufficed to force it open, revealing a narrow corridor beyond. One after another the five crawled through the small aperture and following the corridor ascended an acclivity, lighting their way with candles taken from the den of the carnivores. At the top a door opened into a wide corridor, a short distance down which stood a warrior, evidently on gaurd before a door.

Janzara looked through the tiny crack that Tarzan had opened the door and saw the corridor and the man. "Good!" she exclaimed. "It is my own corridor and the warrior is on guard before my door. I know him well. Through me he has escaped payment of his taxes for the past thirty moons. He would die for me. Come! we have nothing to fear," and stepping boldly into the corridor she approached the sentry, the others following behind her.

Until he recognized her there was danger that the fellow would raise an alarm, but the moment he saw who it was he was as wax in her hands.

"You are blind," she told him.

"If the Princess Janzara wishes it," he replied.

She told him what she wished—five diadets and some heavy, warriors' wraps. He eyed those who were with her, and evidently recognized Zoanthrohago and guessed who the two other men were.

"Not only shall I be blind for my princess," he said; "but tomorrow I shall be dead for her."

"Fetch six diadets, then," said the princess.

Then she turned to Komodoflorensal. "You are Prince Royal of Trohanadalmakus?" she asked.

"I am," he replied.

"And if we show you the way to liberty you will not enslave us?"

"I shall take you to the city as my own slaves and then liberate you," he replied.

"It is something that has seldom if ever been done," she mused; "not in the memory of living man in Veltopismakus. I wonder if your sire will permit it."

"The thing is not without precedent," replied Komodoflorensal. "It has been done but rarely, yet it *has* been done. I think you may feel assured of a friendly welcome at the court of Adendrohahkis, where the wisdom of Zoanthrohago will not go unappreciated or unrewarded."

It was a long time before the warrior returned with the diadets. His face was covered with perspiration and his hands with blood.

"I had to fight for them," he said, "and we shall have to fight to use them if we do not hurry. Here, Prince, I brought you weapons," and he handed a sword and dagger to Zoanthrohago.

They mounted quickly. It was Tarzan's first experience upon one of the wiry, active, little mounts of the Minunians; but he found the saddle well designed and the diadet easily controlled.

"They will be following me from the King's Corridor," explained Oratharc, the warrior who had fetched the diadets. "It would be best, then, to leave by one of the others."

"Trohanadalmakus is east of Veltopismakus," said Zoanthrohago, "and if we leave by the Women's Corridor with two slaves from Trohanadalmakus they will assume that we are going there; but if we leave by another corridor they will not be sure and if they lose even a little time in starting the pursuit it will give us just that much of an advantage. If we go straight toward Trohanadalmakus we shall almost certainly be overtaken as the swiftest of diadets will be used in our pursuit. Our only hope lies in deceiving them as to our route or destination, and to accomplish this I believe that we should leave either by the Warriors' Corridor or the Slaves' Corridor, cross the hills north of the city, circle far out to the north and east, not turning south until we are well past Trohanadalmakus. In this way we can approach that city from the east while our pursuers are patrolling the country west of Trohanadalmakus to Vetlopismakus."

"Let us leave by the Warriors' Corridor then," suggested Janzara.

"The trees and shrubbery will conceal us while we pass around to the north of the city," said Komodoflorensal.

"We should leave at once," urged Oratharc.

"Go first then, with the princess," said Zoanthrohago, "for there is a possibility that the guard at the entrance will let her pass with her party. We will muffle ourselves well with our warriors' cloaks. Come, lead the way!"

With Janzara and Oratharc ahead and the others following closely they moved at a steady trot along the circular corridor toward the Warriors' Corridor, and it was not until they had turned into the latter that any sign of pursuit developed. Even then, though they heard the voices of men behind them, they hesitated to break into a faster gait lest they arouse the suspicions of the warriors in the guard room which they must pass near the mouth of the corridor.

Never had the Warriors' Corridor seemed so long to any of the Veltopismakusians in the party as it did this night; never had they so wished to race their diadets as now; but they held their mounts to an even pace that would never have suggested to the most suspicious that here were six people seeking escape, most of them from death.

They had come almost to the exit when they were aware that the pursuit had turned into the Warriors' Corridor behind them and that their pursuers were advancing at a rapid gait.

Janzara and Oratharc drew up beside the sentry at the mouth of the corridor as he stepped out to bar their progress.

"The Princess Janzara!" announced Oratharc. "Aside for the Princess Janzara!"

The princess threw back the hood of the warrior's cloak she wore, revealing her features, well known to every warrior in the Royal Dome—and well feared. The fellow hesitated.

"Aside, man!" cried the princess, "or I ride you down."

A great shout arose behind them. Warriors on swiftly galloping diadets leaped along the corridor toward them. The warriors were shouting something, the sense of which was hidden by the noise; but the sentry was suspicious.

"Wait until I call the Novand of the guard, Princess," he cried. "Something is amiss and I dare let no one pass without authority; but wait! here he is," and the party turned in their saddles to see a Novand emerging from the door of the guard room, followed by a number of warriors.

"Ride!" cried Janzara and spurred her diadet straight for the single sentry in their path.

The others lifted their mounts quickly in pursuit. The sentry went down, striking valiantly with his rapier at the legs and bellies of flying diadets. The Novand and his men rushed from the guard room just in time to collide with the pursuers, whom they immediately assumed were belated members of the fleeing party. The brief minutes that these fought, before explanations could be made and understood, gave the fugitives time to pass among the trees to the west side of the city, and, turning north, make for the hills that were dimly visible in the light of a clear, but moonless night.

Oratharc, who said that he knew the hill trails perfectly, led the way, the others following as closely as they could; Komodoflorensal and Tarzan bringing up the rear. Thus they moved on in silence through the night, winding along precipitous mountain trails, leaping now and again from rock to rock where the trail itself had been able to find no footing; sliding into dank ravines, clambering through heavy brush and timber along tunnel-like trails that followed their windings, or crept up their opposite sides to narrow ridge or broad plateau; and all night long no sign of pursuit developed.

Came the morning at last and with it, from the summit of a lofty ridge, a panorama of broad plain stretching to the north, of distant hills, of forests and of streams. They decided then to descend to one of the numerous parklike glades that they could see nestling in the hills below them, and there rest their mounts and permit them to feed, for the work of the night had been hard upon them.

They knew that in the hills they might hide almost indefinitely, so wild and so little traveled were they and so they went into camp an hour after sunrise in a tiny cuplike valley surrounded by great trees, and watered and fed their mounts with a sense of security greater than they had felt since they left Veltopismakus.

Oratharc went out on foot and killed a number of quail and Tarzan speared a couple of fish in the stream. These they prepared and ate, and then, the men taking turns on guard, they slept until afternoon, for none had had sleep the night before.

Taking up their flight again in midafternoon they were well out upon the plain when darkness overtook them. Komodoflorensal and Zoanthrohago were riding far out upon the flanks and all were searching for a suitable camping place. It was Zoanthrohago who found it and when they all gathered about him Tarzan saw nothing in the waning light of day that appeared any more like a good camping place than any other spot on the open plain. There was a little clump of trees, but they had passed many such clumps, and there was nothing about this one that seemed to offer any greater security than another. As a matter of fact, to Tarzan it appeared anything but a desirable camp-site. There was no water, there was little shelter from the wind and none from an enemy; but perhaps they were going into the trees. That would be better. He looked up at the lofty branches lovingly. How enormous these trees seemed! He knew them for what they were and that they were trees of but average size, yet to him now they reared their heads aloft like veritable giants.

"I will go in first," he heard Komodoflorensal say, and turned to learn what he referred to.

The other three men were standing at the mouth of a large hole, into which they were looking. Tarzan knew that the opening was the mouth of the burrow of a ratel, the African member of the badger family, and he wondered why any of them wished to enter it. Tarzan had never cared for the flesh of the ratel. He stepped over and joined the others, and as he did so he saw Komodoflorensal crawl into the opening, his drawn sword in his hand.

"Why is he doing that?" he asked Zoanthrohago.

"To drive out, or kill the cambon, if he is there," replied the prince, giving the ratel its Minunian name.

"And why?" asked Tarzan. "Surely, you do not eat its flesh!"

"No, but we want his home for the night," replied Zoanthrohago. "I had forgotten that you are not a Minunian. We will spend the night in the underground chambers of the cambon, safe from the attacks of the cat or the lion. It would be better were we there now—this is a bad hour of the night for Minunians to be abroad on the plain or in the forest, for it is at this hour that the lion hunts."

A few minutes later Komodoflorensal emerged from the hole. "The cambon is not there," he said. "The burrow is deserted. I found only a snake, which I killed. Go in, Oratharc, and Janzara and Talaskar will follow you. You have candles?"

They had, and one by one they disappeared into the mouth of the hole, until Tarzan, who had asked to remain until last, stood alone in the gathering night gazing at the mouth of the ratel's burrow, a smile upon his lips. It seemed ridiculous to him that Tarzan of the Apes should ever be contemplating hiding from Numa in the hole of a ratel, or, worse still, hiding from little Skree, the wildcat, and as he stood there smiling a bulk loomed dimly among the trees; the diadets, standing near, untethered, snorted and leaped away; and Tarzan wheeled to face the largest lion he ever had seen—a lion that towered over twice the ape-man's height above him.

How tremendous, how awe-inspiring Numa appeared to one the size of a Minunian!

The lion crouched, its tail extended, the tip moving ever so gently; but the ape-man was not deceived. He guessed what was coming and even as the great cat sprang he turned and dove headforemost down the hole of the ratel and behind him rattled the loose earth pushed into the burrow's mouth by Numa as he alighted upon the spot where Tarzan had stood.

21

For three days the six traveled toward the east, and then, upon the fourth, they turned south. A great forest loomed upon the distant southern horizon, sweeping also wide upon the east. To the southwest lay Trohanadalmakus, a good two-days' journey for their tired diadets. Tarzan often wondered what rest the little creatures obtained. At night they were turned loose to graze; but his knowledge of the habits of the carnivores assured him that the tiny antelope must spend the greater part of each night in terrified watching or in flight; yet every morning they were back at the camp awaiting the pleasure of their masters. That they did not escape, never to return, is doubtless due to two facts. One is that they have been for ages bred in the domes of the Minunians—they know no other life than with their masters, to whom they look for food and care—and the other is the extreme kindness and affection which the Minunians accord their beautiful beasts of burden,

and which have won the love and confidence of the little animals to such an extent that the diadet is most contented when in
the company of man.

It was during the afternoon of the fourth day of their flight
that Talaskar suddenly called their attention to a small cloud
of dust far to their rear. For a long time all six watched it
intently as it increased in size and drew nearer.

"It may be the long-awaited pursuit," said Zoanthrohago.

"Or some of my own people from Trohanadalmakus," suggested Komodofiorensal.

"Whoever they are, they greatly outnumber us," said Janzara, "and I think we should find shelter until we know their
identity."

"We can reach the forest before they overtake us," said
Oratharc, "and in the forest we may elude them if it is
necessary."

"I fear the forest," said Janzara.

"We have no alternative," said Zoanthrohago; "but even now
I doubt that we can reach it ahead of them. Come! we must
be quick!"

Never before had Tarzan of the Apes covered ground so
rapidly upon the back of an animal. The diadets flew through
the air in great bounds. Behind them the nucleus of the dust
cloud had resolved itself into a dozen mounted warriors,
against whom their four blades would be helpless. Their one
hope, therefore, lay in reaching the forest ahead of their pursuers, and now it seemed that they would be successful and
now it seemed that they would not.

The recently distant wood seemed rushing toward him as
Tarzan watched ahead between the tiny horns of his graceful
mount, and, behind, the enemy was gaining. They were Veltopismakusian—they were close enough now for the devices
upon their helmets to be seen—and they had recognized their
quarry, for they cried aloud upon them to stop, calling several
of them by name.

One of the pursuers forged farther ahead than the others.
He came now close behind Zoanthrohago, who rode neck and
neck with Tarzan, in the rear of their party. A half-length
ahead of Zoanthrohago, was Janzara. The fellow called aloud
to her.

"Princess!" he cried. "The king's pardon for you all if you
return the slaves to us. Surrender and all will be forgiven."

Tarzan of the Apes heard and he wondered what the Veltopismakusians would do. It must have been a great temptation
and he knew it. Had it not been for Talaskar he would have

advised them to fall back among their friends; but he would not see the slave girl sacrificed. He drew his sword then and dropped back beside Zoanthrohago, though the other never guessed his purpose.

"Surrender, and all will be forgiven!" shouted the pursuer again.

"Never!" cried Zoanthrohago.

"Never!" echoed Janzara.

"The consequences are yours," cried the messenger, and on they rushed, pursuers and pursued, toward the dark forest, while from just within its rim savage eyes watched the mad race and red tongues licked hungry lips in anticipation.

Tarzan had been glad to hear the reply given by both Zoanthrohago and Janzara whom he had found likable companions and good comrades. Janzara's whole attitude had changed since the very instant she had joined them in their attempted escape. No longer was she the spoiled daughter of a despot; but a woman seeking happiness through the new love that she had found, or the old love that she had just discovered, for she often told Zoanthrohago that she knew now that she always had loved him. And this new thing in her life made her more considerate and loving of others. She seemed now to be trying to make up to Talaskar for the cruelty of her attack upon her when she had first seen her. Her mad infatuation for Tarzan she now knew in its true light—because she had been refused him when she wanted him, and she would have taken him as her prince to spite her father, whom she hated.

Komodoflorensal and Talaskar always rode together, but no words of love did the Trohanadalmakusian speak in the ear of the little slave girl. A great resolve was crystallizing in his mind, but it had as yet taken on no definite form. And Talaskar, seemingly happy just to be near him, rode blissfully through the first days of the only freedom she had ever known; but now all was forgotten except the instant danger of capture and its alternative concomitants, death and slavery.

The six urged their straining mounts ahead. The forest was so near now. Ah, if they could but reach it! There one warrior might be as good as three and the odds against them would be reduced, for in the forest the whole twelve could not engage them at once and by careful maneuvering they doubtless could separate them.

They were going to succeed! A great shout rose to the lips of Oratharc as his diadet leaped into the shadows of the first trees, and the others took it up, for a brief instant, and then it died upon their lips as they saw a giant hand reach down and snatch Oratharc from his saddle. They tried to stop and wheel their mounts, but it was too late. Already they were in the forest and all about them was a horde of the hideous Zertalacolols. One by one they were snatched from their diadets, while their pursuers, who must have seen what was taking place just inside the forest, wheeled and galloped away.

Talaskar, writhing in the grip of a she-Alali, turned toward Komodoflorensal.

"Good-bye!" she cried. "This, at last, is the end; but I can die near you and so I am happier dying than I have been living until you came to Veltopismakus."

"Good-bye, Talaskar!" he replied. "Living, I dared not tell you; but dying, I can proclaim my love. Tell me that you loved me."

"With all my heart, Komodoflorensal!" They seemed to have forgotten that another existed but themselves. In death they were alone with their love.

Tarzan found himself in the hand of a male and he also found himself wondering, even as he faced certain death, how it occurred that this great band of male and female Alali should be hunting together, and then he noticed the weapons of the males. They were not the crude bludgeon and the slinging-stones that they had formerly carried; but long, trim spears, and bows and arrows.

And now the creature that held him had lifted him even with his face and was scrutinizing him and Tarzan saw a look of recognition and amazement cross the bestial features, and he, in turn, recognized his captor. It was the son of The First Woman. Tarzan did not wait to learn the temper of his old acquaintance. Possibly their relations were altered now. Possibly they were not. He recalled the doglike devotion of the creature when last he had seen him and he put him to the test at once.

"Put me down!" he signed, peremptorily; "and tell your people to put down all of my people. Harm them not!"

Instantly the great creature set Tarzan gently upon the ground and immediately signaled his fellows to do the same with their captives. The men did immediately as they were bid, and all of the women but one. She hesitated. The son of The First Woman leaped toward her, his spear raised like a whip, and the female cowered and set Talaskar down upon the ground.

Very proud, the son of The First Woman explained to Tarzan as best he could the great change that had come upon the Alali since the ape-man had given the men weapons and the son of The First Woman had discovered what a proper use of them would mean to the males of his kind. Now each male had a woman cooking for him—at least one, and some of them —the stronger—had more than one.

To entertain Tarzan and to show him what great strides civilization had taken in the land of the Zertalacolols, the son of The First Woman seized a female by the hair and dragging her to him struck her heavily about the head and face with his clenched fist, and the woman fell upon her knees and fondled his legs, looking wistfully into his face, her own glowing with love and admiration.

That night the six slept in the open surrounded by the great Zertalacolols and the next day they started across the plain toward Trohanadalmakus where Tarzan had resolved to remain until he regained his normal size, when he would make a determined effort to cut his way through the thorn forest to his own country.

The Zertalacolols went a short distance out into the plain with them, and both men and women tried in their crude, savage way, to show Tarzan their gratitude for the change that he had wrought among them, and the new happiness he had given them.

Two days later the six fugitives approached the domes of Trohanadalmakus. They had been seen by sentries when they were still a long way off, and a body of warriors rode forth to meet them, for it is always well to learn the nature of a visitor's business in Minuni before he gets too close to your home.

When the warriors discovered that Komodoflorensal and Tarzan had returned they shouted for joy and a number of them galloped swiftly back to the city to spread the news.

The fugitives were conducted at once to the throne room of Adendrohahkis and there that great ruler took his son in his arms and wept, so great was his happiness at having him returned safely to him. Nor did he forget Tarzan, though it was some time before he or the other Trohanadalmakusians could accustom themselves to the fact that this man, no bigger than they, was the great giant who had dwelt among them a few moons since.

Adendrohahkis called Tarzan to the foot of the throne and there, before the nobles and warriors of Trohanadalmakus, he made him a Zertol, or prince, and he gave him diadets and riches and allotted him quarters fitted to his rank, begging him to stay among them always.

Janzara, Zoanthrohago and Oratharc he gave their liberty

and permission to remain in Trohanadalmakus, and then Komodoflorensal drew Talaskar to the foot of the throne.

"And now for myself I ask a boon, Adendrohahkis," he said. "As Zertolosto I am bound by custom to wed a prisoner princess taken from another city; but in this slave girl have I found the one I love. Let me renounce my rights to the throne and have her instead."

Talaskar raised her hand as though to demur, but Komodoflorensal would not let her speak, and then Adendrohahkis rose and descended the steps at the foot of which Talaskar stood and taking her by the hand led her to a place beside the throne.

"You are bound by custom only, Komodoflorensal," he said, "to wed a princess; but custom is not law. A Trohanadalmakusian may wed whom he pleases."

"And even though he were bound by law," said Talaskar, "to wed a princess, still might he wed me, for I am the daughter of Talaskhago, king of Mandalamakus. My mother was captured by the Veltopismakusians but a few moons before my birth, which took place in the very chamber in which Komodoflorensal found me. She taught me to take my life before mating with anyone less than a prince; but I would have forgotten her teachings had Komodoflorensal been but the son of a slave. That he was the son of a king I did not dream until the night we left Veltopismakus, and I had already given him my heart long before, though he did not know it."

Weeks passed and still no change came to Tarzan of the Apes. He was happy in his life with the Minunians, but he longed for his own people and the mate who would be grieving for him, and so he determined to set forth as he was, pass through the thorn forest and make his way toward home, trusting to chance that he might escape the countless dangers that would infest his way, and perhaps come to his normal size somewhere during the long journey.

His friends sought to dissuade him, but he was determined, and at last, brooking no further delay, he set out toward the southeast in the direction that he thought lay the point where he had entered the land of the Minuni. A kamak, a body consisting of one thousand mounted warriors, accompanied him to the great forest and there, after some days' delay, the son of The First Woman found him. The Minunians bid him good-bye, and as he watched them ride away upon their graceful mounts, something rose in his throat that only came upon those few occasions in his life that Tarzan of the Apes knew the meaning of homesickness.

The son of The First Woman and his savage band escorted Tarzan to the edge of the thorn forest. Further than that they could not go. A moment later they saw him disappear among the thorns, with a wave of farewell to them. For two days Tarzan, no larger than a Minunian, made his way through the thorn forest. He met small animals that were now large enough to be dangerous to him, but he met nothing that he could not cope with. By night he slept in the burrows of the larger burrowing animals. Birds and eggs formed his food supply.

During the second night he awoke with a feeling of nausea suffusing him. A premonition of danger assailed him. It was dark as the grave in the burrow he had selected for the night. Suddenly the thought smote him that he might be about to pass through the ordeal of regaining his normal stature. To have this thing happen while he lay buried in this tiny burrow would mean death, for he would be crushed, strangled, or suffocated before he regained consciousness.

Already he felt dizzy, as one might feel who was upon the verge of unconsciousness. He stumbled to his knees and clawed his way up the steep acclivity that led to the surface. Would he reach it in time? He stumbled on and then, suddenly, a burst of fresh night air smote his nostrils. He staggered to his feet. He was out! He was free!

Behind him he heard a low growl. Grasping his sword, he lunged forward among the thorn trees. How far he went, or in what direction he did not know. It was still dark when he stumbled and fell unconscious to the ground.

22

A WAZIRI, returning from the village of Obebe the cannibal, saw a bone lying beside the trail. This, in itself, was nothing remarkable. Many bones lie along savage trails in Africa. But this bone caused him to pause. It was the bone of a child. Nor was that alone enough to give pause to a warrior hastening through an unfriendly country back toward his own people.

But Usula had heard strange tales in the village of Obebe the cannibal where rumor had brought him in search of his beloved master. The Big Bwana. Obebe had not seen nor heard anything of Tarzan of the Apes. Not for years had he seen the giant white. He assured Usula of this fact many times; but from other members of the tribe the Waziri learned that a white man had been kept a prisoner by Obebe for a year or more and that some time since he had escaped. At first Usula thought this white man might have been Tarzan but when he verified the statement of the time that had elapsed since the man was captured he knew that it could not have been his master, and so he turned back along the trail toward home; but when he saw the child's bone along the trail several days out he recalled the story of the missing Uhha and he paused, just for a moment, to look at the bone. And as he looked he saw something else—a small skin bag, lying among some more bones a few feet off the trail. Usula stooped and picked up the bag. He opened it and poured some of the contents into his palm. He know what the things were and he knew that they had belonged to his master, for Usula was a headman who knew much about his master's affairs. These were the diamonds that had been stolen from The Big Bwana many moons before by the white men who had found Opar. He would take them back to The Big Bwana's lady.

Three days later as he moved silently along the trail close to The Great Thorn Forest he came suddenly to a halt, the hand grasping his heavy spear tensing in readiness. In a little open place he saw a man, an almost naked man, lying upon the ground. The man was alive—he saw him move—but what was he doing? Usula crept closer, making no noise. He moved around until he could observe the man from another angle and then he saw a horrid sight. The man was white and he lay beside the carcass of a long-dead buffalo, greedily devouring the remnants of hide that clung to the bleaching bones.

The man raised his head a little and Usula, catching a better view of his face, gave a cry of horror. Then the man looked up and grinned. It was The Big Bwana!

Usula ran to him and raised him upon his knees, but the man only laughed and babbled like a child. At his side, caught over one of the horns of the buffalo, was The Big Bwana's golden locket with the great diamonds set in it. Usula replaced it about the man's neck. He built a strong shelter for him nearby and hunted food, and for many days he remained until the man's strength came back; but his mind did not come back. And thus, in this condition, the faithful Usula led home his master.

They found many wounds and bruises upon his body and his head, some old, some new, some trivial, some serious; and they sent to England for a great surgeon to come out to Africa and seek to mend the poor thing that once had been Tarzan of the Apes.

The dogs that had once loved Lord Greystoke slunk from this brainless creature. Jad-bal-ja, the Golden Lion, growled when the man was wheeled near his cage.

Korak The Killer paced the floor in dumb despair, for his mother was on her way from England, and what would be the effect upon her of this awful blow? He hesitated even to contemplate it.

Khamis, the witch doctor, had searched untiringly for Uhha, his daughter, since The River Devil had stolen her from the village of Obebe the cannibal. He had made pilgrimages to other villages, some of them remote from his own country, but he had found no trace of her or her abductor.

He was returning from another fruitless search that had extended far to the east of the village of Obebe, skirting The Great Thorn Forest a few miles north of the Ugogo. It was early morning. He had just broken his lonely camp and set out upon the last leg of his homeward journey when his keen old eyes discovered something lying at the edge of a small open space a hundred yards to his right. He had just a glimpse of something that was not of the surrounding vegetation. He did not know what it was; but instinct bade him investigate. Moving cautiously nearer he presently identified the thing as a human knee just showing above the low grass that covered the clearing. He crept closer and suddenly his eyes narrowed and his breath made a single, odd little sound as it sucked rapidly between his lips in mechanical reaction to surprise, for what he saw was the body of The River Devil lying upon its back, one knee flexed—the knee that he had seen above the grasses.

His spear advanced and ready he approached until he stood above the motionless body. Was The River Devil dead, or was he asleep? Placing the point of his spear against the brown breast Khamis prodded. The Devil did not awaken. He was not asleep, then! nor did he appear to be dead. Khamis knelt and placed an ear above the other's heart. He was not dead!

The witch doctor thought quickly. In his heart he did not believe in River Devils, yet there was a chance that there might be such things and perhaps this one was shamming unconsciousness, or temporarily absent from the flesh it assumed as a disguise that it might go among men without arousing suspicion. But, too, it was the abductor of his daughter. That thought filled him with rage and with courage. He must force the truth from those lips even though the creature were a Devil.

He unwound a bit of fiber rope from about his waist and, turning the body over upon its back, quickly bound the wrists behind it. Then he sat down beside it to wait. It was an hour before signs of returning consciousness appeared, then The River Devil opened his eyes.

"Where is Uhha, my daughter?" demanded the witch doctor.

The River Devil tried to free his arms, but they were too tightly bound. He made no reply to Khamis' question. It was as though he had not heard it. He ceased struggling and lay back again, resting. After a while he opened his eyes once more and lay looking at Khamis, but he did not speak.

"Get up!" commanded the witch doctor and prodded him with a spear.

The River Devil rolled over on his side, flexed his right knee, raised on one elbow and finally got to his feet. Khamis prodded him in the direction of the trail. Toward dusk they arrived at the village of Obebe.

When the warriors and the women and the children saw who it was that Khamis was bringing to the village they became very much excited, and had it not been for the witch doctor, of whom they were afraid, they would have knifed and stoned the prisoner to death before he was fairly inside the village gates; but Khamis did not want The River Devil killed—not yet. He wanted first to force from him the truth concerning Uhha. So far he had been unable to get a word out of his prisoner. Incessant questioning, emphasized by many prods of the spear point had elicited nothing.

Khamis threw his prisoner into the same hut from which The River Devil had escaped; but he bound him securely and placed two warriors on guard. He had no mind to lose him again. Obebe came to see him. He, too, questioned him; but The River Devil only looked blankly in the face of the chief.

"I will make him speak," said Obebe. "After we have finished eating we will have him out and make him speak. I know many ways."

"You must not kill him," said the witch doctor. "He knows what became of Uhha, and until he tells me no one shall kill him."

"He will speak before he dies," said Obebe.

"He is a River Devil and will never die," said Khamis, reverting to the old controversy.

"He is Tarzan," cried Obebe, and the two were still arguing after they had passed out of hearing of the prisoner lying in the filth of the hut.

After they had eaten he saw them heating irons in a fire near the hut of the witch doctor, who was squatting before the entrance working rapidly with numerous charms—bits of wood wrapped in leaves, pieces of stone, some pebbles, a zebra's tail.

Villagers were congregating about Khamis until presently the prisoner could no longer see him. A little later a black boy came and spoke to his guards, and he was taken out and pushed roughly toward the hut of the witch doctor.

Obebe was there, as he saw after the guards had opened a way through the throng and he stood beside the fire in the center of the circle. It was only a small fire; just enough to keep a couple of irons hot.

"Where is Uhha, my daughter?" demanded Khamis.

The River Devil did not answer. Not once had he spoken since Khamis had captured him.

"Burn out one of his eyes," said Obebe. "That will make him speak!"

"Cut out his tongue!" screamed a woman. "Cut out his tongue."

"Then he cannot speak at all, you fool," cried Khamis.

The witch doctor arose and put the question again, but received no reply. Then he struck The River Devil a heavy blow in the face. Khamis had lost his temper, so that he did not fear even a River Devil.

"You will answer me now!" he screamed, and stooping he seized a red-hot iron.

"The right eye first!" shrilled Obebe.

The doctor came to the bungalow of the ape-man—Lady Greystoke brought him with her. They were three tired and dusty travelers as they dismounted at last before the rose-embowered entrance—the famous London surgeon, Lady Greystoke, and Flora Hawkes, her maid. The surgeon and Lady Greystoke went immediately to the room where Tarzan sat in an improvised wheelchair. He looked up at them blankly as they entered.

"Don't you know me, John?" asked the woman.

Her son took her by the shoulders and led her away, weeping.

"He does not know any of us," he said. "Wait until after the operation, mother, before you see him again. You can do him no good and to see him this way is too hard upon you."

The great surgeon made his examination. There was pressure on the brain from a recent fracture of the skull. An operation would relieve the pressure and might restore the patient's mind and memory. It was worth attempting.

Nurses and two doctors from Nairobi, engaged the day they arrived there, followed Lady Greystoke and the London surgeon, reaching the bungalow the day after their arrival. The operation took place the following morning.

Lady Greystoke, Korak and Meriem were awaiting, in an adjoining room, the verdict of the surgeon. Was the operation a failure or a success? They sat mutely staring at the door leading into the improvised operating room. At last it opened, after what seemed ages, but was only perhaps an hour. The surgeon entered the room where they sat. Their eyes, dumbly pleading, asked him the question that their lips dared not voice.

"I cannot tell you anything as yet," he said, "other than that the operation, as an operation, was successful. What the result of it will be only time will tell. I have given orders that no one is to enter his room, other than the nurses for ten days. They are instructed not to speak to him or allow him to speak for the same length of time; but he will not wish to speak, for I shall keep him in a semiconscious condition, by means of drugs, until the ten days have elapsed. Until then, Lady Greystoke, we may only hope for the best; but I can assure you that your husband has every chance for complete recovery. I think you may safely hope for the best."

The witch doctor laid his left hand upon the shoulder of The River Devil; in his right hand was clutched a red-hot iron.

"The right eye first," shrilled Obebe again.

Suddenly the muscles upon the back and shoulders of the prisoner leaped into action, rolling beneath his brown hide. For just an instant he appeared to exert terrific physical force, there was a snapping sound at his back as the strands about his wrists parted, and an instant later steel-thewed fingers fell upon the right wrist of the witch doctor. Blazing eyes burned into his. He dropped the red-hot rod, his fingers paralyzed by the pressure upon his wrist, and he screamed, for he saw death in the angry face of the god.

Obebe leaped to his feet. Warriors pressed forward, but not near enough to be within reach of The River Devil. They had never been certain of the safety of tempting Providence in any such manner as Khamis and Obebe had been about to do. Now here was the result! The wrath of The River Devil would fall upon them all. They fell back, some of them, and that was a cue for others to fall back. In the minds of all was the same thought—if I have no hand in this The River Devil will not be angry with me. Then they turned and fled to their huts, stumbling over their women and their children who were trying to outdistance their lords and masters.

Obebe turned now to flee also, and The River Devil picked Khamis up, and held him in two hands high above his head, and ran after Obebe the chief. The latter dodged into his own hut. He had scarce reached the center of it when there came a terrific crash upon the light, thatched roof, which gave way beneath a heavy weight. A body descending upon the chief filled him with terror. The River Devil had leaped in through the roof of his hut to destroy him! The instinct of self-preservation rose momentarily above his fear of the supernatural, for now he was convinced that Khamis had been right and the creature they had so long held prisoner was indeed The River Devil. And Obebe drew the knife at his side and plunged it again and again into the body of the creature that had leaped upon him, and when he knew that life was extinct he rose and dragging the body after him stepped out of his hut into the light of the moon and the fires.

"Come, my people!" he cried. "You have nothing to fear, for I, Obebe, your chief, have slain The River Devil with my own hands," and then he looked down at the thing trailing behind him, and gave a gasp, and sat down suddenly in the dirt of the village street, for the body at his heels was that of Khamis, the witch doctor.

His people came and when they saw what had happened they said nothing, but looked terrified. Obebe examined his hut and the ground around it. He took several warriors and searched the village. The stranger had departed. He went to the gates. They were closed; but in the dust before them was the imprint of naked feet—the naked feet of a white man. Then he came back to his hut, where his frightened people stood waiting him.

"Obebe was right," he said. "The creature was not The River Devil—it was Tarzan of the Apes, for only he could hurl Khamis so high above his head that he would fall through the roof of a hut, and only he could pass unaided over our gates."

The tenth day had come. The great surgeon was still at the Greystoke bungalow awaiting the outcome of the operation. The patient was slowly emerging from under the influence of the last dose of drugs that had been given him during the preceding night, but he was regaining his consciousness more slowly than the surgeon had hoped. The long hours dragged by, morning ran into afternoon, and evening came, and still there was no word from the sickroom.

It was dark. The lamps were lighted. The family were congregated in the big living room. Suddenly the door opened and a nurse appeared. Behind her was the patient. There was a puzzled look upon his face; but the face of the nurse was wreathed in smiles. The surgeon came behind, assisting the man, who was weak from long inactivity.

"I think Lord Greystoke will recover rapidly now," he said. "There are many things that you may have to tell him. He did not know who he was, when he regained consciousness; but that is not unusual in such cases."

The patient took a few steps into the room, looking wonderingly about.

"There is your wife, Greystoke," said the surgeon, kindly.

Lady Greystoke rose and crossed the room toward her husband, her arms outstretched. A smile crossed the face of the invalid, as he stepped forward to meet her and take her in his arms; but suddenly someone was between them, holding them apart. It was Flora Hawkes.

"My Gawd, Lady Greystoke!" she cried. "He ain't your husband. It's Miranda, Esteban Miranda! Don't you suppose I'd know him in a million? I ain't seen him since we came back, never havin' been in the sick chamber, but I suspicioned something the minute he stepped into this room and when he smiled, I knew."

"Flora!" cried the distracted wife. "Are you sure? No! no! you must be wrong! God has not given me back my husband only to steal him away again. John! tell me, is it you? You would not lie to me?"

For a moment the man before them was silent. He swayed to and fro, as in weakness. The surgeon stepped forward and supported him.

"I have been very sick," he said. "Possibly I have changed; but I am Lord Greystoke. I do not remember this woman," and he indicated Flora Hawkes.

"He lies!" cried the girl.

"Yes, he lies," said a quiet voice behind them, and they all turned to see the figure of a giant white standing in the open French windows leading to the veranda.

"John!" cried Lady Greystoke, running toward him, "how could I have been mistaken? I—" but the rest of the sentence was lost as Tarzan of the Apes sprang into the room and taking his mate in his arms covered her lips with kisses.

ABOUT EDGAR RICE BURROUGHS

Edgar Rice Burroughs is one of the world's most popular authors. With no previous experience as an author, he wrote and sold his first novel—*A Princess of Mars*—in 1912. In the ensuing thirty-eight years until his death in 1950, Burroughs wrote 91 books and a host of short stories and articles. Although best known as the creator of the classic *Tarzan of the Apes* and *John Carter of Mars,* his restless imagination knew few bounds. Burroughs' prolific pen ranged from the American West to primitive Africa and on to romantic adventure on the moon, the planets, and even beyond the farthest star.

No one knows how many copies of ERB books have been published throughout the world. It is conservative to say, however, that of the translations into 32 known languages, including Braille, the number must run into the hundreds of millions. When one considers the additional world-wide following of the Tarzan newspaper feature, radio programs, comic magazines, motion pictures and television, Burroughs must have been known and loved by literally a thousand million or more.